ROYALLY
MATCHED

EMMA CHASE

everafterROMANCE

Also by Emma Chase

THE ROYALLY SERIES
Royally Screwed

THE LEGAL BRIEFS SERIES
Sidebarred
Appealed
Sustained
Overruled

THE TANGLED SERIES
It's a Wonderful Tangled Christmas Carol
Tied
Tamed
Twisted
Holy Frigging Matrimony
Tangled

EverAfter Romance
A Division of Diversion Publishing Corp.
443 Park Avenue South, Suite 1008
New York, New York 10016
www.EverAfterRomance.com

Photography: Michael Stokes Photography
Cover Design: By Hang Le

This is a work of fiction. Names, characters, places and incidents either are the product of the author's imagination or are used fictitiously. Any resemblance to actual persons, living or dead, events or locales is entirely coincidental.

For more information, email info@diversionbooks.com

First EverAfter Romance edition February 2017.
ISBN: 978-1-68230-776-2

For all those who
love books and stories,
heroes and heroines,
romance and adventure,
pages and words.

CHAPTER 1

Henry

"**B**alls."

I sliced it.

At least I think that's the correct term. Spliced? Diced? Minced? I'm not sure. I was never a fan of golf. It's too slow. Too quiet. Too bloody *boring*. I like my sports the way I like to fuck—wild, loud and dirty.

Football is more my game. Or rugby. Full body contact. Polo is all right too.

Hell, at this point, I'd settle for an energetic Quidditch match.

"What was that, Your Highness?" Sir Aloysius inquires.

I pass the club to Miles, my caddie, and turn briskly to face the men responsible for my afternoon of torture.

"I said, *balls.*"

Lord Bellicksbub, pronounced fittingly similarly to Beelzebub, Earl of Pennington, covers his gray beard with his aged hand and coughs, his eyes darting away uncomfortably. Because I'm not supposed to say things like that anymore. It's *inappropriate*. Crass. Beneath the station of the Crown Prince, heir to the throne of Wessco. Which is the title I'm now saddled with, thanks to my older brother falling in love—the bastard—abdicating the throne, and marrying his wonderful American girl.

In the last year, if I've been told once, I've been told a thousand times—the heir apparent must act *properly*.

But I've never been very good at doing what I'm told.

It's a problem.

Or a reflex. If they say left, I go right. If they say sit, I jump. If they say behave, I get drunk and spend the weekend screwing all three of the Archbishop's triplet nieces.

They were nice girls. I wonder what they're doing this Friday?

No—I take that back. I'm not wondering that. Because that was the old Henry. The fun, carefree Henry that everyone wanted to be around.

Now I have to be the Henry no one wants to hang around with. Serious. Scholarly. Upstanding, even if it kills me—and it definitely might. Decorum is what my grandmother, the Queen, demands. It's what Parliament—members like Aloysius and Beelzebub—expect. It's what my people need. They're all counting on me. Depending on me. To lead them into the future. To be good.

To be . . . King.

Christ, my stomach rolls every time I think the word. When someone says it aloud I gag. If I'm supposed to be the Great Royal Hope for my country, we're all well and truly fucked.

"Point well made, Prince Henry," Sir Aloysius says. "The brand of balls makes all the difference."

He's full of it. He knows exactly what I meant. But this is how politics is played. With fakery and false smiles and butcher knives to the back.

I hate politicking even more than I hate golf.

But this is my life now.

Aloysius narrows his eyes at his caddie. "We'd best have decent balls on the next outing or I'll personally ensure you never work the links again. Apologize to the Prince for your incompetence."

The young, now pale-faced boy bows low. "I'm terribly sorry, Your Highness."

And my stomach rolls again.

How did Nicholas put up with this for all those years? I used to think he was a drama king. A downer and a whiner.

Now I understand. I've walked a mile in his shoes—and they're filled with shit.

You would think having your arse constantly kissed would be enjoyable, even just a little. But when it's a nest of snakes trying to latch on—offering a rim job with their flicking, forked tongues—it's revolting.

"No worries," I tell the lad, because I have a feeling if I make an issue out of it, Aloysius will take it out on him.

The caddies fall behind as we walk toward the green.

"What are your thoughts on the repatriation legislation, Your Highness?" Beelzebub asks casually.

"Reparti-what?" I reply without thinking.

"Repatriation," Aloysius says. "Allowing corporations that have been sanctioned for frivolous labor violations to bring back overseas funds to Wessco, without penalty. It will allow them to create thousands of working-class jobs. The legislation has been stalled in Parliament for weeks. I'm surprised Her Majesty hasn't mentioned it to you."

She probably did. Along with ten thousand other facts and figures and bits and pieces of legislation, information, and legalities that I need to know yesterday. I'm not an idiot—I can actually be rather brilliant when I feel like it. I always did well in school.

It's just difficult to be interested in things I have no interest in.

At first my grandmother sent me information via emails— memos. But after we crashed the Palace's server, she began having them printed out for me. Probably a whole forest worth of paper is sitting in my room right now, waiting for me.

Sorry, environment.

I may be shit at politicking, but putting on a happy face and covering up my shortcomings is something I'm a master at. Playing the part. Pretending.

I've been doing it my whole life.

"Yes, of course, repatriation. I thought you said *repetrification*, which I'm just familiarizing myself with, but I believe will be a cause very close to my heart."

At their baffled expressions, I cross my arms, lower my head, and explain solemnly, "Repetrification is the distribution of abandoned pets to the elderly. I'll send you a memo on it."

Lord Bellicksbub nods. "Interesting."

Sir Aloysius agrees. "Indeed."

And that, ladies and gents, is my idea of a hole in one.

Aloysius takes the putter from his caddie and gives it a test swing before approaching his ball. As he sets up he asks me, "And as for repatriation? Does that also sound like a worthy cause to you?"

This time I try to think before I speak. Granny would be so proud.

After a moment, I nod. "More opportunity for the working class is always a positive thing. I think it's a good idea."

Beelzebub smiles slowly, his yellow teeth glinting in the cool afternoon sun.

"Excellent."

"What were you *thinking?*"

Turns out Granny isn't so proud after all.

She slaps the *Sunday Times* on her desk, letting the headline do the yelling for her.

CROWN REVERSES STANCE – SUPPORTS
CONTROVERSIAL REPATRIATION

From my chair, across from the Queen's mighty desk, I point at the paper. "That's not what I said."

I should have known when I was summoned here that something was wrong. Being called to the Queen's office is not so different from being ordered to see the headmaster—no good ever comes from it.

She scowls down at me, the lines around her mouth sharper and deeper than they were a year ago. I have that effect on people.

"We have lobbied for months to derail this legislation. The only thing preventing a passing vote has been our strenuous disapproval. And now you, in one stroke, have undone all of that work."

My skin feels tight and itchy beneath my suit. I push a hand through my hair, which I've been told is in need of a trim. Which is exactly why it's almost touching my shoulders.

"I didn't undo anything! It was an offhand remark. A conversation."

The Queen braces her hands on the desk, leaning forward. "You are the Crown Prince—you don't have the luxury of 'offhand' remarks. You speak for the House of Pembrook and your every word, action, and breath has the potential to be twisted and regurgitated by whichever side finds it useful. We have discussed this, Henry."

I used to be Granny's favorite. We had a special relationship. She was always amused by my stories and adventures. That went up in smoke the day I was named her successor. She's never amused by me anymore—hell, I don't think she even likes me.

"Did you even bother to read our stance on the subject? I had Christopher send it to you weeks ago."

Christopher is the Queen's private secretary—her lackey. In his off time I suspect he walks around with a gimp ball in his mouth with her photo on it.

"I haven't had the time."

"You haven't *made* the time."

When excuses fall flat, deflection is always the way to go.

"You were the one who insisted I attend that stupid golf outing with Arseholes One and Two."

Her words are clipped and quick—like the rapid fire of a machine gun. "Because I foolishly thought you were familiar with the phrase 'keep your friends close and your enemies closer.' Silly me."

My nostrils flare. "I didn't ask for any of this!"

To be put in this position. To be weighed down with this crushing responsibility. I never wanted the keys to the kingdom—I was happy with just coming and going through the damn door.

My grandmother straightens and lifts her chin. Unmoved and unwavering.

"No, you weren't my first choice either."

Ouch.

A gut-punch from a seventy-eight-year-old lady shouldn't do much damage. But coming from a woman I actually admire, who's the closest I've had to a mother since I was ten years old? It hurts.

So I react the way I always have. I lean back in my chair, resting my ankle on my opposite knee, a smirk on my lips as far as the eye can see.

"Well, it looks like we're in the same boat, Granny. We should rename the Palace of Wessco—do you prefer the Titanic or the Hindenburg?"

She doesn't flinch or blink and she sure as hell doesn't smile. Her gray eyes are as sharp and glinting as the blade of a guillotine.

And just as lethal.

"You make jokes. If this legislation passes, it will roll back protections for low-wage workers. Exposing them to unfair and possibly dangerous labor practices. Do you think they'll laugh at your jokes then, Henry?"

Damn, she's good. Mother-guilt is effective—but queen-guilt is a whole other level.

My smirk is slapped from my face.

"I'll put out a statement explaining that I was misled by Sir Aloysius and my words were taken out of context."

She shakes her head. "Which will only serve to tell the world that you're a fool who can be easily misled."

"Then I'll put out a statement saying I've reflected on the issue and changed my mind."

"Which will demonstrate that your word cannot be trusted—that your opinions are fluid and you do not mean what you say."

Christ, it's like a Chinese finger trap—the harder you struggle, the stronger it holds. I don't smoke, but I could sure use a cigarette right about now. Or a shot of whiskey.

A pistol might also be the way to go.

"Then what the hell am I supposed to do?"

"Nothing," she hisses. "I will fix this. You will go to Guthrie House and stay there. Do not speak to anyone; do not entertain guests. Just . . . read, Henry. Educate yourself—for all our sakes."

And that is how a queen sends a prince to his room.

She turns around, gazing out the window, her small, wrinkly hands folded tightly behind her back.

I stand and lift my hand toward her, meaning to say . . . something. An apology or a promise to do better. But after a moment it drops back to my side. Because it won't matter—I've already been dismissed.

I walk purposefully through the door of Guthrie House—the historical home of the Heir Apparent and my residence for the last year. Home Prison Home. I take the stairs two at a time to my bedroom. It feels good to have a purpose, a direction, a plan.

And my plan is to drink until I forget my fucking name. All of them.

The pages that cover the walls flutter like birds' wings as I breeze into the room. I wasn't joking when I said my grandmother had sent me a forest's worth of documents. I taped them all around the room so I can read while I dress, fall asleep, first wake up. I have to keep my eyes closed when I rub one out—governmental doctrines are a boner-killer. I'm also secretly hoping to absorb the information through sheer proximity. Hasn't worked so far; osmosis is bullshit.

I shrug out of my navy suit—a constricting, uncomfortable thing. Though I've been told I wear it like a boss, it's not my style. Every time I put it on it feels like I'm sliding into someone else's skin.

I remember when I was five or six, I tried on one of Dad's suits. Mum took a dozen photos, laughing at my adorableness. I wonder if they're in the attic somewhere or, more likely, in the possession of the royal historian who'll publish them after I'm dead. To prove that Prince Henry was a real boy, once upon a time.

I idolized my father. He always seemed so tall to me . . . larger than life. He was wise and sure, there wasn't a job he couldn't do—but he had a playful streak as well. A bit of a rule-breaker. He'd take Nicholas and me to concerts and amusement parks even though it turned the security team's hair gray. He didn't mind if we played rough or dirty. Once he walked out of a meeting with the Prime Minister to join in a snowball fight we were having in the courtyard.

Some days, it feels like I'm still wearing my dad's suit. And no matter how hard I try . . . it'll never fit.

"What do you think you're doing?" my crusty butler Fergus asks, glaring down at the ball of suit on the floor.

I shrug a faded T-shirt over my head and button my favorite jeans. "I'm going to The Goat."

He harrumphs predictably. "The Queen tol' you to stay put."

I have two theories on how Fergus always seems to know the things he does: either he has the whole palace wired for sound and video, which he observes from some secret control room or it's the all-knowing, all-seeing "lazy" eye. One day I may ask him—though he'll probably just call me a cretin for asking.

I step into a worn pair of combat boots. "Exactly. And we both know I'm rubbish at doing what I'm told. Have the car brought around."

CHAPTER 2

Henry

I f the capital were a uni campus, The Horny Goat would be my safe space. My cocoon. My Snuggie—if those came with bottles of alcohol in their pockets.

It's an historical landmark, one of the oldest buildings in the city—with a leaky roof, crooked walls, and perpetually sticky floorboards. Rumor has it, way back in the day it was a brothel—which is quite poetic. Not because of the debauchery, but because of the secrets these walls have always held. And still do. Not a single news story about my brother or me has ever leaked out from under its rickety door. Not one drunken royal quote uttered here has ever been repeated or reprinted.

What happens in Vegas doesn't always stay in Vegas—but what happens at The Goat never sees the light of day.

The man responsible for the hush-hush environment is the owner, Evan Macalister—The Goat's been in his family for generations. When I slide onto the bar stool, he's the stout, flannel-shirt-wearing bloke who puts a frothy pint in front of me.

I hold up my palm. "Step aside, Guinness—this is a job for whiskey."

He grabs a bottle from behind the bar, pouring me a shot. "Rough day at the Palace, Your Highness?"

"They're all I seem to have lately." I bring the shot to my lips, tilt my head back, and swallow it down.

Most people drink to dull the senses, to forget. But the burn that singes my throat is a welcome pain. It makes me feel awake. Alive. It gives me focus.

I motion for another.

"Where's Meg tonight?" I ask.

She's Macalister's daughter, and a former late-night rendezvous of my brother's before he met little Olive. I'm not picky when it comes to women, I don't mind seconds and there's nothing sloppy about Meg—but I wouldn't fuck her even if the world were ending. My one rule when it comes to the opposite sex is to not dip my wick anywhere remotely near where my brother's has been.

That's just disgusting.

Still, I'd rather be looking at her pretty face—and arse.

"She's out with the lad she's been seeing. Tristan or Preston or some other girl's blouse name like that." He pours a shot for himself, muttering, "He's a useless bastard."

"Aren't we all?"

He chuckles. "That's what the wife likes to remind me of. Accordin' to her I was hopeless before she got her hands on me."

I raise my glass. "To good women—may they never stop seeing us as we could be, and not what we are."

"Amen." He taps his shot glass to mine and we both drain our glasses.

"I'll drink to that."

This quip comes from a petite brunette who slips onto the stool beside me.

I can practically feel James, my light-haired, stalwart security shadow, watching us from his spot near the door. I'm used to security detail, it's not new, but in the last year it's gotten heavier, tighter—like a noose.

"What'll you have, Miss?" Macalister asks.

"Whatever Prince Henry is having," she replies with a smile, dropping enough bills on the bar to pay for both our drinks.

I like women. No, I love women. The way they move, how they think, the sound of their voices, the scent of their skin—their warmth and softness. But there's nothing soft about this woman. She's all angles—prominent cheekbones, taut limbs, a pointy chin and dark hair cut in a severe bob just below her ears. Not unattractive—but slim and sharp like an arrow. She sounds American and looks near my age, but there's an aggressive air about her that I've only encountered in middle-aged women. Cougars. I adore cougars—women who are experienced enough to know exactly what they want and confident enough to say it out loud.

I'm intrigued. And horny. I haven't had a good, thorough shag since . . . Nicholas's wedding. Christ—it's been *months*. No wonder I'm a basket case.

Macalister fills a mug with Guinness and sets a shot in front of her. Then he refills my shot glass and makes himself busy down at the other end of the bar.

I turn in my seat, lifting my glass. "Cheers."

Her eyes are ice blue. "Bottoms up."

I wink. "One of my favorite positions."

She gives a snort, then downs her shot like a pro. Licking her lips, she eyes my left forearm. "Nice tattoo."

It's two tattoos, actually. The Royal Coat of Arms begins below my wrist and under it, the military crest of Wessco. I had the first done when I was sixteen, when I slipped my security detail after curfew at boarding school and went into town with a few friends. I thought I could wear long sleeves and my grandmother would never know. That illusion lasted exactly one day—that's how long it took for photos of me at the tattoo parlor to be splashed across all the papers. I had the second added a few years ago—just after basic training—with the lads from my unit.

"Thanks."

She holds out her hand. "I'm Vanessa Steele."

Definitely American. If she were from Wessco, she would bow. I shake her hand; it's dry and smooth. "Henry. But you already know that."

"I do. You're a difficult man to get in touch with."

I sip my pint. "Then how about I finish my drink and you can touch me till your heart's content, love."

She laughs, eyes gleaming. "You're even better than I imagined." She taps a red fingernail on the wood bar. "I have a proposition for you."

"And I do so enjoy being propositioned. Your place or mine?" Then I snap my fingers, remembering. "We will have to stop by the Palace. There's an NDA you're supposed to sign—a technicality. Then we can get right to the good part."

Vanessa braces her elbow on the bar. "Not that kind of proposition. I don't want to sleep with you, Henry."

"Who said anything about sleeping? I'm talking about sex. Good sex. Lots of it."

That puts a flush on her pretty cheeks and she laughs. "I don't want to have sex with you."

I pat her hand. "Now you're just being silly. The cat-and-mouse game can be tantalizing, but it's not necessary." My voice drops to a whisper. "I'm a sure thing."

Her smile is sly and confident. "So I hear. But this is a business opportunity, and I never mix business with pleasure."

And as quick as that, my interest drops. These days, "business" is the most effective cold shower. "Pity."

"It doesn't have to be. I'm a television producer. *Matched*—have you heard of it?"

I squint, recalling. "One of those reality dating shows, isn't it? *Survivor*, but with cat fights and string bikinis?"

"That's right."

Out of the corner of my eye I notice Macalister motion to one of his bouncers—a strapping, thick-necked bloke. Vanessa must notice as well, because she speaks more quickly.

"I'm putting together a special edition—a *royal* edition— and I want you to be the star. We'll take care of everything, make all the arrangements—twenty beautiful blue bloods in one castle and all you have to do is let them fall all over themselves for you. It'll be a month-long, nonstop party. And in the end, you can check off your most important royal duty: choosing your queen."

As far as pitches go, hers isn't half bad. The slumbering, neglected part of me that remembers easy, simple, laid-back days stirs and stretches. It's that feeling you get in the coldest nights of winter—a yearning for sweet, summer sun.

The bouncer stands behind her. "Time to go, Miss."

Vanessa rises from her stool. "Think of me as the female Billy the Kid." She winks. "I'll make you famous."

"I'm already famous."

"But you're not enjoying it anymore, are you, Henry? I can do something for you that no one else can—I will make famous fun again." She slides her card across the bar. "Think about it, then call me."

I watch her back as she struts across the bar and out the door. And though I have no intention of taking her up on the interesting offer, I slip her card into my wallet. Just in case.

The eighties are a sorely underrated decade in terms of musical composition. They don't get nearly the respect they deserve. I try to use my platform in the world to bring attention to this travesty by singing eighties ballads whenever I get the chance.

Like right now, as I sing "What About Me" by Moving Pictures on the karaoke stage. It was their one-hit wonder and a soul-stirring exercise in self-pity. My eyes are closed as I belt out the lyrics and sway behind he microphone.

Not in time to the music—I'm so pissed, I'm lucky to still be standing at all.

Usually I play the guitar too, but my fine-motor functions fell by the wayside hours ago. I'm a fantastic musician—not that anyone really notices. That talent gets lost in the shadow of the titles, the same way the talented offspring of two accomplished stars get discounted by the weight of their household name.

My mother gave me my love of music—she played several instruments. I had tutors, first for the piano, then the violin—but it was the guitar that really stuck with me. The karaoke stage at The Goat used to be my second home and in the last few hours, I've given serious consideration to moving in beneath it.

If Harry Potter was the Boy Under the Stairs, I could be the Prince Under the Stage. Why the fuck not?

As I delve into the chorus for the second time, voices whisper on the periphery of my consciousness. I hear them, but don't really listen.

"Christ, how long's he been like this?"

I like that voice. It's soothing. Deep and comforting. It reminds me of my brother's, but it's not him. Because Nicholas is in a land far, far away.

"He's had a rough go of it."

And that sounds like Simon—my brother's best mate. He checks up on me from time to time, because he's a good man.

"It's been particularly difficult the last few months," Simon says—not to be confused with the electronic game.

"Months?" the smooth voice chokes.

"We didn't want to concern you until there was something to be concerned about."

That voice is a beauty. It could almost pass for Simon's

stunning and frighteningly direct wife, Franny. I wonder if Franny has a twin sister? I would so hit that, if she does.

"James contacted me when he refused to go home. In the last two days he's gone from bad to—"

"—rock bottom," Franny says, finishing Simon's sentence. They're cute like that.

Hashtag relationship goals.

"Wow. You royal guys don't do anything halfway, do you?" a pretty, distinctly American voice chimes in. "Even your mental breakdowns are historic."

The song ends and after a moment, I open my eyes.

One lone patron at a table in front claps, the ash from the cigarette between his fingers falling in slow motion to the floor.

And then I look up.

And my eyes absorb a glorious sight.

My big brother, Nicholas, standing tall and straight by the bar, his face etched with worry. It may just be a fantasy. A delusion. But I'll take what I can get.

I start to smile and move forward, but I forget about the stage—the fact that I'm standing on it. And that first step is an absolute corker. Because a moment later, my whole world goes black.

The next time I open my eyes, I'm on the floor, on my back, staring at the water-stained ceiling of The Horny Goat. And . . . I think there's gum up there. What kind of demented bastard puts chewing gum on the ceiling? Has to be a health hazard.

My brother's face looms over me, blocking out everything else. And sweet, blessed relief surges in my chest. "Nicholas? You're really here?"

"Yes, Henry," he says gently. "I'm really here." His big hand rests on my head. "You took quite a fall—are you well?"

Well? I could fucking fly.

"I had the most ridiculous dream." I point at my brother. "You were there." I point at Simon beside him. "And you." Then Franny, all of them huddled on the floor around me. "And you too. You . . . abdicated the throne, Nicholas. And they all wanted to make me king." A maniacal laugh passes my lips . . . until I turn to the right and see dark blue eyes, sweet lips, and black, swirling hair.

Then I scream like a girl. "Ahhhh!"

It's Olivia. My brother's wife. His very American wife.

I turn back to Nicholas. "It wasn't a dream, was it?"

"No, Henry."

I lie back down on the floor. "Fuuuuuck."

Then I feel sort of bad.

"Sorry, Olive. You know I think you're top-notch."

She smiles kindly. "It's okay, Henry. I'm sorry you're having a hard time."

I scrub my hand over my face, trying to think clearly.

"It's all right. This is a better, new plan—I won't have to live under the stage now."

"You were going to live under the stage?" Nicholas asks.

I wave my hand. "Forget it. It was Potter's stupid idea. Boy Wonder Wizard, my arse."

And now my brother looks really worried.

I gesture to him. "But you're here now. You can take me with you back to the States."

"Henry . . ."

"Give me your tired, poor, huddled masses yearning to be free—that describes me perfectly! I'm a huddled mass, Nicholas!"

He squeezes my arms, shaking just a bit. "Henry. You can't move to America."

I grasp his shirt. And my voice morphs into an eight-year-old boy's, confessing he sees dead people. "But she's so mean, Nicholas. She's. So. Mean."

He taps my back. "I know."

Nicholas and Simon drag me up, holding on so that I stay on my feet. "But we'll figure it out," Nicholas says. "It's going to be all right."

I shake my head. "You keep saying that. I'm starting to think you don't know what the hell you're talking about."

CHAPTER 3

Henry

After that, things are fuzzy. Reality is reduced to snapshots. The car ride to the palace. Vomiting on the rose bushes that my great-great-great-aunt, Lady Adaline, commanded be planted outside the palace. Nicholas and Simon tucking me into bed as Olive comments on the papers taped to the walls—saying it reminds her of Russell Crowe's shed in *A Beautiful Mind*. Then . . . there's only the gentle abyss.

But the void doesn't last long. Because I'm an insomniac—the affliction of champions. It's been this way for as long as I can remember. I only ever sleep for a handful of hours, even on the nights when my blood is mostly alcohol. With the bedside clock reading one a.m., I drag myself on unsteady legs to the kitchen, using the wall for support. My stomach grumbles with the thought of Cook's biscuits.

I don't recall eating at The Goat—how long was I there? A day? Maybe two. I smell my armpit and flinch. Definitely two. *Bloody hell.*

After stuffing my face and taking a few treats for the road, I stumble along the palace hallways. It's what I do at night—it's given me a new appreciation for American mall-walkers. I can't stay in a room, any room, without the walls closing in. It feels good to move, even if I'm not going anywhere.

Eventually I wander over to the blue drawing room, near the Queen's private quarters. The door's slightly ajar—enough to see that the light is on, smell the firewood burning in the hearth, and hear the voices inside.

I lean my head against the door jamb and listen.

"You look well, my boy," Granny says. And there's a warm affection in her tone that I'm familiar with. Because it used to be reserved for me.

Jealous much? A little bit, yeah.

"Marriage agrees with you."

"Marriage *to Olivia* agrees with me," my brother returns.

"Touché."

I hear the clink of the crystal decanter and liquid being poured. My guess is sherry.

"Is Olivia sleeping?" the Queen asks.

"Yes. She nodded off hours ago. The jet lag hit her hard."

"I was hoping it was because she was pregnant."

My brother chuckle-chokes. "We've been married for three months."

"When I was married three months, I was two and a half months gone with your father. What are you waiting for?"

I can practically hear him shrug. "There's no rush. We're . . . enjoying each other. Taking our time."

"But you plan on having children?"

"Of course. One day."

There's the scrape of a chair on the wood floor and I imagine them sitting side by side, settling in for a fireside chat.

"So tell me, Nicholas, now that the dust has settled—do you have any regrets?"

His voice is soft but his tone is firm as iron.

"Not a one."

My grandmother hums, and I picture her sipping her nightcap in the elegant way she does everything.

"But I am curious," Nicholas says. "If it had been you—if

you had had to choose between Grandfather and the throne, what would you have done?"

"I loved your grandfather deeply—I still do—you know that. But, if I had been forced to choose between the two, I would not have picked him. Besides my children, my sovereignty has always been the love of my life."

There's a heavy pause. Then Nicholas says quietly, "It was never that way for me. You understand that, don't you?"

"I see that now, yes."

"I always knew it was expected, and I was determined to do it well—but I never loved it. I never wanted it, not really."

"But you're content now, yes? With the restaurants, the charity you and Olivia and Mr. Hammond oversee?"

It takes a moment for him to answer and when he does, Nicholas's voice is wistful. "I'm not content—I'm happy. Ridiculously happy. More than I ever dreamed was possible. Every day."

"Good," my grandmother proclaims.

"But there is one thing," Nicholas says, "one chink in the rainbow." His words go soft and scratchy, like they've been waiting in his throat for a long time. "I know I disappointed you. It wasn't my intention, but it happened just the same. I didn't forewarn you or discuss it with you. I defied my queen, and you raised me to do better. And for that I am sorry. Truly."

There's a tap of crystal on wood—the Queen setting her glass down on the side table. "Listen to me very carefully, Nicholas, because I will only say this once. You have never disappointed me."

"But—"

"I raised you to be a leader. You assessed the situation, considered your options, and you made a choice. You didn't falter; you didn't wait for permission. You acted. That . . . is what leaders do."

There's a lightness in his response, a relief.

"All right."

There's another comfortable pause, and I imagine my brother taking a drink. Possibly draining the glass. Because then he says, "Speaking of raising leaders . . ."

"Yes," the Queen sighs. "We may as well address the drunken elephant in the room," she quips sharply. "He's . . . how do they say it in the States? A hot mess."

"He is that."

I turn, bracing my back against the wall and sliding down to sit on the floor. It's not that I'm unaccustomed to people talking about me—hell, my pros and cons are often discussed openly, even when I'm standing in the same room. But this . . . this is going to be different. Worse.

"Do you remember the holiday production Henry was in at school? It was the last Christmas with Mum and Dad—he had the starring role. Scrooge." Nicholas chuckles.

"Vaguely. I didn't attend the performance."

"No, neither did I. Dad spoke with me about it. They were concerned that if I went, the press and his teachers and classmates would be so busy fawning over me that Henry would be lost in the shuffle. And they were right." The chair creaks as my brother shifts. "He's spent his entire life in my shadow. And now he's front and center, in the hot glare of the spotlight. It's only natural he'll squint for a bit. You have to give him time to adjust."

"He doesn't have time."

"Plan on dying any day soon?" Nicholas teases.

"Of course not. But we both know the unexpected happens. He must be ready. You don't understand, Nicholas."

"I understand perfectly. I'm the only person in the world who does."

"No, you do not. Before you could walk, you were trained to take the throne. A thousand small things happened around you daily that you wouldn't have even perceived. It was in the way others spoke to you, the conversations you had, the topics you were taught, and the manner in which they were conveyed. Henry has a lifetime of catching up to do."

"Which he'll never be able to do if you break him," Nicholas says harshly. "If you convince him in a thousand small daily ways that he'll never be enough. That he'll never get it right."

Silence falls for several beats. Until my grandmother quietly asks, "Do you know the worst part about growing old?"

"Erectile dysfunction?" my brother replies dryly.

"Oh, you needn't worry about that," the Queen responds, her tone every bit as dry. "It's in the genes, and your grandfather was a stallion until the day he died."

I smother a grin. Because, like the Americans say, when you mess with the bull . . .

"Right." My brother quips. "No more sherry for you."

"The worst part about growing old," Granny continues, "is knowing that soon you will leave the ones you cherish most to carry on without you. And if they are unprepared . . . vulnerable . . . it is a terrifying prospect."

Only the crackle of the fire breaks the stillness.

Then the Queen declares unequivocally, "They will eat him alive. On his current course, Henry will fail spectacularly."

My chest constricts so tight it feels like my bones may crack.

Because she's right.

"He won't."

"You don't know that," she swipes back.

"I damn well do! I never would have abdicated otherwise."

"What?"

"Don't mistake me—I wouldn't have married anyone but Olivia, and I would've waited a lifetime if I had to, until the laws were changed. But I didn't because I knew in my heart and soul that Henry will not just be a good king, he will be better than I ever could've been."

For a moment I don't breathe. I can't. The shock of my brother's words has knocked the air right out of my lungs.

Granny's too, if her whisper is any indication.

"You truly believe that?"

"Absolutely. And, frankly, I'm disheartened that you don't."

"Henry has never been one to rise to the occasion," she states plainly.

"He's never needed to," my brother insists. "He's never been asked—not once in his whole life. Until now. And he will not only rise to the occasion . . . he will soar beyond it."

The Queen's voice is hushed, like she's in prayer.

"I want to believe that. More than I can say. Lend me a bit of your faith, Nicholas. Why are you so certain?"

Nicholas's voice is rough, tight with emotion.

"Because . . . he's just like Mum."

My eyes close when the words reach my ears. Burning and wet. There's no greater compliment—not to me—not ever.

But, Christ, look at me . . . it's not even close to true.

"He's exactly like her. That way she had of knowing just what a person needed—whether it was strength or guidance, kindness or comfort or joy—and effortlessly giving it to them. The way people used to gravitate to her . . . at parties, the whole room would shift when she walked in . . . because everyone wanted to be nearer to her. She had a light, a talent, a gift—it doesn't matter what it's called—all that matters is that Henry has it too. He doesn't see it in himself, but I do. I always have."

There's a moment of quiet and I imagine Nicholas leaning in closer to the Queen.

"The people would have followed me or Dad for the same reason they follow you—because we are dependable, solid. They trust our judgment; they know we would never let them down. But they will follow Henry because they *love* him. They'll see in him their son, brother, best friend, and even if he mucks it up now, they will stick with him because they will want him to succeed. I would have been respected and admired, but Grandmother . . . he will be beloved. And if I have learned anything since the day Olivia came into my life, it's that more than reasoning or duty, honor or tradition . . . love is stronger."

For a time, there is no sound save for the occasional pop of the fire and tinkling of glasses, as the Queen considers. Contemplates before she acts wisely. It's what she does.

What leaders do.

I've paid enough attention through the years to know that much. And I'm self-aware enough to admit that I never have.

The Queen inhales deeply. "Nothing I have attempted has improved the situation. What do you suggest, Nicholas?"

"He needs space to . . . acclimate. Time outside the spotlight to process the scope of his new situation and duties. To learn what he needs to, in his way. And make it his own."

"Space." The Queen taps her finger on the table. "Very well. If space is what the boy needs, then space he shall have."

I'm not sure I like the sound of this.

Two weeks later, I know I don't.

Anthorp Castle.

She sent me to fucking Anthorp Castle.

It's not the middle of nowhere—it's the end of nowhere. On the coast, with jagged cliffs and icy ocean on one side, forest on the other—the nearest thing resembling a town an hour's drive away. This isn't "space"; it's banishment.

"Banishment! Be merciful, say 'death.' For exile hath more terror in his look."

Romeo was a pussy, but at this moment, I feel him.

I sit in the middle of the massive four-post bed, strumming my guitar to the drumbeat of the moon-soaked waves crashing below my open window. The air is cool, but the fire burning bright in the fireplace makes up for it. My fingers pluck out the familiar notes of Leonard Cohen's "Hallelujah." It's a comforting song. Depressing and sad, but comforting in its easy repetition.

Disgusted with myself, I set my guitar aside and punch my arms into my robe. Then I wander the castle a bit, saying hello to the creepy suits of armor that stand sentry at the end of each hallway. Though I could use the rest, I don't want to even try going back to sleep.

Because the dreams have come back. Nightmares.

They were relentless when I was first discharged from military service—reminders of the attack that killed a group of soldiers at an outpost just after I visited. I got a reprieve after I confessed to Nicholas and Olivia what happened and they suggested I reach out to the families of the fallen men.

But the night I stepped foot in Anthorp Castle they returned with a vengeance—and a cruel new twist. Now, when I crawl to the bodies that litter the ground and turn them over to check for survivors, it's not the soldiers' lifeless faces that stare back at me. It's Nicholas's face, and Olivia's . . . Granny's. I wake up gasping and dripping with cold sweat.

Not fucking fun.

So tonight, I stroll.

Eventually I end up in the library on the first floor. I fall into the chair behind the desk, take a page from one stack of documents, and read over the laws governing the marriage of the Crown Prince, which is basically a list of requirements for the bride:

"Verifiable aristocracy in the lineage, within a recognized marital union."

Though, farther down, it states bastards are acceptable in a pinch. How open-minded.

"Certified documentation of Wessconian citizenship by natural birth."

As opposed to hatchlings or clones, I suppose.

"Virginity as evidenced by the insertion of the trusted Royal Internist's two fingers into the vagina, to confirm intact hymen tissue."

Whoever thought this up was one sick son of a bitch. And definitely male. I doubt they'd be so exacting if the law required a prostate exam for members of Parliament.

"I'm makin' tea. Do you want a cup?"

I look up to see Fergus standing in the doorway, in his robe and slippers, his face scrunched and crabby.

"I didn't know you were awake, Fergus."

"Who can sleep with you prowling around the halls like a randy cat?"

"Sorry."

"Do you want a cup or not?"

I put the paper back in its pile.

"No, thank you."

He turns, then pauses, and looks back at me, quietly adding, "It was the same with the Queen."

"What was the same?"

"The lack of sleep. When she was a lass, after just three hours she'd be up and about like that grotesque rodent with the bass drum."

He means the Energizer Bunny.

"I didn't know that about Granny," I say softly.

He hobbles over to the bookshelf, running his finger along the bindings before sliding a thick book out.

"Reading used to help. This was her favorite."

The heavy volume gets dropped on the desk with a thud.

Hamlet. Interesting.

"You realize they all die? The King, Queen, and sweet Prince are all dead at the end."

Not exactly the stuff of pleasant dreams—especially for my family.

"I said it was your grandmother's choice, not mine."

He shuffles off without another word.

I flip through the pages. And talk to myself.

"*This above all, to thine own self be true*. Easier said than done, Polonius."

Because this isn't supposed to be my life. None of it is me. The title, the responsibility, wandering around this cold, ancient stone behemoth with nothing but the echo of my own damn footsteps for company. And although I'm supposed to be "acclimating," it's just not happening.

Because Nicholas is wrong. I'm his blind spot; I always have been. I used it to my advantage when it suited me. He is good and well-meaning . . . but he is wrong.

And we're all fucked because of it.

The silence closes in, making me twitchy. Reminding me of a damn tomb. And the words repeat in my head like a whispering ghost.

To thine own self be true, Henry.

Maybe that's the problem. And the solution.

I hop to my feet, pacing. Thinking—I think better when I move. I think a lot better after a good fuck, but, if wishes were horses . . .

The point is, I haven't felt like myself in a long time. I need to get my groove back. I need to get my freak on. I need to do me for a while.

And then I need to do ten women—maybe a full dozen.

I'm shit at politicking and golfing, terrible at wise decision-making or doing what I'm told, but what I've always been good at is entertaining. Putting on a show. Making people happy. I'm the life of the party and one hell of a host.

I push and pull at the idea—like Play-Doh—and after a moment, it starts to take shape. I didn't ask for this, but it's time I own it. If I'm going to fail spectacularly, I want to fail my way. Go out with a bang.

And a party. A month-long party, the castle brimming with twenty beautiful women falling all over themselves for my attention. *Matched: Royal Edition* suddenly seems like a bloody fucking brilliant idea.

What could possibly go wrong?

And as if God is speaking to me, the pressure on my shoulders loosens. The weight that's been sitting on my chest, making me think I'm constantly having a goddamn heart attack, relaxes.

And I feel . . . good. In control.

I stand up, leaving the documents and ridiculous laws behind me. I go straight up to my room, grab my wallet off the bureau, and slide out the sharp-edged business card that's still inside.

Then I pick up my mobile and dial.

CHAPTER 4

Sarah

"Oh, balls."

I stare at the email on my mobile—at the summons—from Mr. Haverstrom, my boss. And though the sunny afternoon air is crisp, sweat immediately prickles my forehead.

Annie's blond ponytail snaps like a whip as she turns toward me. "Oh my God, tell me someone sent you a dick pic!" She holds out her hands. "Let me see, let me see! What kind of balls are we talking about? Big balls, odd balls . . .?"

"Schweddy balls?" Willard adds, unhelpfully, from his chair across the small, round patio table.

Annie claps her hands. *SNL* reruns are big in Wessco. "I love that bit." She eats a mouthful of salad off her fork. "Did I ever tell you about Elliot's balls?"

I meaningfully meet Willard's brown eyes, then check the time. Three minutes, seventeen seconds.

That's how long it's been since Annie last mentioned Elliot Stapleworth, her giant douche-canoe ex-boyfriend. He broke it off with her two weeks ago, but she's still hopelessly hung up on him. She deserves so much better. Especially since he's not just any douche-canoe—he's one who's never heard of manscaping.

"They were the hairiest little monsters I'd ever seen. Like

two baby hedgehogs curled between his legs, but not at all in a cute way. I used to get pubes caught in my throat all the time."

There's an image I don't need in my head.

Willard frowns. "What a rude prick. Nothing kills a mood faster. I keep my boys smooth as a baby's bottom."

And that's another one.

I look him straight in the face. "I could've gone my entire life without knowing that."

He winks at me.

Annie leans forward. "But, since we're on the subject, tell us, Willard, are your manly parts . . . proportional?"

Willard is just over four feet ten inches tall, only slightly above the height threshold for dwarfism. But his personality is seven feet high—bold and direct, with clever sarcastic wit to spare. He reminds me of Tyrion Lannister from *Game of Thrones*—only kinder and more handsome.

"Annie!" I gasp, blushing.

She pushes my shoulder. "You know you want to know."

No, I don't. But Willard wants to answer.

"I'm blessedly unproportioned. Just as a blind man's other senses are more developed, God overcompensated me in that department." He wiggles his eyebrows.

She nods. "I'll be sure to tell Clarice when I'm convincing her to let you take her out this Saturday."

Annie is a notoriously bad matchmaker. Though Willard's gotten the business end of her attempts more than once, he keeps letting her try.

What's the definition of insanity again?

Annie looks toward me. "Now, back to your mystery balls, Sarah."

"Mr. Haverstrom—"

She gags. "Mr. Haverstrom? Gross! I bet his bits smell like overcooked green vegetables. You can just tell by that permanently unhappy face. Definitely broccoli balls."

Damn. And I really liked broccoli.

"Sarah wasn't referring to Mr. Haverstrom's literal balls, Annie," Willard explains.

Annie flaps her hands. "Then why'd she bring them up?"

I take off my glasses, cleaning them with the cloth from my pocket. "Mr. Haverstrom sent me an email. I'm to go directly to his office after lunch. It sounds serious."

Saying the words makes my anxiety kick into overdrive. My heart pounds, my head goes light, adrenaline rushes through my veins, and I can feel my pulse in my throat. Even when I know it's silly, even when my brain recognizes there's nothing to be panicked about, in unpredictable situations or when I'm the center of attention, my body reacts like I'm the next victim in a slasher film. The one who's stumbling through the woods with the mask-wearing, machete-wielding psycho just steps behind her. I hate it, but it's unavoidable.

"Remember to breathe slow and steady, Sarah," Willard says. "If anything, he's probably going to offer you a promotion. You're the best in the building; everyone knows that."

Annie and Willard aren't just my friends, they're my coworkers here at Concordia Library. Willard works downstairs in Restoration and Preservation, Annie in the Children's department, while I spend my days in Literature and Fiction. Everyone thinks library science is all about shelving books and sending out overdue notices—but it's so much more.

It's about fostering community and information technology, organization, helping others find the needle in whatever haystack they're looking in. In the same way emergency-room physicians must have diagnoses and treatments at their fingertips, librarians, at least the good ones, need to be familiar with an array of topics.

"I've got the flask I stole from Elliot down in my locker," Annie says.

Time: three minutes, forty-two seconds. And the record of nine minutes, seven seconds continues to hold strong.

"You want a nip before you head over?" Annie offers sweetly.

She's a good friend—like Helen to Jane in *Jane Eyre*. As kind as she is pretty.

I shake my head. Then I pull my big-girl knickers up all the way to my neck. "I'll let you know how it goes."

Annie gives me a thumbs-up with both hands and Willard nods, his brown, wavy hair falling over his forehead like a romance-novel rogue. With a final wave to them both, I leave the small outdoor stone patio where we meet each day for lunch and head inside.

In the cool, shadowed atrium, I close my eyes and breathe in the familiar, comforting scent of books and leather, paper and ink. Before Wessco was its own country, this building was a Scottish cathedral, Concordia Cathedral. There have been updates through the centuries, but wonderfully, the original structure remains—three floors; thick, grand marble columns; arched entryways and high, intricately muraled ceilings. Working here sometimes makes me feel like a priestess—the strong and powerful kind. Especially when I track down a hard-to-find book for someone and the person's face lights up. Or when I introduce a reader to a new series or author. There's privilege and honor in this work—showing people a whole new world, filled with characters and places and emotions they wouldn't have experienced without me. It's magical.

Mark Twain said, *"Find a job you enjoy doing, and you will never have to work a day in your life."*

At Concordia Library, I've yet to work a single day.

My heels click on the stone floor as I head toward the back spiral stairs. I pass the circulation desk, waving to old Maud, who's been volunteering here twenty hours a week since her husband, Melvin, passed away two months ago. Then I spot George at his usual table—he's a regular, a retiree, and lifelong bachelor. I grab two of the local papers off the stack, sliding them in front of him as I go.

"Good afternoon, George."

"It is now, darling," he calls after me.

Along the side wall are a row of computer desks, lined up like soldiers, and I see Timmy Frazier's bright red head bent over a keyboard, where he's typing furiously. Timmy's thirteen years old and a good lad, in the way that good lads still do naughty things. He's got five younger siblings, a longshoreman dad, and a mum who cleans part-time at the estate on top of the hill.

My mother's estate.

Castlebrook is a tiny, beautiful town—one of the smallest in Wessco—an old fishing village that's never thrived, but is just successful enough to keep the inhabitants from leaving in search of greener pastures. We're about a five-hour drive from the capital, and while most of the folks here don't venture too far, we often get visitors from the city looking for a quiet weekend at the seaside.

St. Aldwyn's, where all the local children attend, is just a ten-minute walk away, but I bet Timmy could make it in five.

"Is there a reason you're not in school, Timmy Frazier?"

He smiles crookedly, but doesn't take his eyes off the screen or stop typing. "I'm goin' back but had to ditch fourth and fifth periods to finish this paper due in sixth."

"Have you ever considered completing your assignment the day—or, God forbid, a few days—before it was actually due?"

Timmy shrugs. "Better last moment than never, Sarah."

I chuckle, give his fiery head a rub, and continue up the steps to the third floor.

I'm comfortable with people I know—I can be sociable, even funny with them. It's the new ones and unpredictable situations that tie me up in knots. And I'm about to be bound in a big one.

Damn it to hell.

I stand outside Mr. Haverstrom's door, staring at the black letters of his name stenciled on the frosted glass, listening to the murmur of voices inside. It's not that Mr. Haverstrom is a mean boss—he's a bit like Mr. Earnshaw from *Wuthering Heights*. Even though he doesn't get much page time, his presence is strong and consequential.

I take a breath, straighten my spine, and knock on the door firmly and decisively—the way Elizabeth Bennet would. Because she didn't give a single shit about anything. Then Mr. Haverstrom opens the door, his eyes narrow, his hair and skin pale, his face lined and grouchy—like a squished marshmallow.

On the outside, I nod and breeze into the office, but inside, I cringe and wilt.

Mr. Haverstrom closes the door behind me and I stop short when I see Patrick Nolan in the chair across from Mr. Haverstrom's desk. Pat is the co-head of the Literature and Fiction department with me. He doesn't look like the stereotypical librarian—he looks more like an Olympic triathlete, all taut muscles and broad shoulders and hungry competition in his eyes.

Pat isn't as big of a douche-canoe as Elliot, but close.

I sit down in the unoccupied chair beside Pat while Mr. Haverstrom takes his place behind the desk. "Lady Sarah, I was just explaining to Pat the reason I've asked you both for this meeting."

Don't mistake the "Lady" before my name as a symbol of respect. It's just tradition, the equivalent of "Miss" for the daughter of a countess. There's no real power behind it.

Maybe I'm just being paranoid—that happens—but there's that tight, heavy feeling in my stomach, as if at any moment the thread that's holding it in place is going to snap, sending my vital organ to the floor.

I force myself to speak. "Yes?"

"We have been selected to host this year's Northern District Library Symposium."

This isn't just not good—it's bad. Very, very bad.

"As the host facility, each department is required to give a presentation, and given the size and scope of our Fiction and Literature department, I see no reason why you and Patrick can't give separate but complementary presentations."

And splat goes my stomach. And my spleen. I'm fairly certain the liver's in there somewhere too.

"I'll need your topic and outline by the end of the week to ensure there's no overlap."

My lips open and close, like the mouth of a fish, but there aren't any words. *Breathe!* I need to breathe to talk. *Idiot.*

"Mr. Haverstrom, I'm not sure that I—"

"I'm aware you're not comfortable with public speaking," Mr. Haverstrom says, talking right over me.

That happens. A lot.

"But you're going to have to overcome it. This is an honor and a requirement of your position. Barring an act of God, you will not be excused. If you're unable to fulfill all of your duties, I will unfortunately be forced to replace you with someone who can."

Shit. Damn, damn, shit, shit.

"Yes, sir. I understand."

"Good." He nods. "I'll let you get to it, then."

We all stand, and Pat and I head for the door.

"Lady Sarah," Mr. Haverstrom says, "I'll be happy to go over your presentation with you once it's complete, if that will be helpful to you. I do want you to succeed."

I smile tightly. "Thank you, sir."

Then he shakes Patrick's hand. "Pat, we're still on for racquetball this Saturday?"

"Count on it, Douglas."

Internally, I sigh. More disappointed with myself than

anything else. Because I play racquetball—I'm actually quite good at it. And if I had a shred of Miranda Priestly in me, from *The Devil Wears Prada*, I'd tell them—invite myself along, throw in with the big boys.

But, I don't.

Mr. Haverstrom closes the door, leaving Patrick and me alone in the hallway. Pat smiles slickly, leaning in toward me. I step back until I press against the wall. It's uncomfortable—but not threatening. Mostly because in addition to racquetball I've practiced aikido for years. So if Patrick tries anything funny, he's in for a very painful surprise.

"Let's be honest, Sarah: you know and I know the last thing you want to do is give a presentation in front of hundreds of people—your colleagues."

My heart tries to crawl into my throat.

"So, how about this? You do the research portion, slides and such that I don't really have time for, and I'll take care of the presentation, giving you half the credit of course."

Of course. I've heard this song before—in school "group projects" where I, the quiet girl, did all the work, but the smoothest, loudest talker took all the glory.

"I'll get Haverstrom to agree on Saturday—I'm like a son to him," Pat explains before leaning close enough that I can smell the garlic on his breath. "Let Big Pat take care of it. What do you say?"

I say there's a special place in hell for people who refer to themselves in the third person.

But before I can respond, Willard's firm, sure voice travels down the hall.

"I think you should back off, Nolan. Sarah's not just 'up for it,' she'll be fantastic at it."

Pat waves his hand. "Quiet, midge—the adults are talking."

And the adrenaline comes rushing back, but this time it's not anxiety-induced—it's anger. Indignation.

I push off the wall. "Don't call him that."

"He doesn't mind."

"*I* mind."

He stares at me with something akin to surprise. Then scoffs and turns to Willard. "You always let a woman fight your battles?"

I take another step forward, forcing him to move back. "You think I can't fight a battle because I'm a woman?"

"No, I think you can't fight a battle because you're a woman who can barely string three words together if more than two people are in the room."

I'm not hurt by the observation. For the most part, it's true. But not this time.

I smile slowly, devilishly. Suddenly, I'm Cathy Linton come to life—headstrong and proud.

"There are more than two people standing here right now. And I've got more than three words for you: fuck off, you arrogant, self-righteous swamp donkey."

His expression is almost funny. Like he can't decide if he's more shocked that I know the word *fuck* or that I said it out loud to him—and not in the good way.

Then his face hardens and he points at me. "That's what I get for trying to help your mute arse? Have fun making a fool of yourself."

I don't blink until he's down the stairs and gone.

Willard slow-claps as he walks down the hall to me.

"Swamp donkey?"

I shrug. "It just came to me."

"Impressive." Then he bows and kisses the back of my hand. "You were magnificent."

"Not half bad, right? It felt good."

"And you didn't blush once."

I push my dark hair out of my face, laughing self-consciously.

"Seems like I forget all about being nervous when I'm defending someone else."

Willard nods. "Good. And though I hate to be the twat who points it out, there's something else you should probably start thinking about straight away."

"What's that?"

"The presentation in front of hundreds of people."

And just like that, the tight, sickly feeling washes back over me.

So this is what doomed feels like.

I lean against the wall. "Oh, broccoli balls."

CHAPTER 5

Sarah

After I get off work, I walk to my flat, about half a mile away. My building is plain but well-kept, with a garden and sitting area on the roof. There's a newly married couple with an even newer baby in the unit above me—David, Jessica, and little Barnaby—and an elderly couple, Felix and Belinda, together forty years, in the unit below.

I put my keys in the crystal bowl by the door, like always. Then I slip out of my coat and shoes and put both in the closet. Also, like always.

I don't have a roommate or a pet, so my sitting room is just how I left it this morning, neat and spotless, with its beige sofa and burnt-orange throw pillows, matching drapes, pictures of my mother and sister on the end table and my favorite book covers framed on the walls.

The crowning glory of my sitting room isn't the flat-screen television or the wood-burning stove in the corner. It's the bookcase, poised between the two windows.

Six shelves, as high as the ceiling, made of driftwood. I found it at a Christmas market a few years back. It was a shabby piece then, plain and dull—sort of like me—but I could tell the planks were made of sturdy stuff, and they would not buckle. So I brought it home, sanded and polished it, and placed my dearest and most prized possessions upon it—my collection of first-edition classic novels. The full Jane Austen collection, the Brontë sisters, Dickens—they're all here. Although I enjoy good contemporary romance or chick lit as much as the next woman, these are the ones I come back to—stories that no matter how often I reread them are every bit as moving every time.

The flat is small, with only a sliver of ocean view from the bedroom window, but I pay for it myself—not from the family trust fund.

There's satisfaction in earning one's own money. Self-sufficiency—like knowing how to rub sticks together to start a fire. A survival skill. I could make it in the wilderness if I had to.

Well . . . if the wilderness were Castlebrook, anyway.

The thing is, when you're dependent on others, they hold a part of your happiness in their hands. They can nurture it or crush it at any moment. Your fate doesn't belong to you. I've seen how that works—it's not pretty. My life may be small and simple, but it's all mine.

In the kitchen, I fill the pot for tea. Normally, I'd start dinner now, but it's Wednesday—

Wednesdays and Sundays are dinner days with Mother and Penelope.

I have an hour before I need to leave, so it'll be tea and . . . *Sense and Sensibility* for a bit. It's the perfect read. Just enough drama and angst to be interesting, but mostly light and entertaining, with the happiest ending. Colonel Brandon is my favorite—the ultimate book husband. He made good and upstanding look sexy as all get-out. Someday, I'll meet a man just like him—romantic, steady, and reliable—and I don't give a damn how silly that sounds. How immature or fanciful.

Because I have a theory.

If nightmares can come true, and sometimes they do . . . then so can our happiest dreams.

Once my peppermint tea is ready, I sink into the chaise

lounge in my bedroom, throw a soft, velour blanket over my legs, open my book—and block out the world.

Some people look at their family and wonder if they're adopted. Others hope they are.

I never wonder. Because my mother is so clearly the combination of my and my sister's personalities. Or maybe we're each half of hers. She's reclusive—she hates cities, shuns parties, rarely leaves the estate, and doesn't entertain friends—at least not human ones. She's most content in the greenhouse tending and talking to her flowers. But here, within the confines of her own personal fiefdom, she runs the show. She's colorful and exuberant—just like Penelope. In the last few years she's taken to wearing bright, paisley silk housedresses handmade in China and dyeing her hair a sunrise red—melding into a crossbreed of *Sense and Sensibility*'s Mrs. Dashwood and Shirley MacLaine in her prime.

Some in our social circle call her eccentric. Others call her the Crazy Countess. Penny likes "off her rocker." But I don't think Mother's nutty at all. It's just that she tried living life by other people's rules and it didn't work out. So now, she lives as she likes . . . and everyone else can go to hell.

"Hello, my darling," she greets me in a quiet voice.

My mother's always been soft-spoken, genteel. It's how she was raised. But quiet shouldn't be mistaken for weak. Sometimes the most steely resolve is asserted silently.

Stanhope, our butler, takes my coat, shaking off the raindrops that had started to pour down. Mother guides me toward the dining room with her arm around my lower back, the familiar scent of lilies surrounding her. "Tell me, how are things at the library?"

"Awful."

"Awful? That doesn't sound right. What happened?"

We join Penny at the table, where she taps at her mobile, texting, and over the first course, I recount my tale of woe. Though our weekly dinners are informal, Penelope is dressed to the nines in a royal-blue cocktail dress that flatters her fair skin and light blond hair, swept back in a gentle knot. She always did like to play dress-up and at twenty-three, she'll still take any excuse to glam out.

Unlike other mothers in our station, mine has never pushed me to marry well or date—Penelope dates enough for both of us.

When I finish explaining about the presentation, Mother says, "My poor girl. What are you going to do?"

"I don't really have a choice. I'm going to have to present at the symposium and pray I don't vomit on the audience or pass out."

Penny grins, still gazing at her mobile. "Maybe you should cordon off the first few rows, just in case. You can call them the splash-zone seats."

"That's helpful, Pen, thank you."

She looks up. "This could be good for you, you know. Force you out of your comfort zone."

"The same could be said about your upcoming military service, Penelope," Mother comments.

In Wessco, every citizen, male or female, is required to serve two years in the military.

Penny dramatically slouches back in her chair, throwing her arms wide like Christ on the cross. "It's not the same at all! I'll be a terrible soldier—I'm not cut out for all that marching and climbing and sweating."

She checks her glittery manicure to make sure she hasn't chipped a nail from just talking about it. "I tried convincing them to let me serve my time in the WSO."

The WSO is the Wessco Service Organization—they put on shows and entertain the servicemen. And Penelope has always dreamed of stardom—she's too short to be a model, but certainly melodramatic enough to be an actress.

"That's much more my bag. Sparkly outfits and dancing. But, it's against orders, they said."

"Yes," I smirk. "The military likes to have their orders followed. They're funny like that."

She sticks her tongue out at me.

Before I can decide which obscene gesture to respond with, thunder claps so loudly outside, the china and crystal rattles on the table.

Rain batters the windows and, seconds later, another boom bursts over the house—this one shaking the walls. A shelf gives way, sending decorative plates and figurines falling to the floor, exploding into shards, like tiny glass grenades.

I close my eyes, but it doesn't matter—everything goes gray.

I come to gasping. It's always the way it happens, as if I've been held underwater just until I'm on the cusp of drowning.

"There she is," Mother coos from the chair beside me, while Penelope rubs small circles on my back from the other side.

"It was a long one this time," Penny says with concern. "Over ten minutes."

And the familiar shame tightens and squeezes inside me.

"I'm sorry," I whisper.

"None of that, now," Mother chides, pressing a cool, damp cloth to my forehead.

"Let's go into the parlor, Mother," Penelope says. "Sarah will be more comfortable on the sofa."

I nod, not concerned with missing the rest of the meal—I

think we've all lost our appetites. My sister helps me stand, and though my knees are shaky, I give her a smile.

"It's all right. I'm all right now."

As soon as I'm seated in the parlor, the downstairs maid, Jenny, puts a glass of brandy in my hand. I sip it slowly.

"I've been reading about a new meditation specialist, Sarah. I think you should make an appointment with him," my mother tells me. "He's a Buddhist and rumored to be very good."

Temporary dissociative fugue state is what the doctors call it. Rooted in stress, anxiety, and trauma, triggered by loud noises, most often breaking glass. But it's inconsistent. There are times when I can hear the sound and have no reaction at all; other times the echo of a single dropped glass in a restaurant can cause me to "blink out."

It's not as bad as it could be—for some it can last days or even weeks, and the poor people afflicted wander and act in ways they have no memory of when they come to. My episodes last anywhere from a few seconds to a few minutes. I don't move or speak—it's like I'm just gone . . . dead, but still breathing. I've tried medication, but it doesn't really help and the side effects are unpleasant. I've tried hypnosis, therapy, acupuncture . . . but they've also been mostly ineffective.

"All right, Mother."

We enjoy our drinks in silence for a few minutes and then Stanhope enters the room.

"There is a visitor, Countess."

"A visitor?" Mother looks toward the rain-drenched windows. "Who would be out in this mess? Has their car given out?"

"No, My Lady. The young woman says her name is Nancy Herald. She apologized for not making an appointment and provided her card. It seems to be a business proposition."

My mother makes a sweeping motion with the back of her hand.

"I have no interest or time for business propositions. Send her on her way, please."

Stanhope places a business card on the table, bows, and leaves the room.

Penny picks it up as she sips her drink, looks it over—and then spits her brandy all over the carpet.

"Penelope!" mother yells.

My sister stands up, waving the card over her head like Veruca Salt after she got her hands on the golden ticket to the chocolate factory.

"Stanhope!" she screams. "Don't let her leave! She a television producer!"

Penny turns to me and in a quieter but urgent voice says, "She's a television producer."

As if I didn't hear her the first time.

Then she sprints from the room. Or . . . tries to. Halfway to the door, her heel catches on the carpet and she falls flat on her face with an "Ooof."

"Are you all right, Pen?"

She pulls herself up, waving her hands. "I'm fine! Or I will be, as long as she doesn't leave!"

The second try's the charm, and Penelope scurries out of the room as fast as her four-inch heels will take her.

My mother shakes her head at my sister's retreating form.

"Too much sugar, that one."

Then she drains her glass.

"The producer is most likely interested in filming on the property," my mother adds. "It seems like every few months I get an inquiry."

A few moments later, there's the echo of Penelope's quick, high-pitched chatter from the foyer and, shortly after, she walks back into the parlor. Her arm is linked with a petite, dark-haired woman in a drenched trench coat. Stanhope follows behind them like a frowning shadow.

Penelope introduces her like they're old schoolmates, stealing Stanhope's thunder.

"Mother, Sarah, this is Nancy Herald. She's a television producer."

I stand and offer my hand. "Hello, Miss Herald. Tell me, are you a television producer? I wasn't sure."

I wink at my sister. She sneers back.

"Assistant producer, actually," she replies, shaking my hand. "It's nice to meet you."

Stanhope sniffs. "May I take your coat, Miss Herald? And offer you a hot beverage?"

"Thank you." She hands over the dripping garment. "Coffee would be awesome, if you have it."

Without rising, my mother motions for her to sit. "What brings you out in such terrible weather, Miss Herald?"

She smiles, sits, and pulls out a folder from the briefcase in her hand. "Before I explain, I'm going to have to ask you each to sign a nondisclosure agreement. And I realize that's very odd, but I have a special opportunity for . . ." she checks her paperwork, "Sarah and Penelope Von Titebottum." She glances at my sister and me. "For both of you, but it's a matter of national security, so I need evidence of your confidentiality in writing. You're under no obligation, except to keep my offer to yourselves."

Penelope begs with her eyes . . . and her mouth.

"Please, Mummy! Sarah, please, please, pretty-pretty please?"

My mother huffs and rolls her eyes. "Very well, give it here."

We each sign the short, one-paragraph document. And Stanhope sets a cup and saucer on the table for Miss Herald. She files the form away, takes a sip of the steaming liquid, and after our butler has left the room, closing the door behind him, she leans forward.

"Have you heard of the television series *Matched*?"

"Out of the question," my mother declares the moment Miss Herald finishes telling us about the royally themed reality-TV dating show.

"No!" Penny squeaks. "It most certainly still is in question."

"Not for me." I shake my head. "Thank you for the offer, Miss Herald, but I don't even like having my photo taken. I have no interest in being on a television show."

"What about being queen?" she prods.

"I have no interest in that either."

Penny raises her hand. "But I do! I could still join up, right? Even if Sarah doesn't?"

"Absolutely."

"Absolutely not," Mother says firmly.

Penelope is offended. "Mother, you're acting like you don't trust me at all."

"I don't." She shrugs. "And with good reason. There are plentiful examples of your lack of judgment, darling. Let's see . . . there was the tattoo artist."

"It was a phase."

"The circus performer."

"He was interesting!"

"The convict."

Penny squirms. "Being on the lam wasn't as romantic as I'd thought."

She falls to her knees beside my mother's chair. "But this is different. It's not about a boy . . ."

"Isn't it?"

Penny rolls her eyes. "Henry's a lot of fun and he's fantastic to look at, but he's a playboy—everyone knows that. When he marries he won't have just a mistress; he'll have a whole harem. We would never work."

Then she resorts back to pleading. "But you know how I love to perform. This could open up doors for me, Mother. For a real career in the industry."

My mother closes her eyes. "I'm going to regret this . . . but, all right."

Penny starts to squee, and my mother holds up an ultimatum finger.

"*If* Sarah goes along to keep an eye on you, to be your voice of reason because it's apparent you were born without one, you may participate."

Penelope flings her arms around her. "Thank you, Mummy!"

Then she whips around to me. Looking so hopeful, it just about breaks my heart.

"Sarah?"

"Penny . . . I can't. I have my flat, my work. I just can't blow them off for . . ."

"Six weeks in total," the producer supplies.

"For six weeks. I'm sorry, Pen."

She shuffles on her knees over to me—probably giving herself rug burns.

"*Please*, Sarah. This could change everything."

That's what I'm afraid of.

"It'll be so much fun. The best kind of adventure."

And my chest aches. Because I want this for her—I want to be able to do it for her—but the prospect of so much change, so much unknown, terrifies me.

"I don't think I can do it, Pen," I whisper.

She clasps our hands together. "We'll do it together. I'll have your back and you'll have mine."

I open my mouth . . . but the words stay trapped in my throat.

"Penelope is supposed to report for military service next month," Mother tells the producer.

"We'll be able to get her out of that," Miss Herald says.

"We have a signed edict from Prince Henry excusing all the contestants from work, school, or any other obligations for 'confidential' Palace business. It's an official Act of Royalty."

Her words stop me cold. "What did you just say?"

"An Act of Royalty. It's like a proclamation, an order from the Crown . . ."

"Or an act of God," I whisper.

"Yes, exactly."

And the wheels in my mind turn.

"Could I get one? A letter for my employer if I go with Penny, as her . . . assistant?"

"Of course. Many of the ladies are bringing their own staff—chefs, hairdressers, yoga instructors, dog walkers—it'll be interesting."

"But I could have the letter?" I push. "To be excused from work for six full weeks?"

"Sure."

My eyes meet Penelope's and her eyebrows rise. Because she knows exactly what I'm thinking.

"That does change things, doesn't it?"

It certainly does. Now we're down to the lesser of two evils.

And the choice is clear.

I was never a cheerleader, but if I had pom-poms I'd shake them until my hands fell off. *Yay, reality television!*

"Show us where to sign. We're in."

CHAPTER 6

Henry

'm impressed. Two weeks after I ring Vanessa Steele, I barely recognize the place. The castle is buzzing with activity—crewmen and women swinging figuratively from the rafters, installing lighting and cameras—without damaging the historical integrity, of course. Fergus had a full-out tizzy about that one, but I talked him down.

There's always someone to chat with, someone saying hello or asking me a question or mentioning how excited he or she is to be working with me.

It feels bloody grand.

Set designers are arranging props and baskets of flowers here and there and oohing and ahhing over the antique paintings, suits of armor, and what Nicholas and I always called the Fantastic Wall of Death. It's a large wall in the great room, covered floor-to-ceiling with weapons that were used by our ancestors on the battlefield. Writers and directors walk about the property, creating storyboards and film location lists.

AD's and PA's and Extra PA's flit about, and I'm really hoping we can add DP to the frequently used initials vernacular very soon.

But then, in the library, Vanessa dashes those horny hopes as fast as Cinderella's coach poofed back into a sad little pumpkin.

"No sex."

We're going over my contract. I don't have to sign the $50 million NDA like every single other person who's even remotely involved, but I do have rules.

Sodding rules. Everywhere I look, there are do's, don'ts, musts, and for fuck's sake nevers.

Doesn't anyone know how to have fun anymore?

"What do you mean, no sex? I've seen your show—sex is the whole point. All the good parts are blocked out, but it's picnic sex, candlelight sex, after-hiking-through-the-forest sex. I was really looking forward to that part."

She shakes her head, her shiny, short hair swaying. "Prepare for disappointment. This is the royal edition. It's special. Special rules."

"I don't want to be special. I want to be like all the other average blokes on your show. Only, better-looking. Sucking face in the morning with one contestant, then sex with a different woman in the evening. And no one even gets angry. It's a fascinating study in human behavior." I clap my hands. "Bravo, sweetheart."

And she's still shaking her head. *Damn it.*

"In this case, we're selling the fantasy. The fairy tale. That the woman you choose will be your queen. And in order to keep that fantasy going, you can party, but you can't have sex."

"Are you telling me that you actually found twenty noble virgins?"

Because if that's the case, this isn't going to be nearly as much fun as I thought.

"I'm telling you it doesn't matter if they're virgins, as long as the audience believes they are." She glances out the window, tapping her finger on the desk. "I mean, you're just looking for a good time, right? You weren't actually planning on settling down with one of these girls, were you?"

"I don't plan on settling down for a very long time, sweets.

My brother has the positive publicity covered and while one of my duties is to beget an heir, men can have children well into their fifties, so I have plenty of time for practice shots." I lift my glass of scotch, toasting the Almighty. "Praise the Lord."

Vanessa nods. "Perfect. Then I think we'll both get exactly what we're looking for, Henry."

I skim the rest of the contract.

"You should have your attorney look it over too," she says.

"No need." I glance up, pen poised. "There's no ban on blow jobs, is there?"

Vanessa laughs. "No. Just be discreet."

I wink. "Discreet should have been one of my middle names."

Right after "Ironic."

I sign the final page with an eager flourish that John Hancock would envy. Vanessa picks up the contract and slides it into a leather folder. "Congratulations, you just bought yourself a month's worth of good times."

I lean back in my chair, folding my arms behind my head, content with the world.

"Oh, one more thing," Vanessa adds. "It's about your staff."

Ten minutes later, they're all gathered in the library. Cook, Fergus, James, and his security team, stand in a circle an I'm in the center, like I'm about to lead them onto the football field to victory.

"I've explained to Ms. Steele that there is no need for my private staff to sign nondisclosure agreements. Because the House of Pembrook, of which you are all members, is better and more honorable than that." I meet eyes of each person, peering particularly hard at Fergus. "Aren't we?"

Granny isn't the only one who knows how to manipulate.

"That means we have only one rule: no one tells the Queen. I can't stress this enough."

I continue to slowly turn to each of them. Fergus glares, Cook smiles, James and his lads look like they're going to puke.

I hold out my hand, palm down, and motion for them add their hands on top. "What do you say?"

"Your parents are rolling in their graves, God rest their souls," Fergus grinds out, making the sign of the cross.

And inside, I flinch. Hard.

On the outside, I shrug. "Won't be the first time, old man."

Then it's Fergus's turn to flinch. He glances down, sheepishly.

"Come on," I rally, "don't get depressing on me. This is the way it's done now. The Pope tweets, politicians troll, and the heir to the throne finds his match on reality television."

"It's tasteless and tawdry," he argues.

"Where have you been? The whole damn world is tasteless and tawdry."

My voice changes then, softening, and I almost believe my own words. "But she could be out there, Fergus, just waiting for me to find her. The woman I'm supposed to love, the future mother of my children, the lady who is destined to be Wessco's queen—she could be one of them. And wouldn't that be a tale to tell?"

He looks at my face for a moment, and his expression doesn't soften at all. But then he nods. And steps forward, putting his hand over mine. "Your father would've had a good laugh about this. Always enjoyed a dip on the wild side, that one."

I smile and smack his back. Then I look to Cook. She grins broadly, her cheeks round and full and her brogue thick as molasses.

"I don't tweeter like the Pope, but . . ." And she adds her hand to mine and Fergus's.

James whispers with the other boys, then turns to me, speaking for the group.

"This could be considered treason, Sir."

I scoff. "No. No one's talking about betraying government secrets or overthrowing the monarchy. It's just a case of . . . what she doesn't know won't hurt her."

Poor James rubs the back of his neck, looking like he's going to shit himself.

"I can't lie to the Queen, Prince Henry."

I shake my head. "And I would never ask you to. But . . . if she's not asking you directly, then it's not really lying."

"I email daily reports to Winston. He'll have my arse if he finds out I didn't tell him about this."

Yeah, that's a tricky one. Winston is the head dark suit at the Palace.

"Then we'd best make sure he doesn't find out. Continue your reports . . . just keep them . . . vague. General. 'We're all good here at Anthorp Castle, how the hell are you?'"

He still looks like the weak link.

So I put all my cards on the table.

"Look, James, I am Prince of Pembrook now. And I realize I'm not Nicholas; I never will be. But if this goes south I won't let you or your boys take the fall, I swear it. So, it comes down to trust. Either you believe in me or you don't."

And I really need someone to fucking believe in me. Even for just a little while.

James's blue eyes read mine, like he's delving into my brain. After a long moment, he scrubs his hands down his face. "Fuck it—we're with you, Prince Henry."

The lads nod behind him and I can't not smile.

"You're good men. I've always liked you. You're going places, I can tell."

James and the rest of the security boys add their hands to the pile. And because I don't want to be a full-out wanker, I don't cheer or yell. I just nod to each of them, tap our hands, and say, "I'm proud of all of you. And grateful to each of you. I won't let you down. Go, team."

CHAPTER 7

Sarah

Mr. Haverstrom isn't pleased when I present him with my official Act of Royalty letter, excusing me from work for the next six weeks. But, as he acknowledged, he can't fire me. And while I'll miss the library and the regulars and lunch with Annie and Willard, in the end, it's worth it. The unknown of *Matched* pales in comparison to the stark terror of standing in front of hundreds of people. No contest.

Ten days after Miss Herald showed up at our front door, a car arrives to take Penelope and me to Anthorp Castle. The property is only a little over an hour's drive from Castlebrook. It's guarded grounds, the royal family's private property, so while I've read a few books about the castle's history and have seen photos, I've never actually visited.

When the car pulls up the long, winding drive and stops in front of giant wood-and-iron doors, I decide for the first time that a book just can't compare. The smell of salt and sea is in the air, and the wind coming off the water whips at my hair. It's sunny and cool, and the huge gray stone castle with its points and towers, flags and flowers, drawbridge and moat, is straight out of a fairy tale—like *Cinderella* or *The Little Mermaid*.

Yes, with the waves crashing on the rocks below the cliff,

The Little Mermaid is the perfect comparison. And it's my favorite Disney movie.

A few of the show's crew members collect our bags and carry them in. I notice a few other ladies—in designer clothes and large sunglasses—exiting cars nearby. A couple are familiar to me—the Duchess of Perth, Laura Benningson, and Lady Cordelia Ominsmitch—but the rest I've never met, though I'm sure Penny has. Miss Herald greets us in the main foyer and gives us a quick tour. Penelope chooses her room almost immediately—a large pink room on the second floor, near the main staircase and close to the action.

"I'd like to explore the grounds on my own, if that's all right," I tell Miss. Herald. "I'll select a room after."

"That'll be fine," she replies. "The crew, wardrobe, and makeup are using the whole west wing, but any other empty room is up for grabs."

She hands Penelope her schedule for the day. The first filming session is late this afternoon, in front of the castle with the full cast, including Prince Henry, to shoot the opening scenes of the first episode. Before that, Penny has an interview, a wardrobe consultation, and a cocktail hour meet-and-greet with the other ladies in the castle.

I give my sister a hug before Miss Herald guides her away.

"Have fun, Pen."

Her soft brown eyes dance up at me. "You too. If you spot any ghosts in this old place, try to get a photo!"

When they walk off, I step slowly through the castle, taking it all in, gazing at the ceilings and the walls and everything in between. I think about the people who have stood where I am right now, whose footsteps I could be retracing—grand lords and ladies, powerful soldiers and warriors, mighty kings and commanding queens.

It's humbling and thrilling at the same time. Like their energy and spirit is in the stone itself, speaking to me, showing me—guiding my way. Before I know it, I'm in the corner of the east wing on the third floor. It's quiet here, a bit far from the commotion of the main filming areas. The door creaks when I open it, stepping inside the bedroom.

And my breath catches.

Oh. Hell. Yes. I've found my room. Because for me, this one is perfect—absolutely perfect.

Later, when the sun hangs low in the sky but there are still a few hours until sunset, the full cast of ladies and crew are down in front of the castle. Vanessa Steele, the executive producer, announced that all assistants and non-cast members must remain indoors or off set. Since it's an outdoor shoot, she doesn't want to chance any of us getting caught in the shot.

I've found the perfect spot to watch the taping—on the forested side of the castle, up a hill, near a tree for cover, just in case. I have a stellar view of the castle entrance down below, and in the meantime, I have my book for company. Sitting back against the tree, I sigh with contentment. This is going to be lovely. Then I open my book . . . and practically jump out of my skin when a cough sounds from behind me.

I didn't see anyone when I first walked up here.

Closing my book, I look out from behind the trunk cautiously. Just far enough . . . to see the unmistakable sight of His Royal Highness, Prince Henry, standing a few yards away.

With a gasp, I duck back behind the tree.

I grew up inundated with news stories of the royal family and posters of our handsome princes pinned to my bedroom walls—every girl in Wessco did. Nicholas was the serious one, staid and well-spoken, honorable—just like Mr. Darcy. Henry always seemed more like Fiyero Tigelaar from *Wicked*:

The Life and Times of the Wicked Witch of the West—fun-loving, passionate, and thoughtless, focused only on the next party and his own pleasure.

I stand up and peep back out from behind my tree for another glimpse.

And my heart starts to gallop, my head goes fuzzy, and it feels like my throat is closing in on itself. Because—sweet baby Jesus in a manger—he's coming this way! His long, purposeful strides are aimed right at me. Which means when he gets here, I'll actually have to speak to him. Although we met that one brief time—last year in a pub when he was with his brother and Olivia Hammond, who is now Princess Olivia, the Duchess of Fairstone—and while I'm acquainted with the details of Prince Henry John Edgar Thomas's life, he's still just a handsome stranger. And I don't do well with strangers.

My eyes dart around for an escape. Curling up behind the tree like a snail in its shell is out—he's obviously already spotted me. *Damn.* I glance up at the branches—I'm an excellent climber—but even the lowest one is out of jumping reach. *Double damn.*

He's almost here. *Shit, shit, shit.*

I think I'm hyperventilating. I may pass out. Which would solve the problem of having to talk with him, but it'd be even more embarrassing—I'm speaking from experience.

Mentally, I shake myself. I just need to think of something to say.

And now the only thing filling my mind is *thinkofsomethingtosay, thinkofsomethingtosay, thinkofseomthingtosay.*

My hands turn sweaty and numb.

I could ask about his mother—always a safe bet. Except . . . his mother is dead.

Damn it all to hell.

And . . . he's here.

My eyes drop down and I freeze, like a deer caught in the

biggest, brightest headlights. I stare at his boots, dark and shiny like black mirrors. I force my gaze upward, over his long legs clad in black . . . polyester pants? His hips and waist are covered by a white jacket with garishly shiny buttons, purple accents, and gold-roped tassels on each of his broad shoulders.

It's a ridiculous outfit—like a cheap Prince Charming costume—and yet he still manages to look fantastic.

The top button is clasped at his neck, accentuating a sexy, masculine Adam's apple. He has a chiseled chin; a strong, slightly stubbled jawline; criminally full lips; a straight, regal nose; thick, wild dark-blond hair, and eyes so beautiful they'll steal your breath, words, and thoughts. They're a stormy shade of green, but warm like raw emeralds heated by the sun. I remember, the first time we met, thinking how none of the pictures I'd ever seen of him did his eyes justice. And, at this moment, I second that opinion.

If I weren't naturally speechless, I would be now.

Prince Henry's brow furrows, looking down at me in an almost disgruntled way.

"Did someone die?"

And it's such a ludicrous question, I forget to be panicked.

"What?"

"Or are you a witch?" He clicks his tongue, shaking his head. "Sorry—Wiccan? Pagan? Worshipper of the dark arts? What is the PC term these days?"

Is this really happening?

"Uh . . . Wiccan, I believe, is acceptable."

He nods. "Right. Are you a Wiccan, then?"

"No. Catholic. Not especially devout, but . . ."

"Hmm." He wiggles his finger at my hands. "What are you reading?"

"Oh . . . *Wuthering Heights*?"

He nods again. "Heathcliff, right?"

"Yes."

"So it's about a fat orange cat?"

My mind trips as I try to figure out what he's talking about. The comic! He thinks it's about Heathcliff the comic strip.

"Actually, no, it's about a young man and woman who—"

His eyes crinkle and his lips smirk, making my cheeks go warm and pink.

"Are you teasing me, Your Highness?"

"Yes." He chuckles. "Badly, apparently. And please, call me Henry."

My voice is airy, hesitant, as I try it out.

"Henry."

His smile remains, but softens—like he enjoys hearing the word. And then I remember myself, curtsying as I should have from the start.

"Oh! And I am—"

"You're Lady Sarah Von Titebottum."

Warmth unfurls in my stomach.

"You remembered?"

"I never forget a pretty face."

My cheeks go from pink to bright red. I change colors more often than a chameleon. It's a curse.

"I'm not usually good with names." His eyes drift down to my hips, trying to look behind me. "But Titebottum does stand out."

When nervous, I typically go mute. This moment is the exception to that rule.

Just my luck.

"You would think so, although several of my uni professors had trouble with the pronunciation. Let's see, there was *Teet-bottom, Tight-butt-um,* and one who insisted it should be *Titty-bottom*. It's not everyday you hear a distinguished professor say the word *tit*. That one kept the class entertained for weeks."

He tilts his head back, chuckling again. "That's great."

My face is now approaching purple. I take a deep, slow breath. "Um . . . why did you ask if someone had died?"

He gestures to my clothes. "Both times I've seen you, you've worn black. What's that about?"

"Oh." I glance down at my long-sleeved, knee-length black dress with a crisp white collar and black ankle boots. "Well, black is easy; it goes with everything. And I'm not one for loud colors; I don't like to stand out. You could say I'm a bit . . . shy."

And the award for understatement of the year goes to . . .

"That's a shame. You'd look gorgeous in jeweled tones. Emerald, deep plum." His eyes wander, pausing at my legs, then my breasts. "In a clingy ruby number, you'd bring men to their knees."

I look at the ground. "You're teasing me again."

"No." His voice is rough, almost harsh. "No, I'm not."

My eyes snap up to his, and hold.

There are meetings in books that stand out, that alter the course of the story. Profound encounters between characters when one soul seems to say to the other, "There you are—I've been looking for you."

Of course, life isn't a novel, so I'm probably just imagining the slipping, sliding feeling inside me, like things are shifting around before finally snapping into their rightful place. And I think my mind is playing tricks on me—fancying that it's interest alighting in Prince Henry's eyes.

Heated interest.

My breath catches and I cough, breaking the moment.

Then I gesture to his jacket. "Do you really think you're qualified to give fashion advice?"

He laughs, rubbing the back of his neck. "I thought I looked like an absolute tool—now I'm sure of it."

"Did the producers pick that out for you?"

"Yes. I'm supposed to ride down to the castle on horseback. Make my grand entrance." Briskly, his long fingers unbutton the jacket. He shrugs it off, dropping it on the ground, revealing a snug white T-shirt and gloriously sculpted arms.

"Better?"

"Yes," I squeak.

The teasing smirk comes back, then he grips the back of his T-shirt, pulling it off. And my mouth falls open at the sight of warm skin, perfect brown nipples, and the ridges and swells of muscles up and down his torso.

"What do you think of this?" he asks.

I think this is worse than I thought.

Henry Pembrook isn't a Fiyero—he's a Willoughby. A John Willoughby from *Sense and Sensibility*—thrilling, charming, unpredictable, and seductive. Marianne Dashwood learned the hard way that if you play with a heartbreaker, you can't be surprised when your heart gets shattered into a thousand pieces.

I shrug, trying to seem cool and unaffected. "Might look a bit too 'Putin' on the horse."

He nods, then puts his shirt back on, and my stomach swirls with a strange mix of relief and disappointment.

"Why aren't you down with the other girls?"

"Me? Oh, I'm not part of the show. I couldn't imagine . . ."

"Then why are you here?"

"Penelope. Mother wouldn't let her participate unless I tagged along to keep an eye on her."

"Every family has a wild child. Penny's yours?"

Takes one to know one.

"Yes, definitely."

He tilts his head, the sunlight making his eyes a deeper green, almost simmering. "And what about you? Is there any wild in you, Teet-bottom?"

My cheeks go up in flames. "Not even a little. I'm the boring one. The good one."

His teeth scrape his lower lip and it looks . . . naughty.

"Corrupting the good ones is my favorite pastime."

Oh yes, definitely a Willoughby.

I hug my book to my chest. "I'm not corruptible."

His smile broadens. "Good. I like a challenge."

A crew member suddenly appears, trailing a large white horse behind him. "They're ready for you, Prince Henry."

Keeping his eyes on me, he places one foot in the stirrup and smoothly swings up onto the saddle. With his hands on the leather reins, he winks.

"See you around, Titty-bottom."

I cover my face and groan.

"I never should have told you that."

"Can't blame me. It makes you turn so many lovely shades. Is it just your cheeks that blush?" His gaze drags down my body, as if he can see beneath my clothes. "Or does it happen everywhere?"

I fold my arms, ignoring the question.

"I think you might be a bully, Prince Henry."

"Well, in grade school I did enjoy pulling on the girls' braids. But these days I only tug on a woman's hair in a very specific situation." His voice drops lower. "Let me know if you'd like a demonstration."

His words cause images of slick, entwined limbs and gasping moans to flare in my mind. And as if on cue, the blush blooms hot under my skin.

Henry laughs, the sound deep and manly. Then he spurs his horse and rides away, leaving me glowing like a damn Christmas tree. I open *Wuthering Heights* and press the pages against my face, cringing.

It's going to be a long month.

CHAPTER 8

Henry

Here's something I didn't know before: reality television isn't actually real. I mean, it is in the sense that there are actual people speaking and moving, as opposed to artificially intelligent human-like robots that will eventually become self-aware and kill us all.

Instead of castle-walking in the middle of the night, I've been watching the Terminator series. The first one is still the best.

But my point is, *Matched* and its ilk aren't genuine. The scenes are staged, the shots planned, and "takes" are done multiple times. A few minutes on film could take a few hours of real-life time to shoot.

This is the fourth time we've gone through my "riding up to the castle on horseback" scene, and we haven't even gotten to the front of the castle yet. Something to do with lighting and shadows or whatever the hell. The horse is now cranky and I'm bored.

While the director and Vanessa and the cameraman go over the next shot, I glance toward the hill, thinking about the funny little blusher at the top of it. The way she peeked out from behind the tree, then tried to hide as if I'd caught her doing something dirty.

I could show her what dirty really looks like.

The thought makes me chuckle, imagining the pretty pink her cheeks would turn if she heard what was running through my head. I wonder if her arse would turn the same sweet shade after a good, warm spanking?

I bet it would.

I shift in the saddle, getting hard at the prospect.

Lady Sarah Von Titebottum. A cute, odd bird with—from what I could tell in her well-fitted but drab black dress—a very fitting name. Pretty face, too: big, dark, long-lashed eyes that sparkled behind those prim glasses and a lush mouth made for moaning.

I've known girls like her before. The aristocracy is actually a very small group, and some of the families are all about keeping their offspring—particularly their female offspring—sheltered from the rest of the world. Hidden away in private, all-girl academies where they interact with only their own. It makes for reserved, intelligent, but generally plain and tediously proper young ladies.

Although she's obviously the quiet type, Sarah held her own with me. She was clever, charming in a bashful way—different. People are so disappointingly predictable that being surprised by that shy slip of a girl feels almost . . . tantalizing.

"Just like that, Prince Henry," the director calls. "That smile right there—that's what we've been looking for. Whatever put that look on your face, keep thinking about it."

Well, that's not going to be difficult.

Unlike the show itself, the host of *Matched* is the genuine article. She's authentically crackers. As mad as a box of frogs.

She's Emily Rasputin, an American stage actress who was

known as the Queen of Broadway in her prime. A notorious cocaine addiction, a hit-and-run scandal, and a contemptuous divorce in the nineties knocked her off her throne. But she reappeared a few years back as the host of television's newest, hottest reality show. Her suspenseful hosting skills and the bold, prying questions she poses to the contestants have become as big of a draw as the show itself.

And everyone loves a comeback story. I should know.

But she's a full-on nutter—a method hostess. She insists on doing only one take per scene and refuses to interact with anyone, unless it's on film. Real emotion and reaction, according to Vanessa, is the hardest to capture, and Miss Rasputin thrives on it.

When I, fucking finally, make it up to the courtyard of the castle, where twenty ladies are waiting, the cameras don't stop rolling. There are four . . . no, five cameramen so they can capture every angle and every interaction. They move between us like ghosts through walls, pausing and zooming in to catch something interesting when they find it.

But I ignore the cameras and instead focus on the expression of the lovely ladies all around me, smiling and adoring. Confidence that was once so familiar and has been sorely missing these last months surges back in my chest. This is the life I'm used to. And I think doing this show may turn out to be the best decision I've ever made.

"Here ye, here ye," Emily calls into her microphone, wearing a shiny long gold coat, almost matching blond hair, and big hoop earrings that could fit around a wrist. "I present to you, ladies of Wessco, His Royal Highness, Prince Henry! He comes in search of true love and to make that true love queen of his heart and queen of his country."

Emily lifts up her hand, clutching a group of necklaces with charms dangling from each one. "At the end of this night, Prince Henry will place a glass slipper charm on the pillow of each lady he chooses to remain here at Anthorp Castle. Only ten of you will be chosen. Then, each night after, one lady will leave until His Royal Highness bestows the diamond tiara on the one who will be his royal bride." She looks straight into the camera. "Welcome, ladies and our audience at home, to *Matched—Royal Edition*!"

Ding!

The first event of the show is speed dating. Before the cameras started rolling again, Vanessa told us to "be ourselves," whatever that may be. To not hold back—that any conversation that doesn't work for the show or isn't fit for television can be fixed in the editing room later. I'm sitting at a table with a black-curtained partition across the middle. The curtain lifts and I get two minutes with each lady to see if, as Emily put it, we have an "instant connection." Some of the girls I already know—one or two I've already screwed, not that I wouldn't mind a repeat. But for the moment, I sip my scotch and enjoy the electricity that sparks in my veins from the excitement and the fun that practically lights up the whole damn castle.

Ding!

And the first lady up is . . . the Duchess of Perth, Laura Benningson. I've known Laura for years; she's beautiful, with thick light-brown hair and sparkly light-blue eyes.

She was engaged to Mario Vitrolli, a professional race car driver and a good man, up until last year when he was tragically killed in an accident on the track. Laura was pregnant at the time and lost the baby a few weeks after Mario's death, though thankfully, that part was kept out of the papers.

I lean over the table and kiss her cheek. "How are you, dove?"

She gives me a smile still tinged with sadness. "I'm all right. This is a bit crazy, though, isn't it? I don't know how they plan to address my obvious non-virginity. Everyone we know knows about the miscarriage."

"According to the producer, that's the magic of reality television. A bit of creative editing and they can make any reality they want. If it makes you feel any better, I'm not a virgin either. They were shocked when I told them. Just shocked."

Laura laughs, and it feels good to make someone really laugh for a change.

"Anyway, you can relax, Henry, I'm not vying for the throne—I think I'd make a terrible queen. I'm too lazy and self-absorbed."

"And too honest."

"Exactly." She sighs. "But, when they approached me, I just felt like it was time, you know. To try to move forward. Maybe have some fun. It's a strange thing to do, but I decided to give it a try."

I put my hand over hers. "I'm glad you did."

She squeezes back. "So am I, now."

Laura's a yes.

Ding!

Lady Cordelia Ominsmitch. She's the daughter of an earl, and while she's known in my circles as a serious partier, she maintains a stellar reputation to the outside world. And she's drop-dead gorgeous. Big blue eyes, bouncy hair, and even bouncier tits. My type of girl.

As soon as the curtain lifts, she gets right to it.

"We've never met, Your Highness, but we could be good together. Hot together. I'm everything you need in a wife and a queen. I have the looks, the education, the pedigree, and the temperament. I'm also a virgin." She winks. "Tight as a drum. Until I marry, I've promised myself and the Lord to only do anal."

I choke on my drink.

Definitely a yes.

Ding!

Jane Plutorch. Cousin to a duke and heiress to a fortune built on wart cream—Wart Away is the official name, I think. She's also seriously Goth. Black lipstick, black hair, ivory skin, piercings, and ink up and down her arms.

"I hate my family," she says without any inflection at all. "And they hate me. They made me come here, mostly because they didn't want to look at me. I only agreed because I thought it'd be fab to live in a castle. Like a vampire."

"I can respect that," I say. "And you have great taste in tattoos."

She glances at her arms, and it's as if it takes all her energy just to keep breathing.

"Thanks."

She's a yes.

Ding!

Lady Elizabeth Figgles. Her father's a viscount and a member of Parliament, and she's also Sam Berkinshire's—an old schoolmate and one of my dearest friends—girlfriend.

"Elizabeth? What the hell are you doing here? Where's Sam?"

"Sam can go fucking die." She looks right at the camera. "Are you getting this? You can go fucking die, Sam! I hope your prick gets caught in a wood chipper, you cheating bastard!"

"He cheated on you? Sam?"

Sam's a great guy. The kind of guy even really good guys want to be more like. He makes Abraham Lincoln look like a lying shit.

"Your face right now, that's exactly how I looked when I found out—but a hell of a lot angrier. I found receipts, knickers that weren't mine, rubbers. Faithless, worthless son of a bitch."

She bangs the table and her nails are long enough to double as claws.

"Now I want Sam to see what it feels like. So I'm going to fuck you. On television. A lot. Hopefully live. You'd better rest up, Henry. I brought lube—a whole bucket of it."

Wow.

Ding!

Penelope Von Titebottum. Her mother's a reclusive countess, but Penny is pleasant, fun, attractive. And her sister is . . . interesting.

"Hello, Henry, how've you been?"

"I'm good, Penelope. You look well."

She bounces in her seat and smooths her hair. "Thank you! I'm just so excited to be here. We're going to have so much fun."

"That's the plan."

"And I can't believe we're going to be on television! All over the world. It's amazing."

"I saw Sarah earlier. We said hello."

"Oh good. She didn't want to come at first, but I'm glad she did. We have to get her out of her shell. Not too much, just enough to show her a good time, right?"

I nod. "Count me in."

Penelope stays.

And that means Sarah does too.

Ding!

Princess Alpacca, pronounced like the animal, first in line to the throne of Alieya Island, a small nation below the south of France. The Queen invited her to Wessco after an attempted coup forced her family into exile last year. She doesn't speak English and I don't know a word of Aliesh. This is going to be a challenge.

Guermo, her translator, glares at me like I'm the bubonic plague in human form—with a mixture of hatred, disgust, and just a touch of fear.

She speaks in Aliesh, looking at me.

And Guermo translates. "She says she thinks you are very ugly."

Princess Alpacca nods vigorously.

She's pretty in a cute kind of way. Wild curly hair, round hazel eyes, a tiny bulbous nose, and full cheeks.

"She says she doesn't like you or your stupid country," Guermo informs me.

Another nod and a blank but eager smile.

"She says she would rather throw herself off the rocks to her death in the waves and be devoured by the fish than be your queen."

I look him in the face. "She barely said anything."

He shrugs. "She says it with her eyes. I know these things. If you weren't so stupid you would know too."

More nodding.

"Fantastic."

She says something to Guermo in Aliesh, then he says something back—harshly and disapproving. And now, they're arguing.

But they can stay.

Guermo is obviously in love with Alpacca and she clearly has no idea. My presence will force him to admit his feelings . . . but does she return his infatuation? It'll be like living in a Latin soap opera—dramatic, passionate, and over the top. I have to see how it ends.

Ding!

Lady Libadocious Loutenhiemer. Track and Field Olympian in the last two games. The youngest Wessconian to ever win a gold medal, cousin of a marquess.

"You can call me Libby. Or Libs. Lulu. Or LL—I pretty much answer to anything."

She's in amazing shape—everything tight and toned, but still definitely feminine. Wavy blond hair frames an attractive face with high cheekbones and great eyes.

"In my spare time, I like biking, swimming, running, fucking . . ."

I smirk. "What a coincidence—those are all my favorite hobbies too."

Oh, yes.

Ding!

And so it goes. Some are bubbly and upbeat, some more ambitious and dramatic, but I enjoy meeting and chatting with all of them. It's difficult to make cuts, but the show must go on. After the dating game, Vanessa hands me a map of the castle, marking the rooms where each of the ladies is staying.

I do my bit and leave the glass-slipper charms on the pillows of the girls I've chosen. Then I exit filming as the cameras continue to roll, capturing the reactions. Screams of joy and disappointment race down the halls of the stone castle. And then there were ten.

CHAPTER 9

Henry

D*rrrrrrrrrrrrr.*
 "Stop."
Drrrrrrrrrrrrrr.
"Go away."
Drrrr. Drrrr. Drrrr. Drrrr.
"Bloody hell."
DRRRRRRRRR.
"Shut the fuck up!"

I'm talking to the cameras mounted in the corners of my room. I'm contractually obligated to let them be there, and while they were installed over a week ago, tonight's the first night they've been on. Boy, are they ever on.

Drr. Drr. Drr. Drr. Drr. Drr.

It's the audio version of Chinese water torture. It's slowly and surely driving me mad. Every time I blink, breathe, roll over, scratch my nose or my nuts, the fucking things move. And they're not quiet about it.

DRRRRRRR. DRRRRRRR. DRRRRRRR.

I throw my pillow at the one on the left, which seems to be the most active. But the launch falls short. And now I have no pillow. I just lie flat, looking at the ceiling.

Listening to the last sound I'll hear before I die.

Drrdrrdrrdrrdrrdrrdrrdrrdrrdrrdrrdrrdrrdrrdrrdrrdrrdrrdrrdrrdrrdrrd rrdrrdrrdrrdrrdrr . . .

I've been trying to sleep for the last three hours, and now it's a quarter past two in the morning and I have to be dressed and downstairs for filming at half past six. Even for a practiced insomniac like myself, this is going to be rough. I need a few hours at least. At this point, I'd take a few minutes.

DRRRRRRRRRRRRRRRRRRRR.

And I can't even play my guitar. Because of that fucking sound.

Knock, knock.

That's new. I sit up, looking at the cameras to see who's making the strange noise.

Knock, knock.

But it's coming from the door. I swing out of bed and cover my bare arse with a pair of sleeping pants—careful not to give the cameras a show. Then I swing the door open.

And Lady Elizabeth stands on the other side, her vixen-red lips stretched into a salacious smile. "Hello, love. Time to fuck!"

She's in a black leather bustier and teeny, tiny black knickers that look . . . well, they look fabulous on her. Elizabeth has a stripper's body—a high, firm rack, trim waist, legs for days. She saunters into the room, hips swinging, waving a dildo in one hand and a pair of handcuffs in the other.

She spots the cameras and squeals. "How bloody perfect! They can get us from all angles!"

"Elizabeth . . ." I sigh.

But any further words are momentarily caught in my throat when she bends over the edge of the bed, slapping her arse for the camera. "Go to hell, Sammy."

Now, my head and my heart are not at all interested . . . but my dick certainly is. He's up for a party. He's a bit of an arsehole.

Still, I cross my arms over my chest. "This isn't happening, Elizabeth. Sam is a good friend—one of only a few that I have."

She bats her long, fake eyelashes and tosses her hair. "It's so happening."

When she tries to put her arms around me, I hold her forearms and step back.

She pouts. "Then why did you give me a slipper charm? Why am I still here, Henry?"

"So you don't go out and revenge-fuck anyone else. Not until you and Sam straighten out this misunderstanding."

She stomps her foot, slips out of my grasp, and lies back in the center of the bed.

"Fuck me, Henry. I'll beg if you want me to."

My cock nods. Sick bastard.

I rub my eyes. "You need to leave."

She smiles coyly. "Make me, my Prince."

O-kay.

I open the door, walk down the hall to the two security men stationed at the top of the stairs, and hook my thumb toward my room. "Make her leave."

Sometimes being me isn't so bad.

Like moments later, when they're gently but physically escorting Elizabeth out the door, so I don't have to.

"All right," she calls over her shoulder. "Tomorrow then!"

And I slam the door behind them.

This isn't how I thought it'd be. The cameras mock me in stereo sound.

Drrr. Drrr. Drrr. Drrr.

Christ, I'm tired. I need sleep. I need peace. I need for my balls to not be so blue they're practically purple. As purple as Sarah Von Titebottum's—

My mind comes to a screeching halt with the unexpected thought. And the image that accompanies it—the odd, blushing lass with her glasses and her books and very tight bottom.

Sarah's not a contestant on the show, so I'm willing to bet both my indigo balls that there's not a camera in her room. And, I can't believe I'm fucking thinking this, but, even better—none of the other girls will know where to find me—including Elizabeth.

I let the cameras noisily track me to the lavatory, but then, like an elite operative of the Secret Intelligence Service, I plaster myself to the wall beneath their range and slide my way out the door.

Less than five minutes later, I'm in my sleeping pants and a white T-shirt, barefoot with my guitar in hand, knocking on Sarah's bedroom door. I checked the map Vanessa gave me earlier. Her room is on the third floor, in the corner of the east wing, removed from the main part of the castle. The door opens just a crack and dark brown eyes peer out.

"Sanctuary," I plead.

Her brow crinkles and the door opens just a bit wider. "I beg your pardon?"

"I haven't slept in almost forty-eight hours. My best friend's girlfriend is trying to praying-mantis me and the sound of the cameras following me around my room is literally driving me mad. I'm asking you to take me in."

And she blushes. *Great.*

"You want to sleep in here? With me?"

I scoff. "No, not *with* you—just in your room, love."

I don't think about how callous the words sound—insulting—until they're out of my mouth. Could I be any more of a dick?

Thankfully, Sarah doesn't look offended.

"Why here?" she asks.

"Back in the day, the religious orders used to give sanctuary to anyone who asked. And since you dress like a nun, it seemed like the logical choice."

I don't know why I said that. I don't know what's wrong with me. Somebody just fucking shoot me and be done with it.

Sarah's lips tighten, her head tilts, and her eyes take on a dangerous glint.

I think Scooby-Doo put it best when he said, *Ruh-roh*.

"Let me make sure I've got this right—you need my help?"

"Correct."

"You need shelter, protection, sanctuary that only I can give?"

"Yes."

"And you think teasing me about my clothes is a wise strategy?"

I hold up my palms. "I never said I was wise. Exhausted, defenseless, and desperate."

I pout . . . but in a manly kind of way.

"Pity me."

A smile tugs at her lips. And that's when I know she's done for. With a sigh, she opens the door wide. "Well, it *is* your castle. Come in."

Huh. She's right—it is my castle. I really need to start remembering that.

I stand a bit taller as I walk in and look around. It's one of the smaller rooms, not as ornate as the ones on the second floor—it's used for servants when the castle is fully staffed. But the bed is large—a king—and takes up much of the room, with a small sofa and side table near the fireplace.

"How did you get stuck in here?" I ask. "Weren't any other rooms available?"

"They were, but I picked this one."

"Why?"

Her eyes go wide and light. "Because it has the best feature ever." She extends her right arm, presenting the cushioned window seat like a game-show hostess presenting a brand-new automobile.

"A window seat is the best feature ever?"

She shakes her head at me in a pitying way and I remember it—last year when we first met in that little pub, she did the exact same thing.

"It's not just a window seat—it's a nook!"

My eyebrows rise. "A nook?"

"A reading nook!"

It's only then that I notice the curved arch above the window, creating a little alcove, the worn leather satchel in the corner and a carefully stacked pile of old books at one end of the cushioned seat, that must belong to Sarah.

"A reading nook is a magical thing," Sarah explains, color rising in her pale cheeks from excitement. It's a nice look on her. "Every true reader appreciates a comfy, quiet space built just for reading."

I nod. "A nook. Got it."

I prop my guitar up against the nightstand. Then I turn toward the bed and fall into it face first. The mattress is soft but firm, like a sheet of steel wrapped in a cloud. I roll around, moaning loud and long.

"Oh, that's good. Really, really good. What a grand bed!"

Sarah clears her throat. "Well. We should probably get to sleep, then. Big day tomorrow."

The pillow smells sweet, like candy. I can only imagine it's from her. I wonder if I pressed my nose to the crook of her neck, would her skin smell as delicious?

I brush away the thought as I watch her stiffly gather a pillow and blanket from the other side of the bed, dragging them to . . . the nook.

"What are you doing?"

She looks up, her doe eyes widening. "Getting ready for bed."

"You're going to sleep there?"

"Of course. The sofa's very uncomfortable."

"Why can't we share the bed?"

She chokes . . . stutters. "I . . . I can't sleep with you. I don't even know you."

I throw my arms out wide. "What do you want to know? Ask me anything—I'm an open book."

"That's not what I mean."

"You're being ridiculous! It's a huge bed. You could let one rip and I wouldn't hear it."

And the blush is back. With a vengeance.

"I'm not . . . I don't . . ."

"You don't fart?" I scoff. "Really? Are you not human?"

She curses under her breath, but I'd love to hear it out loud. I bet uninhibited Sarah Von Titebottum would be a stunning sight. And very entertaining.

She shakes her head, pinning me with her eyes.

"There's something wrong with you."

"No." I explain calmly, "I'm just free. Honest with myself and others. You should try it sometime."

She folds her arms, all tight, trembling indignation. It's adorable.

"I'm sleeping in the nook, Your Highness. And that's that."

I sit up, pinning her gaze right back at her.

"Henry."

"What?"

"My name is not Highness, it's fucking Henry, and I'd prefer you use it."

And she snaps.

"Fine! Fucking Henry—happy?"

I smile.

"Yes. Yes, I am." I flop back on the magnificent bed. "Sleep tight, Titebottum."

I think she growls at me, but it's muffled by the sound of rustling bed linens and pillows. And then . . . there's silence. Beautiful, blessed silence.

I wiggle around, getting comfy.

I turn on my side and fluff the pillow.

I squeeze my eyes tight . . . but it's hopeless.

"Fucking hell!" I sit up.

And Sarah springs to her feet. "What? What's wrong?"

It's the guilt. I've barged into this poor girl's room, confiscated her bed, and have forced her to sleep in a cranny in the wall. I may not be the man my father was or the gentleman my brother is, but I'm not that much of a prick.

I stand up, rip my shirt over my head. and march toward the window seat. I feel Sarah's eyes graze my bare chest, arms. and stomach, but she circles around me, keeping her distance.

"You take the bloody bed," I tell her. "I'll sleep in the bloody nook."

"You don't have to do that."

I push my hand through my hair. "Yes, I do." Then I stand up straight and proper, an impersonation of Hugh Grant in one of his classic royal roles. "Please, Lady Sarah."

She blinks, her little mouth pursed. "Okay."

Then she climbs onto the bed, under the covers. And I squeeze onto the window bench, knees bent, my elbow jammed against the icy windowpane, and my neck bent at an odd angle that I'm going to be feeling tomorrow.

The light is turned down to a very low dim, and for several moments all I hear is Sarah's soft breaths.

But then, in the near darkness, her delicate voice floats out on a sigh.

"All right, we can sleep in the bed together."

Music to my ears. I don't make her tell me twice—I've fulfilled my noble quota for the evening. I stumble from the nook and crash onto the bed.

That's better.

The light on the bedside table next to Sarah brightens. "I'm awake now. I'm going to read for a bit, if it doesn't bother you."

"*Wuthering Heights*?" I yawn.

"Yes. Sleep well, Henry."

And something about the way she says my name this time—the sweetness of her voice—makes me smile. Until . . .

"*Hmm, hmmm, hmmm, hmmm, hmmmmm, hmm, hmm* . . ."

And I'm once again staring at the ceiling. "What is that sound?"

"What? Oh, that's me—sorry—I hum when I read." The bed shakes as she shrugs. "Habit."

"Well for Christ's sake, don't."

I'm being an arse. When she doesn't reply for a few seconds, I start to worry I've upset her. It's not Sarah's fault I'm tired—and horny. So horny. She doesn't deserve to have her head ripped off.

But before I can apologize, she says, "And here I thought you were the type who'd enjoy a good hummer."

And for a moment I'm stunned. And then I laugh, turning on my side, facing her. "Was that a joke, Sarah Titty-teet-butt-um?"

"It was supposed to be, yes."

"And it was a dirty joke. I'm impressed. I'll have to completely reevaluate my impression of you."

She covers her lovely mouth with her hands. "They slip out from time to time, but usually only with Penny or Willard and Annie."

And suddenly, I don't feel tired anymore.

"Willard and Annie?"

"My best friends. They work with me at the library."

"You're a librarian?"

She nods. "Mmm-hmm. At Concordia Library."

I fold my hands behind my head. Letting my imagination run wild.

"I've always wanted to fuck standing up in the stacks. Have you ever tried it?"

And without looking, I can feel her blush—like the rays of the red sun of Krypton.

"No."

I glance at her, my eyes raking up and down her body.

"I can see it. The long dark hair, the glasses, a tight gray pencil skirt and a snug white blouse with the top two . . ." I glance down at her impressive breasts, ". . . three buttons undone. You're the epitome of the sexy librarian."

She giggles, like I've said something silly.

"What?"

"I've never been called sexy a day in my life."

"Then you're sorely overdue."

Sarah closes her book and sets it on the nightstand, and a victorious feeling simmers in my chest. Like I've accomplished something.

"I've already said you can sleep in here. You don't have to butter me up."

I look into her eyes, smirking. "If I'm trying to butter up any part of you, you'll know it." Before she has time to flush, I ask, "If you're a hot librarian in your real life, what are you doing here for the next month? And don't say it's for Penelope. I've met Penelope—she's a wily one. She would've figured out a way to get here with or without you. There must be another reason."

Sarah crosses her arms and nods. "You're very perceptive, you know."

"Thank you. You're deflecting."

With a loud groan that goes straight to my cock, Sarah throws herself back onto her pillow, her head sinking in, partially obscuring her face.

"I was supposed to present at a symposium. In front of hundreds—*hundreds*—of people!"

"Ah . . . I'm going to take a wild guess and say public speaking is not your favorite thing?"

She turns on her side, tucking her hands under her cheek innocently. "It's paralyzing. I'm not an admirer of Edgar Allan Poe, but public speaking is my own personal "Premature Burial.""

I've never been big on Poe either—talk about a downer—but I understand what she means.

And I have the perfect solution.

"You should imagine me naked." I snap the waist of my sleeping pants. "I could take this off, if you like. The vivid image will heal all that ails you, sweets."

She shakes her head. "I believe the traditional strategy is to imagine the audience in their underwear."

"But imagining me naked is much more fun."

And we both laugh, even though it's true.

Sarah sits up and reaches over, plucking a string on my guitar. It's propped against the nightstand on her side of the bed. "So . . . do you actually know how to play this thing?"

"I do."

She lies down on her side, arm bent, resting her head in her hand, regarding me curiously. "You mean like, 'Twinkle, Twinkle, Little Star,' the 'ABC's,' and such?"

I roll my eyes. "You do realize that's the same song, don't you?"

Her nose scrunches as she thinks about it, and her lips move as she silently sings the tunes in her head. It's fucking adorable. Then she covers her face and laughs out loud.

"Oh my God, I'm an imbecile!"

"You shouldn't be so hard on yourself, but if you say so."

She narrows her eyes. "Bully." Then she sticks out her tongue.

Big mistake.

Because it's soft and pink and very wet . . . and it makes me want to suck on it. And then that makes me think of other pink, soft, and wet places on her sweet-smelling body . . . and then I'm hard.

Painfully, achingly hard.

Thank God for thick bedcovers. If this innocent, blushing bird realized there was a hot, hard, raging boner in her bed, mere inches away from her, she would either pass out from all the blood rushing to her cheeks or hit the ceiling in shock—clinging to it by her fingernails like a petrified cat over water.

"Well, you learn something new every day." She chuckles. "But you really know how to play the guitar?"

"You sound doubtful."

She shrugs. "A lot has been written about you, but I've never once heard that you play an instrument."

I lean in close and whisper, "It's a secret. I'm good at a lot of things that no one knows about."

Her eyes roll again. "Let me guess—you're fantastic in bed . . . but everybody knows that." Then she makes like she's playing the drums and does the sound effects for the punch-line rim shot. "*Ba dumb ba, chhhh.*"

And I laugh hard—almost as hard as my cock is.

"Shy, clever, a naughty sense of humor, and a total nutter. That's a damn strange combo, Titebottum."

"Wait till you get to know me—I'm definitely one of a kind."

The funny thing is, I'm starting to think that's absolutely true.

I rub my hands together, then gesture to the guitar. "Anyway, pass it here. And name a musician. Any musician."

"Umm . . . Ed Sheeran."

I shake my head. "All the girls love Ed Sheeran."

"He's a great singer. And he has the whole ginger thing going for him," she teases. "If you were born a prince with red hair? Women everywhere would adore you."

"Women everywhere already adore me."

"If you were a ginger prince, there'd be more."

"All right, hush now smartarse-bottum. And listen."

Then I play "Thinking Out Loud." About halfway through, I glance over at Sarah. She has the most beautiful smile, and I think something to myself that I've never thought in all my twenty-five years: this is how it feels to be Ed Sheeran.

Sarah bites her bottom lip when I finish. And she claps. Her voice is quieter, scratchier with sleepiness. "You play beautifully, Henry."

I wag my finger. "Told you. Never doubt me."

She yawns big and wide. "Do it again."

And though I feel exhaustion tugging on me, I don't want to say no.

I think a moment. "Here's one of my favorites."

I play "Hallelujah."

"I love this song, too." Sarah smiles serenely and hums softly along as I play.

Afterward, I grunt out a yawn of my own. As I lay my guitar on the floor, I tell Sarah, "You have excellent pitch. Do you sing?"

She stretches, pushing her awesomely full tits against her dark navy sleeping shirt, and my mouth goes dry.

"Only in the shower."

Big mistake number two.

I groan.

Sarah puts her glasses on the end table, frowning. "Are you all right?"

"I will be. Some day. I'm just really tired."

"Sorry. You came here for rest and I've kept you up."

I grin as I lie back on the pillow. "I didn't mind."

Although she's at the other end of the huge bed, it feels . . . nice, comforting . . . lying here like this.

"Good night, Henry."

"Sweet dreams, Sarah."

CHAPTER 10

Henry

When I wake up in the morning, Sarah is nowhere to be seen. And the ghost of being blown off after a one-night hookup walks over my grave. But I brush the feeling aside.

Because today's the day that the fun really starts. I have a workout date with Libby Loutenhiemer down at the beach, which means sweat and panting and her in some tight, scanty spandex outfit. Maybe we'll have an after-workout cocktail . . . which will hopefully lead to an equally sweaty but different kind of physical exertion, off camera.

My morning wood is particularly persistent, probably due to the delectable scent that filled my nostrils as I slept and still clings to my skin. But I don't have time to rub one out, so I head to my room, quickly change into a sweatshirt, running shorts, and cross-trainers, and jog to the beach.

An hour later, I discover yet again that none of this is how I envisioned it.

And I'm not in nearly as good of shape as I fucking thought.

Because Libby is an animal, and I don't mean the doggie-style type. The woman is an Olympian, but still . . .

A three-mile beach run, rope-jumping, sit-ups, push-ups, and a hundred mountain climbers later, I think I may actually be having a heart attack.

Which means if Granny kicks it, the throne goes to dumb Cousin Marcus—the only person less suited to rule than I am. For that reason, I power through, but it's not easy. I may not give Libby the diamond tiara, but I'm having serious thoughts of giving her the position of being my personal trainer.

Finally, we stop to catch our breath. We're on the beach, both bent at the waist, hands on our knees, the cold sea blowing on our heated, dripping skin.

"This was so fun!" Libby chirps. "You're the first man who's ever been able to keep pace with me."

I give her a thumbs-up. It's all I can manage, because my muscles and vital organs would very much like to lie down and die now.

She moves in closer and whispers in my ear, "I want to suck your big, sweaty cock, Henry."

Scratch that—not *every* organ is ready to die just yet.

"That's the best damn thing I've heard in ages."

She giggles, taking me by the hand, turning around . . . and walking straight into Vanessa Steele.

No.

"That was great, you two—hope you had a good time. Libby, we need you in hair and makeup for your after-date, hot-seat session."

Fuck no.

"And Henry, you have to be showered and dressed for your afternoon date." She taps her wrist. "We're on a schedule."

Talk about a royal cock-block.

Libby looks just as disappointed as I feel. She toys with the collar of my shirt.

"Later on, yeah?"

I nod, and she gives me a quick peck on the cheek.

Behind her, someone on the beach in the distance grabs my attention. I squint, peering closer. She's alone, in an oversized T-shirt and black leggings, doing what appears to be a martial arts routine, and looking very fine doing it. Just when I think I have this girl pegged . . .

Libby notices and turns around too.

"Sarah knows aikido," she says. "She's quite good."

When Vanessa ushers Libby away, I stay right there for a while longer.

Watching.

Later in the afternoon I have a dog-walking, picnic date with Cordelia Ominsmitch.

We meet in the courtyard of the castle and while the other ladies and crew are several yards away, behind the cameras, if I keep my back to them, it feels almost normal. Cordelia walks up to me, smiling, carrying a well-fed white miniature poodle with beady, angry black eyes.

The cameras roll as Cordelia reaches me, wearing snug blue jeans, high brown leather boots, and a flowy, flower-patterned blouse with a revealing neckline. She's lovely. I stand straight, one arm folded across my lower back, and nod.

"Hello, Henry."

"How are you, Cordelia?"

"I'm very well now." She flutters her lashes coyly. "But I've been thinking, I'd like to get our first kiss out of the way. Then, I won't be nervous thinking about it, and I'll already know how magical we are together."

She's playing for the cameras—I've seen it done enough to know. But I don't care.

"I'm game if you are."

And I lean in, she reaches up—then the unpleasant mongrel in her arms growls and tries to bite my face off. Luckily, I pull back just in time.

"Oh! Walter, no!"

She smiles apologetically. "This is Walter."

I wave. "Good to meet you, Walter."

He snarls back.

Cordelia bites her lip. "Sorry. He's very protective of me." She gazes down at the dog and he starts to lick her chin. "Aren't you, precious?" she coos to him. "You love your mummy. You want to give Mummy a kiss? Okay, give Mummy all your kisses."

And then Walter plants one on Cordelia—with tongue. And she lets him. He licks her chin, her lips, and as she laughs . . . it looks like her teeth and tongue get a thorough cleaning too.

Then she puts him on the ground and turns to me, starry-eyed and smiling.

"Now . . . about that kiss?"

I look at Cordelia's lush, perfect mouth, and then down at the pudgy pooch . . . voraciously licking his own arsehole. And I grimace.

"Maybe later."

Or . . . not.

"Cut!" the director yells.

And Vanessa walks forward, with a clipboard in hand. "That was great. Lots of simmering, sexual tension with a tease for more to come. Love it. Let's freshen up and we'll get some shots of Henry and Cordelia in the convertible for the montage and voice-over piece. Then we'll move to the picnic area; it's almost ready."

But then, from behind the camera, someone knocks into the lighting tripod. It tilts over and crashes, the lens bursting with a loud pop and splintering shatter. A minute later, there's a commotion, the ladies crowding together. There are whispers and concerned looks, and Laura Benningson asks if someone should get a doctor.

"No," I hear Penelope answer. "No, she'll be all right in a few minutes."

I push through the crowd to the center, where Sarah stands unnaturally still. Her skin is ashen, her face is frozen in terror, and her eyes are flat and blank. And I feel like I've been punched in the gut, because I remember this. From last year at the pub, the very first time I spoke to her. When someone dropped a tray of glasses, and she froze up in fear.

Penny has her arm around Sarah's lower back, softly whispering words I can't hear. And it's like my heart stops in my chest and my stomach roils at the sight of her so still and afraid. I go to move closer but before I get to her, she comes to. Waking up gasping and blinking, reaching for her sister.

What the hell was that?

Penny catches my eye and shakes her head, telling me silently not to come closer. To pretend that everything is fine.

Eventually, everyone goes back to their tasks—the crew prepares for the next taping, the ladies chat and drink Champagne.

But Sarah remains off on the side. And she looks smaller somehow, like she's trying to sink into herself. Fold up and disappear. I don't like it. Sarah's too pretty to not be standing straight and tall so everyone can see. And she's . . . nice. Believe it or not, that's rare in my circle. She helped me last night. Even though it made her uncomfortable, she did it anyway.

And now I want to do something for her.

I want to see Sarah Titebottum smile. A brazen, bold, unselfconscious smile. But more than that, there's a small, selfish part of me that wants to make her smile. Be the one she's smiling for.

I glance around the set—everyone is buzzing like worker bees getting ready for the shot. Cordelia's getting primped and powdered by a makeup girl, Vanessa is speaking with a few of the cameramen, and the convertible I'm supposed to drive is just sitting there . . . all by its lonesome.

And look at that—someone left the keys in the ignition.

Stealthily, I sidle up to Sarah.

"Have you ever driven in a convertible?"

She looks up sharply, like she didn't see me approach. "Of course I have."

My hands slide into my pockets and I lean back on my heels.

"Have you ever been in a convertible driven by a prince?"

Her eyes are lighter in the sun, with a hint of gold. They crinkle as she smiles.

"No."

I nod. "Perfect. We do this in three."

Now she looks nervous. "Do what?"

I spot James across the way, eyes scanning the crowd—far enough away that he'll never get over here in time.

"Three . . ."

"I don't know what you mean."

"Two . . ."

"Henry . . ."

"One."

"I . . ."

"Go, go, go!"

"Go where?" she asks, loud enough to draw attention.

So I wrap my arm around her waist, lift her off her feet, carry her to the car, and swing her up and into the passenger seat. Then, I jump into the driver's side.

"Shit!" James curses. But then the engine is roaring to life. I back out, knocking over a food service table, and the tires screech as I turn around and drive across the grounds . . . toward the woods.

"The road is that way!" Sarah yells, the wind making her long, dark hair dance and swirl.

"I know a shortcut. Buckle up."

We fly into the woods, sending a flurry of leaves in our wake. The car bounces and jostles, and I feel Sarah's hand wrapped around my arm—holding on. It feels good.

"Duck."

"What?"

I push her head down and crouch at the same time, to avoid getting whipped in the face by the low-branch of a pine tree.

After we're past it, Sarah sits up, owl-eyed, and looks back at the branch and then at me.

I smirk. "If you wanted me to push your head down, love, you could've just said so."

"You're insane!"

I hit the gas hard, swerving around a stump. "What? You're the only one who gets to make dirty jokes?"

We have a sharp turn coming up ahead. I lay my arm across Sarah's middle. "Hold on."

And as quick as that, we emerge from the trees, up a steep slope, and onto the smooth asphalt of the highway. I check the rearview mirror, and the coast is clear.

Sarah blinks at me. Her glasses are crooked, so I fix them for her.

"I get the feeling you've done that before."

I tilt my head up, enjoying the feel of the sun and breeze— like a dog on a joyride. "Ditching security is one of the thrills of my life."

She shakes her head, flabbergasted. "Why?"

"Because I'm not supposed to."

And then she smiles. Just like I wanted her to. Big and shamelessly. And my chest goes warm and my heart beats hard.

I flick the knob on the radio, and "Setting the World on Fire" by Pink and that country bloke comes from the speakers.

"This is a good song," Sarah says.

"Then turn it up," I tell her.

She does, then she holds her hands out, trying to catch the wind.

We both decide we're hungry. And though Sarah's hometown, Castlebrook, is the town nearest to the castle, there's no Mega Burger in Castlebrook. So, we head in the opposite direction, because Mega Burger is worth the extra forty-five-minute driving time.

When I pull up to the order window, the lad in the pointy paper hat jumps.

"Holy fuck!"

I glance at Sarah. "I get that a lot."

"Damn, man . . . you're Prince Henry."

I nod. "Good to meet you."

"Hey, can I get a photo?"

"Sure."

He leans out the window and I lean out of the car, and he snaps a selfie.

"Do me a favor," I ask, "don't post it on social media. I'm supposed to be working and if the Queen finds out I'm slacking off, she'll be angry. You wouldn't like her when she's angry."

He laughs, nodding.

After the boy brings our order and I pay, I slip him an extra wad of cash. "Use this to treat as many cars as possible that come after me. If there's any left over, it's yours."

His head bobs. "Awesome. I always thought you were cool."

"I try." We bump fists and then I pull out.

I feel Sarah watching warmly as I drive.

"That was very nice."

"That was easy." I shrug. "My mother used to say that

kindness is contagious. It only takes one person to start the best kind of epidemic."

I pull up to a deserted lot near the beach, kill the engine, and Sarah and I perch on the hood of the car to eat our flaming-hot heart-attack-waiting-to-happen with fries.

Hesitantly, I ask about her earlier episode. "Are you feeling all right now?"

Her smile is small and embarrassed. "Yes."

"Does what happened . . . happen often?"

She tilts her head. "Not too frequently."

I'm in unfamiliar territory here. I don't want her to be uncomfortable, but at the same time I want to know more about those episodes. More about her, full stop.

"Look, Sarah, feel free to tell me to piss off, but is it . . . a medical condition?"

"Temporary fugues, brought on by loud noises. I've tried a few treatments, but it's just something I live with. If there's a crash, sometimes I just . . . blink out."

"You looked so frightened. Where do you go when you blink out?" I ask very gently.

Sarah swallows, staring at the ground. "Nowhere. It's just . . . gray. There's no floor, no ceiling or walls, no sound. It's just as if I'm . . . suffocating in gray."

I cover her small, warm hand with mine. "I'm sorry. Do you know why? What caused them to start?"

Sarah's smile is tight. "Everyone has their quirks."

Then she breathes deep and deftly changes the subject. "Are you enjoying filming the show?" Sarah asks. "Narrowing down your choice for queen?"

I nod. "So far, Guermo's my top pick."

She chuckles.

"What do you think of the show, so far?" I ask.

She grunts. "I think it's a glorified beauty pageant."

"You don't approve?"

She shrugs. "I suppose it could be worse. At least they're including a variety of women, not just those who check the boxes of those disgusting laws on who a crown prince can marry."

"Are you a virgin?" I ask.

"Well . . . yes."

"Then why are you complaining? You qualify."

Sarah's eyes flash with annoyance and she practically growls at me. "Because I'm more than my hymen, Henry! To base the value of an accomplished, intelligent, passionate woman on a flimsy piece of skin is degrading. How would you feel if your worth rested on your foreskin?"

I think it over. And then I grin. "I'd be all right with that, actually. I've heard it was an impressive foreskin—all the nurses were fawning over it. It's probably being showcased in a museum right now."

She stares at me for a beat, then she laughs out loud—a rich, throaty, sensual sound.

"You're a terrible human being."

"I know." I shake my head at the calamity of it all.

"And you're an even worse feminist."

"Agreed. That's something I need to work on. You'll help me, won't you? We should spend as much time together as possible—every minute of the day and night. I'm hoping you'll rub off on me."

Sarah pushes my shoulder. "Ha! You're just hoping I'll rub you off."

Now it's my turn to laugh. Because she's not even a little bit wrong.

"But there's never been anyone? Really?"

Sarah shrugs. "Penny and I were tutored at home when we were young . . . but in year ten, there was this one boy."

I rub my hands together. "Here we go—tell me everything. I want all the sick, lurid details. Was he a footballer? Big and strong, captain of the team, the most popular boy in school?"

I could see it. Sarah's delicate, long and lithe, but dainty, beautiful—any young man would've been desperate to have her on his arm. In his lap. In his bed, on the hood of his car, riding his face . . . all of the above.

"He was captain of the chess team."

I cover my eyes with my hand.

"His name was Davey. He wore these adorable tweed jackets and bow ties, he had blond hair, and was a bit pale because of the asthma. He had the same glasses as I and he had a different pair of argyle socks for every day of the year."

"You're messing with me, right?"

She shakes her head.

"Argyle socks, Sarah? I am so disappointed in you right now."

"He was nice," she chides. "You leave my Davey alone."

Then she laughs again—delighted and free. My cock reacts hard and fast, emphasis on hard. It's like sodding granite.

"So what happened to old Davey boy?"

"I was alone in the library one day and he came up and started to ask me to the spring social. And I was so excited and nervous I could barely breathe."

I picture how she must've looked then. But in my mind's eyes she's really not any different than she is right now. Innocent, sweet, and so real she couldn't deceive someone if her life depended on it.

"And then before he could finish the question, I . . ."

I don't realize I'm leaning toward her until she stops talking and I almost fall over.

"You . . . what?"

Sarah hides behind her hands.

"I threw up on him."

And I try not to laugh. I swear I try . . . but I'm only human. So I end up laughing so hard the car shakes and I can't speak for several minutes.

"Christ almighty."

"And I'd had fish and chips for lunch." Sarah's laughing too. "It was awful."

"Oh you poor thing." I shake my head, still chuckling. "And poor Davey."

"Yes." She wipes under her eyes with her finger. "Poor Davey. He never came near me again after that."

"Coward—he didn't deserve you. I would've swam through a whole lake of puke to take a girl like you to the social."

She smiles so brightly at me, her cheeks maroon and round like two shiny apples.

"I think that's the nicest thing anyone's ever said to me."

I wiggle my eyebrows. "I'm all about the compliments."

Sarah shakes her head. "Anyway. Once word got around school, no one else wanted to come near me. And here I am—twenty-five and probably more of a virgin than the Virgin Mary was."

Sarah makes the sign of the cross, just in case that's blasphemous, I guess.

"But you have some experience, don't you?" I slide my fingers together meaningfully. "Even . . . just with yourself? Rubbing one out is good for the soul."

Her reaction is a level-five blush . . . crimson.

"That's private," she murmurs.

"That's a yes."

And holy hell, the images that come to my mind. My cock moans—willing to give up a neighboring nut for a peek at Sarah Von Titebottum pleasuring herself.

"Since I'm staying in your room, we should work out a system. A sock on the door or such. I don't want to deprive you. Or . . . you could let me watch—I'm a fantastic audience member."

She glares, still blushing. "I don't like you anymore."

I tap her nose. "Liar."

When we pull back into the castle courtyard, James is waiting. And he does not look happy. Actually he looks like a blond Hulk . . . right before he goes smash. Sarah sees it too.

"He's miffed."

"Yep."

We get out of the car and she turns so fast there's a breeze. "I should go find Penny. 'Bye."

I call after her. "Chicken!"

She just waves her hand over her shoulder.

Slowly, I approach him. Like an explorer, deep in the jungles of the Amazon, making first contact with a tribe that has never seen the outside world. And I hold out my peace offering.

It's a Mega Pounder with cheese.

"I got you a burger."

James snatches it from my hand angrily. But . . . he doesn't throw it away.

He turns to one of the men behind him. "Mick, bring it here."

Mick—a big, truck-size bloke—brings him a brown paper bag. And James's cold blue eyes turn back to me.

"After speaking with your former security team, I had an audience with Her Majesty the Queen last year when you were named heir. Given your history of slipping your detail, I asked her permission to ensure your safety by any means necessary, including this."

He reaches into the bag and pulls out a children's leash—the type you see on ankle-biters at amusement parks, with a deranged-looking monkey sticking its head out of a backpack, his mouth wide and gaping, like he's about to eat whoever's wearing it.

And James smiles. "Queen Lenora said yes."

I suspected Granny didn't like me anymore; now I'm certain of it.

"If I have to," James warns, "I'll connect this to you and the other end to old Mick here."

Mick doesn't look any happier about the fucking prospect than I am.

"I don't want to do that, but . . ." He shrugs, no further explanation needed. "So the next time you feel like ditching? Remember the monkey, Your Grace."

He puts the revolting thing back in its bag. And I wonder if fire would kill it.

"Are we good, Prince Henry?" James asks.

I respect a man willing to go balls-to-the-wall for his job. I don't like the monkey . . . but I respect it.

I flash him the okay sign with my fingers.

"Golden."

CHAPTER 11

Sarah

The *Matched* crew wakes us up before dawn, banging on doors like drill sergeants, to the vocal disgruntlement of the contestants. If there's one thing the female aristocracy values above all else, it's beauty sleep. Staff have been fired—and in the past, killed—for less.

I think the producer intentionally wants them on edge, moody, and pissed off—ready to snap at each other.

Drama sells, almost as well as sex.

They tell us to pack an overnight bag quickly. Only one bag per person, which for this group is a challenge. They don't tell us our destination, only to bring clothes appropriate for a pool party. Danish pastries and tea are laid out on the dining room table, but we have to grab and go, to the airport.

Once there, we're ushered into a very large back waiting room, separate and shielded from the public. The rear wall is all windows, facing the tarmac where private planes sit. Henry gazes out the window, in a white button-down shirt and tan slacks, his broad back to the room of ladies, leaning one hand on the glass. He seems fixed on something, staring.

I come up beside him, peeking under his arm, to see what he sees.

And my heart drops.

Because it's a military plane. Four uniformed soldiers have deplaned, and with practiced, almost beautiful precision, they carry a casket, draped in the gold-and-purple Wessco flag, and place it onto a silver-wheeled table.

I'm transfixed as they move, marching in time, one man at each of the corners—reverently escorting the remains toward the waiting hearse. Three of the soldiers stay behind, while one of them walks through the door at the far end of the waiting room we now occupy.

It's only then that I turn my head and see a dark-haired, middle-aged woman in a wrinkled beige coat, holding the hand of the small boy beside her. He seems to be about ten years old. The soldier bends his head, speaking softly, handing the woman a manila envelope.

Henry watches for a moment, and then he's walking toward them. I follow behind.

The soldier's eyes flare when he sees him, immediately going stiff with a salute. Henry pauses a few feet away, snapping a salute in return. And then the soldier bows low and Henry nods. The soldier straightens up, gives some final words to the woman, and tells her they'll wait for her at the car until she's ready.

The woman watches him walk away, bringing a tissue to her nose. And it's only then that she notices Henry—realizes who he is.

"Oh, Your Highness." She bows, and the boy beside her mimics the motion. "Hello. I didn't know you were here."

"It's an unannounced trip. Ms. . . .?"

"Campbell. Mrs. Margery Campbell." She strokes the boy's hair. "And this is Louis."

"Mrs. Campbell. Hello, Louis."

"Hello, Prince Henry," the boy says without smiling.

"I want to offer my condolences for your loss."

Mrs. Campbell dabs at her eyes with the tissue. "Thank

you." She gazes lovingly at the casket through the window. "That's my oldest, Charlie."

"Charlie Campbell," Henry says, like he's committing the name to memory.

"That's right. Charlie's captain told me that it was an ambush that took him, said he was very brave. He drew the fire on himself so the other boys could take cover."

"A heroic act that I'm sure those boys will never forget," Henry offers.

Mrs. Campbell nods. "He was always a good lad. Protective. And now he's in heaven with his da, watching over us all."

I lean down toward Louis. "I bet Charlie loved having you for a little brother."

The boy sniffs and nods. "He taught me how to fly-fish. I've been practicing and I'm real good at it now."

I nod, just barely able to hold back my tears. "And whenever you fish, you'll think of him and so he'll always be with you."

Louis nods again.

Henry takes his wallet from his pocket and hands Mrs. Campbell his card. "If there's anything I can do for you—anything at all—I want you to call my office. Please."

She takes the card, smiling with wet eyes. "I will, thank you." Then she gazes up at Henry, contemplatively. "You've grown into such a fine young man, Prince Henry. Princess Calista would be so proud."

Henry looks down. "I hope so," he says, his voice soft and rough.

"Oh, I'm sure of it. We mums know these things. She would be as proud of you as I . . ." Her voice drifts off as she turns to gaze at the flag-draped casket. And her face crumples. "Oh my boy . . . my poor, sweet Charlie . . ."

She covers her face, sobbing into her hands, and the tears leak through her fingers.

Without hesitating, Henry pulls her into his arms and presses her head to his chest.

It's a break in protocol—common citizens aren't supposed to hug royalty—but Henry doesn't seem to care.

"I'm sorry," he whispers, smoothing her hair down. "I'm so, so sorry."

When little Louis's face twists, I hug him to me, soothing him with soft, rambling words that I can only hope will bring him comfort.

And we stay just like that for a time, until the tears calm and deep breaths are taken. Henry leaves Mrs. Campbell with a squeeze of her hands and a reminder to call his office if she needs anything. Then together, we rejoin our waiting group.

"That was television gold!" Vanessa Steele practically bounces in her stilettoes. "When that footage airs—the dashing prince comforting the grieving mother—it'll be the biggest cross-continental panty drop the world has ever seen."

At first Henry looks ill, and then . . . angry.

"You filmed that?"

"Of course we filmed it. I told you, everything is copy—and that was fucking phenomenal. Real emotion; you can't stage that kind of thing."

Henry's finger lashes out, pointing toward the exiting hearse. "That boy died for his country. For *my* country. He gave his life protecting the ground beneath your feet."

Vanessa stands straight, meeting his discontent head on.

"And when I'm done with him, everyone will know his name. His story and sacrifice."

Horseshit. I'm naïve, but not even I am *that* naïve. The producer's motivations have nothing to do with honoring the dead.

Henry nods, tensely rubbing his lips together. He motions to the cameraman. "Can I see it?"

The cameraman hands over the silver device—small, as

Penny had explained to me, to unobtrusively capture the shot in public, but powerful enough to film from long distances in the highest definition. Henry turns it over in his hands.

Then he drops it to the ground and stomps it to pieces beneath his boot—paying special care to pulverize the memory card.

"Henry!" Vanessa screeches. "God damn it!"

"This is one of the worst days of their lives, in a string of horrific days," he bites back. "You don't get to turn that into entertainment."

The producer seethes. "Do you know how expensive that equipment is?"

Henry sneers. "Bill me."

And then he strides away.

Out on the tarmac as we file up the steps onto the plane, Henry is last in line. I double back and slip behind him. He's still furious—his face tight, shoulders tense, and fists clenched.

"That was amazing," I tell him softly. "I think what you did was amazing."

He shakes his head bitterly.

"No. It was just decent." His eyes burn with a green, thrashing fire. "Your expectations shouldn't be so low."

"My expectations of you?"

"Of everyone." His words are clipped and sharp. "Set your bar higher, Sarah."

Then he turns around, dismissing me, and steps onto the plane.

We touch down in Hampton Hills, a posh destination for the rich and famous in the northernmost region of Wessco. A black window–tinted caravan whisks us to The Reginald Hotel, where *Matched* has reserved the indoor pool for a private party. Upon entering, Henry strips down to his swim trunks and heads straight for the bar. The camera follows him as he moves to a reclining lounge chair, a whiskey in each hand.

My chest pinches as I watch him watching the ladies frolic in the pool, in their colorful array of barely-there string bikinis. I push up the sleeves of my black shirt, feeling sticky and uncomfortable in the steamy, humid room. Until Vanessa Steele whips out her obnoxious bullhorn again, ordering all assistants and non-cast members to leave the area.

"Come play, Henry!" Lady Cordelia calls, holding a beach ball over her head and moving closer to the cameraman who stands at the edge of the pool.

He gulps his drink, grinning. "I'll join you just as soon as I finish this, sweets."

I look away and move toward Penelope, where she's comparing manicures with Laura Benningson near the diving board.

"I'm going up to the room, Pen," I tell her. "Behave yourself, yeah?"

My sister nods and waves.

And my head wants to swivel in Henry's direction for one last look, to see if he's gone to "play" with Cordelia. But I force myself to keep my eyes trained on the door.

And then I walk out.

Later, after a dinner of fish and chips in my room, I lie in bed trying to read *Jane Eyre*, but my heart's just not in it. The words blend together and the only thing I see in my mind is Henry Pembrook, lying half-naked on a pool chair, giggling and laughing and drinking. I wonder—did he stay at the pool? Or did he move to one of the girls' rooms—Cordelia or Elizabeth or, hell, Penelope's—for a more private party?

My book closes with a clap.

I slip on my shoes and take the lift down to the pool. It's

late, and the hotel halls are quiet and empty. James, Henry's personal security guard, stands outside the pool area door.

"Is he still in there?" I ask.

"He is, Lady Sarah."

I try to sound nonchalant, but don't think I pull it off.

"Is he alone?"

James's blue eyes are soft with sympathy; I just can't tell if it's for Henry or for me.

"Aye. Filming wrapped hours ago but he hasn't left. Hasn't eaten, either."

I nod. And against my better judgment, allow my feet to pull me inside.

He's in the deep end, his upper body floating on an inner tube, a half-full glass of whiskey in his hand. And he's singing. *"Rubber ducky, you're the one. You make bath time lots of fun."*

"You do realize it's a swimming pool and not a bathtub, don't you?"

His eyes are cloudy. Drunk.

"There she is. Where did you float off to, little duck? You missed the party. It was a good time."

"I was in my room."

He holds up his glass, sloshing the contents into the pool. "Don't tell me—you were *reading*. What was on the menu this evening?"

"Jane Eyre."

A disgusted sound comes from his throat. "That's depressing. Not even a good mummy porn or a nice, old-fashioned bodice ripper?"

I snort, because Prince Henry knowing those terms is funny.

"Not tonight."

"Well, let me know when you've got one of those—I want you to read it to me. Out loud."

As expected, I blush, and Henry chuckles.

Then he lowers his face to the water, sucks up a mouthful, and spits it out in a high, arched stream. "Look, I'm a fountain."

I shake my head. "You're an arse."

He pouts. "Is that any way to speak to the heir to the throne?"

"Right now? Yes." I cross my arms. "You should get out—you're all pruned."

"Or you could join me? Come on, jump in—show me your best cannonball."

"I'm not wearing a suit."

"So swim naked. I'll keep my eyes closed, I swear."

He holds up his hand, fingers crossed, to show me he's lying. And I laugh. "I don't think so."

"What are you frightened of?"

"Dying. I don't know how to swim."

If he's surprised by the admission he doesn't show it.

"You shouldn't be afraid of dying, Sarah—everyone does it. The only thing to be scared of is not living before you do."

I move closer, my shoes stopping at the edge. "That's very poetic, Henry. Now come out—it's dangerous to drink and swim alone."

"Then don't let me swim alone! The water's lovely. Come in, let me carry you to the other end of the pool—face your fear—and then I'll get out like a good lad, I promise."

This time his fingers are spread wide, uncrossed. He slips out of the inner tube, holding his drink above the water, and kicks over to me. Waiting.

He's going to be stubborn about this, I can tell. And there's a foreign, blooming bud inside me that wants to try. It's a quiet but insistent voice, a gentle nudge. I'm starting to think of it as the Henry Effect, because he makes me feel so many . . . things. Safe and wild and maybe just a little bit mad all at once.

Henry makes me want to take a chance. On new experiences. And on him.

So, I take a deep breath and slide out of my shoes. Trying to control my shaking limbs, I turn around and lower myself over the edge, into the water. My cotton sleeping pants and shirt mold to my body, but they're light, so they don't drag me down. Still, I hold onto the edge with white-knuckled hands.

And Henry is right there, his skin slick and warm, his arm like an iron band around my waist—strong and solid.

"That's a brave girl," he whispers against my ear.

I turn in his arms, squeezing mine around his neck. My legs kick, and the sensation of nothing beneath them sends me veering toward panic.

"Easy, I've got you."

Henry shifts to his back, arranging me on his torso, like he's my own personal royal floaty. Then he reaches for his drink on the pool's edge. "Hold onto this for me?"

Smoothly, he pushes us off from the wall, and the water makes little currents against his shoulders and arms as we glide toward the middle. My trembling eases a bit.

"See?" Henry teases. "Water is your friend. Do you want to learn to swim? I could teach you."

"I don't know." I eye the water suspiciously.

"Why are you afraid all the time?" he asks, not in a nasty way but with simple curiosity.

"I'm not. I just like . . . consistency."

"Consistency is boring."

"It's safe. If you know what's coming, you're never caught off guard."

Henry rolls his eyes.

"Why are you sad all the time?" I ask.

"I'm not sad—I'm pitiful. There's a difference."

He's quiet for a moment, and the only sound between us is the gentle swish of water.

"Do you think Charlie Campbell lived?" Henry wonders. "Before he died?"

Droplets glitter on his lashes like diamonds. I try to focus on that and not the heartache wrapped in the question.

"I hope so. Sometimes, that's all there is. Hope."

Henry nods. "I suppose you're right."

I hold up his drink and toast, "To Charlie."

Henry smiles softly as I take a sip, before holding the glass to his lips.

"To Charlie," he says, then drinks.

He takes the empty glass from my hand and sends it floating away. Then he strokes his arms through the water, pushing us gently forward.

And then, he just . . . looks at me. With warmth and enjoyment. My glasses fog and I slip them off.

"Fuck, but you're pretty," Henry murmurs.

Instinctually, my chin dips and I glance down at his chest.

"Hasn't anyone ever told you that?"

I shrug. "Not really."

"They should have," he insists softly. "You should've been told every day how pretty you are—inside and out."

And there's a great swelling of tenderness in my chest, around my heart, that almost feels too large to contain. Not because of the compliment, but because of him. This beautiful, broken, pitiful prince. Was Henry ever told how brilliant he is? Kind and strong, generous, and good? I don't think he was and they should've told him. Every single day.

Before I know it, we're across the pool at the shallow end. Henry's shoulder brushes the slick, tiled edge.

"There." He stands upright and my feet touch the pool's bottom. "That wasn't so bad, was it?"

We're close enough that I can taste his breath—smoky wood, whiskey, and man.

"No. Not so bad."

And I feel like I'm in a daze, like I'm in a dream. Our gazes lock and Henry's finger runs from my forehead, down my cheek to my chin, stroking back a damp lock of hair.

"Sarah . . ." he says, almost groaning.

He leans in closer, slowly . . .

And I blink and turn away.

Because maybe he's right after all. Maybe I *am* afraid all the time.

I move to the edge of the pool, out of his embrace. A waterfall pours from my sopping clothes as I lift myself out, my voice quickly chirping with cheeriness.

"Come on now, out we go."

I wrap one towel from the lounge chair around my chest and unfold the other, holding it open for him. Henry hesitates, looking ready to argue.

"You promised," I remind him.

He sighs dramatically and lowers his lips into the water, blowing out a wet raspberry. But then he climbs up the steps, holding the railing, and takes the towel from me, rubbing it over his shoulders and down his arms.

I try not to look, but when he dries his stomach my eyes drop—and the clear, hard outline of his thick erection against his swim trunks is unmistakable. And magnificent.

I know he's caught me looking when he teases, "Will you tuck me into bed, Titebottum? Give me a good-night kiss . . . somewhere?"

I tighten the towel at my chest, hating how prim the action must look, but still replying, "No. That honor goes to James."

He scoffs. "Spoilsport."

CHAPTER 12

Henry

After our night at the pool, things are different between Sarah and me. More. Closer. I still make her blush prettily—but it's a soft pink that blooms on her cheeks now, not the intense deep scarlet that resulted from my first teasings. She still keeps to herself mostly, reading in a corner or under a tree, but she comes out to watch as we film, and more than once I've spotted her chatting and laughing with Laura Benningson and Princess Alpacca, with Guermo's broody translating assistance.

I haven't slept in my own room—or attempted to—since that first night. I thought the producers would give me shit for that, but Vanessa explained they're not counting on the cameras catching anything interesting there—they're there in case something good just happens to occur.

And while my days are spent ziplining and bungee jumping, shearing wool on a sheep farm and swimming in hot springs with a different lady every time, before bestowing a dwindling number of glass-slipper charms—like a randy male tooth fairy—my nights are spent in a blissful hell of unrequited lust.

Because I can't forget the feel of Sarah pressed against me in the water, slick and soft and wet. She's almost constantly in my thoughts.

She haunts my dreams.

And she's caused me, more than once, to wake up painfully hard and snuggled up against the sweetest, tightest of Titebottums—using every ounce of self-restraint I have to keep from humping her in her sleep.

At night, when Sarah hums while reading her bland, classic novels in bed, I yearn to feel those lovely lips humming around my cock. When she sighs in her sleep, I think of how she would sound moaning for more. When she absentmindedly twirls her hair around her finger, I imagine fisting my hand in those dark, silky tresses and teaching her every filthy delight I know—and I know a lot.

The other evening when I walked into the room, Sarah was in the bath. I stood outside the locked bathroom door, listening to the drip and swish of the water as she moved, washing herself—touching herself—and I almost came in my pants like a sodding twelve-year-old boy.

It's becoming a problem.

But I don't consider, for even a moment, staying in my own room. Because the best part and the hardest part—pun intended—is that after we're in bed, with Sarah in her plain cotton sleeping clothes, both of us bundled under the covers to keep out the drafty frigid air, and the lights are low . . . we chat. About everything and nothing and all the things in-between.

She talks about her mother with her greenhouses and flowers; Penny with her Hollywood dreams; her grouchy boss, who sounds like he could be a relation of old Fergus; her library and tidy little flat and simple, organized life. I tell her about Nicholas and all the misplaced faith he has in me, though Sarah insists it's not misplaced at all. I talk about spunky, spirited Olive and how I wish they didn't live so far away. And in soft, shamed tones, I tell her about Granny—and how thoroughly I've disappointed her time and again.

And Sarah Titebottum, as timid and bashful as she appears to be, is an honest-to-God optimist. She has no patience for self-pity or regret, but instead, like the little train that could, she believes in onward and upward, in moving forward one small step at a time.

Though I'm familiar with the basic history, Sarah tells me excitedly about Lady Jane Grey, the nine-day Queen of England, whom she read a book about once. It was a romanticized account of how she ended up falling in love with Guildford Dudley, the man her family forced her to marry. And when dark-intentioned powers illegitimately propped Lady Jane up as Queen, it was that love that gave her the strength to dream grand dreams about the things she could do for her people and her country. Sarah's smile is so delightful, her face so animated as we talk, I don't have the heart to point out that young Lady Jane never had the chance to implement any of her plans. Because they cut her fucking head off.

Sarah doesn't ask me about my own future, my thoughts on becoming King, and I'm grateful for that. Because I still don't want to think about it. But there's a light in her eyes and an admiration in her voice that makes me feel, deep inside, that Sarah believes I could be good at it.

And it's different than with Nicholas. Or Granny.

For reasons I can't put my finger on, the fact that this pure, unadulterated lass believes it—that she believes in me—makes me think that the day could come when I believe it too.

Midway through the second week of filming, we wrap an outdoor shoot on the balcony at around eight p.m. As soon as the director calls cut, Elizabeth twines herself around me like a vine of poison ivy, whispering the deviant things she wants to do to me on camera—some of which I'm not sure the laws of physics will allow.

I disentangle myself and charge toward my room. Well . . . Sarah's and my room. But when I walk in, I find her filling her worn satchel with her books—looking like she's on her way out the door. I saunter over to the nook, bracing my hand on the wall behind her, and lean in.

"And just where are you sneaking off to so late at night?"

She looks up at me, her mouth tightening into an amused bow.

"I'm not sneaking and it's hardly the middle of the night, Henry."

She smells like sweets and I want to lick her. Up, down, and all around.

So I pretend she hasn't spoken and continue with my train of thought—it's much more interesting anyway.

"Are you on your way to a hot date with a secret lover, perhaps? Or maybe you belong to a sex club? A seedy, back-alley place you visit every chance you can, but not nearly as often as you'd like, where every fetish—no matter how depraved—is rapturously indulged."

My eyes travel down her body, visually caressing the sumptuous curves beneath her tight black turtleneck and leggings. "Maybe a naughty librarian fantasy? Or is it a cat-burglar role play? You're caught sifting through some wealthy, well-hung aristocrat's bedroom and have to beg, *'Oh please don't turn me in, My Lord—however can I persuade you? I'll do anything . . .'*"

Delicate eyebrows rise above the wire frame of her glasses. "That's very . . . specific. Seems like you've given this a lot of thought."

"You have no idea." I lean in closer. "Where are we going, love?"

"We?" Her eyes are darker—dilated, and her chest rises and falls in quick, excited pants. I wonder if she even realizes it. "*I* have a meeting. Mother's sent her car to take me. You can't come, Henry."

"I can come lots of times. My stamina is legendary. Do you want me to show you?"

Her voice comes out soft, husky. "You can't come with me."

"That sounds like a challenge." I smirk slowly. "I bet I could time it just right."

Her mobile pings, alerting her to the text that her car is out front. She blinks and ducks under my arm, scooting away—and like the dog I am, I want to chase her.

"What kind of meeting?"

Sarah slips into her coat. "A club meeting."

And I'm about to bring up the sex club again and ratchet up the raunchy—but then it all becomes clear.

"It's a book club, isn't it?"

Of course it is.

Sarah nods. "The bi-monthly meeting of The Austenites."

And here I am, again, trying not to laugh.

She takes one look at my face and jabs her finger into my chest. And the small, sharp contact makes my cock grow thick and hard.

Celibacy is making me crazy.

"Don't you dare laugh."

I bite my lip and catch her gazing at my mouth.

"The Austenites," I repeat, clearing my throat. "What do the Austenites do, exactly?"

"Character discussions, read-alouds, community events . . . sometimes we put on plays."

"Sounds riveting. I've never been to a book club meeting. Seems like something everyone should try at least once."

She crosses her arms, making her breasts squeeze and lift. "You'll hate it."

I cross my arms, and her eyes fall to my biceps—she's been doing that a lot lately, the naughty virgin voyeur.

"I'm getting the feeling you don't want me to go. Are you ashamed of me? That hurts, Titty-bottum—I'm wounded."

She laughs disdainfully. "No you're not. And it has nothing to do with me not wanting you to go—you can't go. There are about thirty Austenites. As soon as they spot you, word will get out that you were in Castlebrook."

"Oh the horror, because Castlebrook is the hub of the social scene and media elites."

That was sarcasm, in case you weren't sure. Sarah is, which is why her eyes rolls behind her glasses. "It only takes one set of loose lips for the Queen to find out you were there when you're supposed to be here. And the producers don't want you going anywhere, anyway."

"I could ditch?"

She blows a puff of breath up at her dark bangs, which have fallen too close to her eyes.

And now I'm thinking about Sarah blowing things.

"And then you'll have to wear the monkey."

"I fear no man or monkey. But it is sort of creepy, isn't it?" I groan. "Fucking James."

Sarah mocks me. "Right, fucking James is trying to keep you safe and alive and not kidnapped, like it's his job or something. Bastard."

Huh, look at that. Sarah can do sarcasm too. That's sexy. And she said the word *fucking*—which makes me think about fucking her—on the bed, the sofa . . . Christ, *in the nook*. She would be absolutely wild in the nook.

Talk about a fantasy—that one's going straight to the top of the wank bank.

"I'll be bored here by myself," I whine, just to see her smile. "I guess I'll rub one out. Or . . . five. Because that's how I roll. And how I rub."

But the thing is, this time . . . Sarah doesn't blush. She just looks at me, eyes glazing over like she's seeing an alternate version of me. A me that's whacking off. And judging from the way she swallows hard and runs her tongue along her bottom lip, she likes what she sees.

Fuck, that is so hot.

She blinks, snapping out of it, adorably flustered. "I . . . ah . . . I have to go."

I wave.

Halfway through the door, Sarah stops and turns around. "Henry?"

"Mmm?"

She points her finger at me. "Stay."

I smile and salute her.

With narrowed eyes, she backs out of the door, closing it behind her.

And I sit on the uncomfortable sofa for five whole minutes, thinking. And then I get up.

Because I still don't like doing what I'm told.

Two hours later, the car pulls up to Concordia Library—I'm assuming this is where the holy book club meeting is held. Sarah had a valid point about it not being good if word got around that I was in town, so I gave her a healthy head start and plan to slip in undetected in the back to see her in action.

She also had a point about the sodding monkey.

Which is why James is driving and good ole Mick is riding shotgun.

Out of the tinted SUV window, I glance up at the large ivory building. A library built for a queen. I can see her working here—I can see her loving it here. It suits her, this almost magical house of worship built for books.

The main roadway is nearly deserted and there's not a single person in front of the dimly lit library. As I follow Mick up the ivory stone steps, for a moment I wonder, *is this stalker territory? Does it cross a line? A boundary?* But then—fuck it, I'm a prince, we don't have boundaries—it's one of the perks. Anyone who says otherwise is doing it wrong.

The door's unlocked and we go in. I'd never noticed how eerie a library is at night—large and echoed—like a mausoleum. But I notice it now as I glance about the main floor, listening. I head down a set of stairs near the circulation desk, with light coming from small windows in the doors at the bottom of it. I glance through the windows and spot a room at the end of a long hallway. It's about classroom size, the kind of place where a Bible study or Sex Addicts Anonymous meeting might be held. Or a book club.

The door's open just enough to hear, but closed enough that I'll remain undetected if I stand outside of it. I lean back against the wall, listening to the charming lilt and fall of Sarah's unmistakable voice. And I discover a whole different side of her—another version to add to all the others. I don't think I'll ever completely figure her out.

She sounds confident, efficient, and sure, almost businesslike. I wonder if it's this place, if it's because this is her domain, and she thrives here. It almost reminds me of my grandmother in her office or while addressing Parliament.

When it seems as if they're wrapping up, Mick and I duck into a room next door. It's filled with odd-smelling boxes, a bag of ski masks, cans of red paint, poster boards and signs—one says "Free the Butterwald Ducks."

What in the bloody hell is a Butterwald Duck?

When the last trickle of bookworms slinks down the hall, and only three distinct voices remain in the room—and I know who those voices belong to—I have Mick wait outside while I pop my head in.

"Don't tell me I missed it? Over already—damn."

Sarah's entire face lights up. It makes me feel a bit drunk.

"Henry! What are you doing here?"

"I couldn't stay away."

And I'm only half joking.

A gorgeously round little piece with bright blue eyes and blond hair approaches from across the room and curtsies, sighing, "Wow. Wow, wow, wow."

This must be Annie—Sarah talks about her and Willard often.

"This is Annie," Sarah says.

She's the type I'd usually go for—perky and easily happy with a look of pure hero worship on her face. The funny thing is, she's Sarah's friend, and that fact puts up an immediate roadblock in my brain, muting any attraction to her.

"And this," Sarah gestures to a short bloke in a large chair with an enormous smoking pipe between his lips, "this is Willard."

Willard doesn't stand, but dips his head instead of bowing. It's not proper—but given my own derision for all things "proper," it doesn't bother me.

"Impressive pipe," I tell him. "Should I call you Sherlock?"

He grins. "Only if I can call you Princess."

My head toddles as I think it over. "I'm secure enough in my manhood to stand that."

"Excellent."

Willard motions to the decanter of amber liquid on the table beside him.

"Brandy? It's cheap, but it gets the job done."

"Please."

While he pours me a glass, Annie chirps, "For God's sake, Sarah, when you told Haverstrom you had official Palace business to tend to, I was sure you were pulling all our legs. What kind of business does Sarah do for you, Your Highness?"

"She's helping me reorganize the Palace library." I press

my finger to her lips and she almost passes out. "But that's a secret—a surprise gift for the Queen."

I glance over at Sarah where she's packing up a box of papers, and she smiles gently at the lie.

"Did you have a good meeting, love?" I ask her.

And there's that pretty pink blush again, though I'm not sure why it appears this time.

"Yes, it went very well."

Sipping my brandy, I tease, "Do you open the meeting with a sacrifice to the book gods? An animal or a nonreader, perhaps?"

Smoke puffs from Willard lips as he answers, "Only on Tuesdays."

"Have you ever thought about writing a book, Prince Henry?" Annie whispers. "My ex-boyfriend, Elliot, always said he wanted to."

Willard checks his watch.

Then Annie goes on.

"You could write under a pen name about the behind-the-scenes secrets of the palace. Or," a sly look comes over Annie's face while she glances at Sarah, then back to me, "it could be a sexier tale. About a young virgin who tames the wild, worldly prince—like *Fifty Shades* but with royalty."

"I'd read it." Willard shrugs.

Come to think of it, so would I.

Back at Anthorp Castle, Sarah and I get ready for bed—we each brush our teeth and change in the bathroom. Me, in my usual sleeping pants and bare chest, Sarah in her cotton pants and simple top—it's a thin-strapped tank top tonight, and her tits look amazing. Then we sit on the bed. I pick up my guitar and strum a few notes.

"By the way, what's a Butterwald Duck?" I ask. "I saw supplies and a sign mentioning it in one of the other rooms at the library."

"Oh, those are for next month." She takes off her glasses and sets them on the bedside table. "For the protest we're holding to allow the ducks penned in at Butterwald Park free rein."

"Protest?" I ask.

She nods. "The Austenites are very active in the community."

I set my guitar down, leaning it against the wall. "You're terrorists?"

Sarah rolls her pretty eyes. "Don't be silly. We're . . . an organization committed to bringing awareness to social issues, through what may be seen as semi-controversial methods at times."

"Exactly." I nod. "Terrorists."

Sarah pinches my arm.

"Ow . . . violent terrorists," I tease.

She tilts her head up and laughs, her dark hair falling over her shoulder and down her back. And it's mesmerizing. Was there a time when I actually thought she was plain? I'm an imbecile—she's stunning. I've never known anyone like her.

And I want to kiss her, right now.

And then I want to go back to the library, to that place she loves, and kiss her there too. In front of her friends, in front of mine . . . Christ, Nicholas would *adore* her.

I want to be that man to her.

She catches me staring and tilts her head. "What is it?"

And my mouth suddenly goes dry. Because I've never done this before. The only time I've talked about feelings with a girl involved direction or appreciation and a whole lot of screwing: *harder, tighter, faster, yes that's good, just like that—don't stop.*

I try to swallow and my voice comes out low and rough, like an unpracticed lad in the schoolyard.

"I like you, Sarah. I like you so much."

She continues to look at me, and I see when comprehension darkens her big, round eyes.

"I . . . I like you too, Henry."

She watches as I pick up her hand from where it rests on the bed and bring it to my lips. Softly, I kiss the back of it and each of her little knuckles. Even her hands are fucking pretty.

Her breath catches when I turn her hand over and place an open-mouthed kiss on the inside of her sensitive wrist, suctioning just slightly.

And then, I need her mouth. I can't remember the last time I needed anything so much.

Maybe I never have.

I lean in and Sarah's eyes flutter closed. I stroke her smooth cheek, and cup her jaw in my palm, and then I press my lips against hers. She's so soft and warm, so fucking sweet. I angle my mouth and turn our heads, changing direction—sucking the smallest bit of her plump lower lip, then tracing it with my tongue.

And that's when she pulls away, turns her head, and looks down at her hands. Sarah's breathing hard and her cheeks are flushed, and she looks beautiful.

And then . . . it all goes to bloody hell.

"I can't do this with you, Henry." She gazes down at the bed. "I can't be with you."

"You're with me right now."

She shakes her head. "Not in that way."

"Of course you can. I think you're amazing."

She looks up at me then, with fear and sadness slashed across her face. "You do now, but you're a Willoughby."

I scratch my head. "Isn't that like, a kangaroo?"

She squeezes her eyes tight and it's almost like she's

stuttering. Like she can't make the words come out. And when they do, I wish they'd stayed where they were.

"No, a Willoughby—from *Sense and Sensibility*. He was the character Marianne fell in love with. He was wild and inappropriate, selfish and thoughtless, and he crushed her."

"Sarah, you're not making any sense."

"I can't be with you because I'm waiting for a Colonel Brandon."

"Who the fuck is Brandon?"

"He's serious and maybe a little boring, but he loves Marianne. He's dependable and steady, romantic and proper. That's what I want; that's who I'm supposed to be with."

"Proper?" The word sticks in my throat like a thorn. I slide off the bed and pace, going over her ramblings. "Let me make sure I have this right: you can't kiss me because some wanker from a book named Willoughby fucked over some other girl from a book named Marianne?"

She gives a little huff and wags her hands. "When you say it like that, it sounds mad."

"That's because it *is* mad!"

Sarah twists her hands together. "He broke her heart. It almost killed her."

I look down at her, feeling something breaking inside my own chest.

"And you think I would do that to you?"

"I know you would."

"Because I'm a Willoughby?"

Her chin jerks in a nod.

"Because I'm thoughtless and selfish and just don't measure up. And because you're waiting for someone better to come along."

Sarah shakes her head. "This isn't coming out right."

There's a different kind of pain when you're injured by someone you truly care about. It runs deeper, hurts longer, like a burn—it starts off stinging and smarting, then it blisters and spreads inside you, eating away at tender flesh.

Leaving in its wake a gaping hole.

I cross my arms and smirk, like I don't give a flying fuck about anything.

"How's the view from that ivory tower, Sarah? Must be lovely judging everyone beneath you, while keeping yourself too high to touch."

She rises to her knees on the bed. "It's not like that. I care about you, it's just—"

"I'm selfish and irresponsible and inappropriate—I heard you the first time. You could've saved yourself all those syllables and just called me a dick."

"Henry . . ."

"I think you're a coward. See what I did there? Simple, concise."

Her eyes snap up to me. She blinks and glances away.

"I'm not a coward. I just . . . like my life how it is. I like . . ."

I wander over to the "nook" and grab the first book I see. "You don't have a life. You hide in this room and you cower behind these books. It's fucking sad."

Sarah's voice is gentle, but staunch. "I realize I've hurt your feelings, but there's no need to be cruel."

I laugh. "You think you've hurt my feelings?"

"If this temper tantrum is any indication, I'm sure of it."

"This isn't a temper tantrum—this is a wake-up call." I wave the book at her. "These aren't your friends, Sarah—there's no sodding Colonel Brandon popping off the page coming to love you."

"I know that!" And then her eyes follow the book in my hand. "Henry, be careful—it's fragile."

And that just pisses me off more. Her concern for this inanimate, stupid thing.

"Do you even see me? Christ, I'm standing right here—real

and, unlike you, actually living." I wave my arms around, swinging the book by its back cover. "And you're more concerned with fucking paper and ink!"

And that's all she wrote.

With a crack, the spine of the book snaps in half, and loose pages fly off, fluttering all over the room, then falling to the floor like a flock of wounded white birds.

"No!"

The absolute heartbreak in Sarah's voice cuts through my own, vanquishing my anger and leaving behind a residue of regret.

She falls to her knees, gathering the pages and snatching the broken book from my hand.

"I didn't mean to do that," I say quietly, in case she didn't know.

Her dark hair falls over her shoulders, hiding her face.

"Sarah, did you hear me? I'm sorry."

Why does it feel like that's all I end up saying lately?

Her shoulders shudder; I think she's crying. And my stomach feels as if it's full of worms—wiggling and squirming disgustingly.

"I'll give you the money to replace it. It's a book. I mean . . . there's more than one." I stumble on like an utter fucking prat.

"Was it very valuable?"

When she still doesn't respond, I put my hand on her back. She jerks up, wrenching away from me. Her eyes are wet and furious and wounded.

"Get out," she hisses.

"What?"

"Get. Out!" she shouts, louder this time, gathering the last of the pages in her arms and placing them gently on the bed.

I nudge the floor with the tip of my foot, murmuring, "It's my castle."

And that pushes her over the edge.

She shoves me, harder than I expect. Her cheeks are high with color, her hair mussed, and her eyes wild. I'd be as hard as a steel rod right now, if I weren't so concerned that I'd truly hurt her.

"Sarah, come on . . ."

When I don't move fast enough, she shoves my chest again.

"Get out of my room, you mean, childish son of a bitch!"

I'm about to reply with some flippant comment, but before I can, her breath catches, breaking on a hiccup, and I realize with horror that she's trying very hard not to burst into tears.

I reach out. "I'm—"

Sarah throws her hand up, looking away and closing her eyes.

"Just go, Henry. Please."

And since it's the least I can do, I leave.

CHAPTER 13

Sarah

I wake up late the next day, at least late for me—my eyes are puffy and my chest is sore. Heavy. I don't leave my room until I know he's off the property. I hear the helicopter come in for his date with Cordelia—mountain climbing or ice fishing or herding cattle or something equally ridiculous. After the helicopter has departed, I head to Penelope's room with my poor, damaged book. She hovers over it like it's a baby bird with a broken wing, cooing that it'll be good as new in no time and touching it so gently. Because she's a good sister.

She really doesn't care about *Sense and Sensibility*, but she cares about me. She knows how much this book means to me—even if it doesn't mean much to her.

Unlike a certain handsome, heartless prince who shall not be named.

I don't think about the gentle brush of his lips against mine before it all turned bad. I refuse to remember the simmering in his dark green eyes while he looked at me like no man has ever looked at me before—like I was something precious, a treasure that he wanted more than his next breath. And I definitely don't focus on that wonderful, thrilling feeling that spread in my lower stomach. Filled with desire and excitement and joy.

I block that all out and focus on my poor, battered book. It's simpler that way.

We ask one of the crew members for tape and repair the damage as best we can. Then Penny spends the rest of the day in hair and makeup and then in her "hot seat" one-on-one interview while I spend it walking around the castle grounds. And I think about leaving, going back to my flat and my job . . . and my life.

I mean, really, what the hell am I doing here?

But, it's entirely possible Mother will force Penny to come home if I do. She's having so much fun and she's actually learning a few things about television production—making friends with the crew, developing contacts. So, for the time being anyway, I'm stuck like a mouse in a trap. In a castle.

I take a sandwich to my room for dinner and watch the news instead of reading. By sunset, I'm exhausted and fall asleep early.

Late that night, there's a knock on my bedroom door. And I hate the thrill that zings through me, hate the delicious swoop of my stomach and uptick in my pulse as I walk to answer it. Because my body knows who's on the other side. And it— traitorous thing that it is—can't wait to drink in the sight of him, feel the strength of his presence, smell the warmth of his skin. My blood urges my heart to forgive and forget—it says I'm being silly, that the still sore wound in my chest is only a scratch.

I inhale when my hand touches the doorknob—bracing for the overwhelming sensual onslaught that is Henry Pembrook.

He looks tired. And sad. And my wound throbs more painfully.

His usually dancing green eyes are dull and guarded. The blond stubble on his chin, which typically gives him an irresistible roguish allure, now seems almost war-weary. I pull the top of my robe tighter and secure the knot on the belt, as if that might protect me from his charm.

"What do you want?"

Thick, long lashes blink innocently—he knows what he's doing.

"It's bedtime. I'd like to sleep. Or we can chat if you prefer? I could play something soft for you on the guitar . . . or you could hum while I try to drift off and I won't complain once, I swear."

There's a heartbreakingly hopeful note in his voice as he recounts what has become our nightly routine. And I want to open the door to him. And my arms. The way I would embrace a lad who's so sorry he broke my favorite toy.

But I don't—I can't. It's self-preservation. Henry is no mere lad—and his thoughtlessness is capable of shattering so much more than a toy.

I adjust my glasses because it makes me feel intelligent and strong.

"You're not sleeping here, Henry."

He shifts gears and changes tactics. Smirking devilishly. Persuasively. He braces his hand on the door jamb, leaning in. "Come on, Sarah. It was an accident—I've already said I'm sorry. Why are you making such a fuss about it?"

This is good. This is what I need. His flippancy and derision. It shores up my anger, and anger builds a stronger wall than hurt.

His eyes scan my puckered mouth, tight jaw and hard, unyielding eyes. He pushes a hand through his hair, tugging at the strands.

"This is fucking stupid—it's a book! I'll have a new one delivered for you first thing tomorrow. What else do you want me to do? Tell me and I will."

"Anything?"

"*Anything.*"

I open the door a bit wider, leaning closer, and looking straight into his eyes.

"Leave. Me. Alone."

He flinches, brows falling helplessly. "I can't do that."

I shrug, channeling Miss Havisham's cruel protégé, Estella, from *Great Expectations*.

"Then you're not really sorry, are you?"

His fists clench and his body coils, like he wants to punch something. Strange, but I'm not the least bit afraid. Because to the depths of my soul I know without question that while Henry has hurt me, he would never, ever *hurt* me.

"If you didn't mean to let me in, why the hell did you open the door in the first place?"

Estella's smile tugs at my lips. "So I could do this."

Then together, Estella and I slam the door in the Crown Prince's face.

Henry

I went back to my room, lay in bed and tried to sleep through the annoying racket of the cameras—and failed. I'm scheduled to spend the morning filming with Penelope, which I take as a sign that perhaps God hasn't completely written me off. Because Penelope is bubbly and outgoing and, unlike her sister, she likes me—she's always liked me. Having her on my side may not get me into Sarah's pants—though a man can dream—but it could help get me back into Sarah's good graces.

Vanessa arranges us like Beach Barbie and Ken dolls. "Hold hands and walk slowly down the beach. Talk to each other and laugh like you're having fun."

I can't believe I thought this shit-show would be a good time. Christ, I'm a moron.

Vanessa backs off and calls to the cameraman, "Hold the wide shot. Make sure you get that sunrise in the background."

I take my chance with the younger Titebottum sister. "I wanted to talk to you about Sarah—"

"Are you miked?" She cuts me off, her smile frozen in place.

"Uh . . . no. Vanessa just wants the visual, no sound."

"Good." She stares off across the water. "Then there'll be no one to witness me saying you're a piece-of-shit bastard and I hope you die screaming."

It's conceivable Penelope doesn't like me as much as I thought.

"Come again?"

"Prince or no prince, if I could, I would cut your balls off, ground them into a fine powder, mix them in water, and make you drink them."

I swallow hard.

"That's . . . creative."

She's still smiling serenely, making the entire exchange all the more bizarre. And unnerving.

"Have you all gone mad? Christ, it's a bloody book!"

"Not to her. You see, Prince Prick," she continues, "your family loves you. Whatever fucked-up intrigue or drama goes on in the palace, they truly love you. Not everyone has that. Our mother is off her rocker and our family wouldn't give two shits if Sarah and I rolled off a cliff and disappeared forever. It's always been that way. Except for dear Auntie Gertrude. She's the only one who ever gave a damn about us. Before she died, she summoned Sarah and me to her estate to give us our inheritance, because she knew, despite her will, her arsehole children wouldn't have."

Penelope's hand holds mine in a strangling death grip.

"Aunt Gertie gave me her jewels, because she said I was hard and sparkly. She gave Sarah her rare collection of books, because she said Sarah was a dreamer. She told her she could sell them for a pretty penny or keep them for herself—but either way, Sarah would have her dreams. They mean the world to my sister, and you tore one apart. Which makes you a big, fat, limp, useless dick."

"I . . ."

Have no clue what to say.

The chance to reply passes when Vanessa moves in front of us, framing us with her fingers for the photographer beside her. "Get the still shots, Jerry. Gorgeous."

Without missing a beat, Penny turns into my side, throws her arms around my neck, kicks up one leg behind her, and smiles bigly for the clicking camera.

Like a professional sociopath.

Fucking hell.

In the afternoon, I'm supposed to picnic with Laura in a flowered valley straight out of that awful *Twilight* film. I can't bring myself to call these orchestrated excursions "dates," even in my own mind. My sense of humor is not quite that delusional. In any case, the picnic is not happening. I have more important plans to execute.

Covert, off-camera plans.

And for them to happen, I need James.

He stands between the lighting tripods, arms crossed, eyes ever watchful.

"Here's the deal," I tell him quietly, "I'm bugging out for the afternoon. I'll let you tail me as long as you hang back and," I point toward Vanessa's custom camera-pimped SUV, "as long as your men keep them from following. This one's strictly off the grid. Agreed?"

His nod is quick and tight. "Of course, Sir."

Half an hour later, Mission Ditch *Matched* is implemented successfully. And I'm in the convertible, with only James following behind, on my way to the library.

I find Willard in the catacombs of Concordia Library—Sarah explained this is where they do the preservation and restoration work. It's two floors below ground level, but a surprisingly modern, well-lit, and dust-free white room. A precious little old woman with—thankfully for me—poor eyesight directed me here from the otherwise empty front desk area.

He looks up when I walk in, sliding thick, red-tinted, science fiction–like goggles to the top of his head. "Princess. This is surprising. To what do I owe the pleasure?"

"I need your help."

He chuckles. "Oh how the mighty have fallen. I love it. How can I be of service?"

I've never met another man who could so artfully convey in his tone the opposite of what his words mean. Sarcasm, thy name is Willard.

"Sarah's pissed off at me."

The corner of his mouth ticks upward.

"Sarah rarely gets angry and when she does it never sticks. Did you kick a puppy?"

"No. I broke one of her books."

He freezes in place and his voice is stunned into softness. "Which one?"

My intestines squirm with shame. "*Sense and Sensibility.*"

"Why . . . would you do that?"

I rub the back of my neck. "I didn't mean to . . . I lost my temper—"

"Get out."

He takes the goggles off his head, slamming them onto the table.

"No, you don't understand—"

"I understand perfectly. What you don't seem to comprehend is that Sarah is my best friend. The only one I've got. I'm not fucking helping you. Piss off, Princess."

He turns to walk away.

And I shout, "She's hurt!"

That makes him pause mid-step, his back stiffening.

"I haven't just made her angry, I've hurt her terribly. She's still hurting . . . and I can't stand it, Willard." My hands find their way into my hair.

I move in front of him, bending my knees to catch his eyes, which seems quite apropos.

"Help me make it better. Not for me, but for her. Please."

Willard regards me for several moments. And then he sighs.

"What do you need?"

"I need your connections, your contacts. I need to find a book."

After a three-hour drive, Willard and I stand in a cramped, dusty rare-book shop between two boarded-up buildings, one block from a homeless encampment. Under the suspicious eyes of the shop owner, I check out the merchandise.

It feels like a drug deal.

"What do you think?"

Willard speaks around the large, curved pipe between his lips.

"Depends. What do you think, Princess?"

I turn the shiny first edition of *Sense and Sensibility* over in my latex-gloved hands—the owner insisted. Carefully, I flip through the pristine pages . . . with Sarah's soft, airy voice in my head—from the very first time we met, in that pub more than a year ago.

"The only thing that smells better than a new book is an old one."

I put the book down.

"This isn't it. She'd want a book that's been read—dog-eared and held and sighed over—not one that's been caged in glass its whole life. She'll want one that's been loved."

Ever so slowly, Willard smiles. "There's hope for you yet."

I step over the threshold of Anthorp Castle at two in the morning—exhausted and, yet, triumphant. The rooms are still and empty, all of my guests greedily sucking at the tit of beauty sleep. I head for the stairs, but a form steps out from the music room—and a voice.

"You missed two call times today."

Not as empty as I thought.

I turn to face Vanessa, still in her pantsuit and heels, a scotch and soda in her hand.

"I had something important to take care of."

"More important than the show?"

I would laugh, but I'm too damn tired.

"Much more, yes."

She sips her drink as she steps toward me, deliberately. "We needed those shots, Henry."

"You'll get them tomorrow."

Her lips pucker like her drink's gone sour. "You'll be in the dining room, dressed and ready to have breakfast with Princess Alpacca, at six a.m. sharp, is that clear? I've whipped more difficult talent than you into shape, Your Highness. If you know what's good for you, you'll remember that."

My shoulders straighten, and my voice drops low, and without even trying . . . I sound just like my father. "I'm not *talent*, Vanessa—and I don't respond well to orders. For the sake of your show, you really ought to try remembering *that*."

Sarah

I'm a coward. This shouldn't come as a surprise, but it does.

I'm a fool. That's new. And bothersome.

By the evening —or morning, I guess would be more accurate—I lie in bed, staring at the ceiling, and come to grips with these cold, hard truths. Henry broke my book and that's upsetting, but that's not why I've kicked him out and refused to see him. It's not why I've rejected his apology.

It's because of the kiss. I keep thinking about it, no matter how desperately I try to forget—my lips still tingle with the remembered caress of his mouth. It was more lovely than I'd imagined or hoped it could be. My stomach spun and my head went light, and my heart thudded fast and thrilled like I was going to die—while feeling the most alive I'd ever felt.

Because I wanted him to kiss me. I wanted to kiss him back. And I didn't want to stop at just a kiss. I wanted to push myself against him and feel the bulging strength of him everywhere. His stunning arms surrounding me, his large hands touching me. I wanted to know the hard press of his chest against my breasts, the taut, flat plane of his stomach, the bite of his hips against mine as he covered me on the bed.

I want to know the flavor of his skin, the scratch of his stubble, the taste of his mouth.

He's not what I envisioned for myself—I was truthful about that part. Henry is wild and careless, but that's not all he is. He's also gentle and kind and patient and giving and intelligent and clever . . . and wonderful. I left those parts out.

He could crush me; the foreshadowing is clearly written. It's a tale as old as time: the inexperienced bluestocking and the bed-hopping rogue.

Bloody hell, I'm a trope.

But the biggest part of my heart doesn't care. It says it would be worth it. It shouts at me that we're strong enough to survive the breaking. Marianne did. We'll glue ourselves back together again and have the amazing, tender memories of a dashing whirlwind romance, the likes of which I have never known.

My heart asks me if I'm tired yet—tired of being too afraid to jump and leap, tired of keeping my feet so firmly on the ground. I groan and cover my face with a pillow. And Henry's scent surrounds me, fills me. I press it closer and inhale, smothering myself with him.

And now I've become a cliché too.

Damn it all to hell.

I put the pillow aside and drag myself up and out of bed. Big-girl knickers time. I'm going to find him, accept his apology, and give him one of my own. I don't bother with my robe or slippers; I just rush to the door and step out into the hallway— directly on the hard, thick item outside my door.

Emotions are mysterious things. Sometimes they build slowly, surging like a wave before cresting to a peak and crashing all over you.

But that's not what I'm experiencing now.

As I reach down to pick up the worn, aged book off the hallway floor, my emotions hit like a bullet. Hard and piercing, blowing a hole right through the center of me. I smile as tears rise in my eyes. It's like the dual symbol masks of the theater— relief and pain, joy and sadness. I could say it's one of the nicest things anyone's ever done for me, and that would be true. But that's not why it means the absolute world to me.

It only means so much because Henry did this. And he did it for me.

I trace the lettering on the cover, shaking my head. And then I open the book and gasp.

He wrote in it. A first-edition copy of *Sense and Sensibility* that has survived the centuries relatively unscathed, and the mad bastard wrote in it.

Of course he did.

I laugh as tears trickle down my cheeks, feeling a bit unhinged.

> *Now you can dream a new dream.*
> *-H*

I hold the book against my heart, wrapping my arms around it, bringing it with me as I walk straight to his room. But he's not there. For an awful moment I wonder if he's found a different room to sleep in—maybe Cordelia's or Libby's.

And the pain that lances through me takes my breath away.

But would Henry do that? And I know the answer before I finish the thought.

The Henry I know—not the wild lad in the papers or the would-be king who, as my sister said, will have a harem, but the boy who likes to talk in soft whispers about silly things late at night; the one who plays his guitar and listens to me hum and takes me on joyrides through the woods; the man who wants to teach me to swim and wants to be sure I live before I die—he would not.

God, I'm such an idiot.

I want to find him, I need to see him—now. I check the library first, the dining room and music room, and I hear the buzz of cameras, mounted on the walls, following me as I go. I get to the kitchen . . . and there he is, like a tired lump at the table, bent over, his head resting on his arms. His eyes are closed, his mouth soft and his jaw lax.

He looks younger like this. Peaceful.

I've seen Henry playful and teasing. I've seen him frustrated and tense. But peaceful is his most beautiful state. My hand reaches out, tracing the strong crest of his brow and cheeks, nose and chin, without actually touching him.

With an intake of breath, his long lashes flutter and dark green eyes gaze up at me.

"Sarah?" he asks drowsily.

I love how he says my name, warm and soothing like a snuggling embrace.

"Thank you for the book, Henry," I whisper. "Thank you."

He sits up, smiling adorably and rumpled. "You like it?"

"I love it." And I hope he hears the sincerity in my tone. "It's my new favorite."

"*Sense and Sensibility* was always your favorite."

"But now it's my favorite for a better reason." I reach out for him. "Come on. Time for bed."

He takes my hand, but when I give him a tug to pull him up, he pulls harder and a second later, I'm standing between his spread knees. He stares at my hand in his, brushing his thumb across my knuckles, sending warm, spiraling tingles to my very core.

"I'm sorry about the things I said." His voice is raspy and the tingles tighten. "I didn't mean them."

"I'm sorry too." My words rush out because there's so much I want to say. "I don't think you're selfish or thoughtless. I don't think you're a Willoughby. I don't believe you'd hurt me."

"I did hurt you."

My heart breaks, not for me, but for him.

"Only because I hurt you first."

His lips tug up at the corners and his head gives a little nod. "You've become . . . important to me, Sarah. I mess up a lot; I always have. I don't want to mess this up."

What a strange pair we are. The sad boy and the frightened girl.

I look into his eyes, moving closer, putting my hands on his shoulders. "I won't let you mess it up."

"We're friends then?" he asks. "I'm usually pretty good at that."

Is that what I really want to be—Henry's friend?

Again, I know the answer before I finish the thought. And the answer is no. But I can't just blurt it out. How would that even work? What would it look like? I've never been good with speaking and I can't see how this time would be any different. My stomach churns threateningly.

I have to think it through, figure it out, organize the words in just the right way. Figure out what Elizabeth Bennet would have said if she had to give the speech instead of Mr. Darcy.

So I nod. "Yes, of course we're friends."

Balls, balls, balls.

Henry

We go to bed, but neither of us goes to sleep. I don't know about Sarah, but I'm too relieved to be near her again. Excited. It's like Christmas night after you've opened your presents and you've gotten exactly what you wanted more than anything. No one wants to sleep after that; you just want to keep touching and holding and looking at the lovely new toy.

"Did you think I was silly, getting so upset over a book?" she asks me, lying on her back, looking at the ceiling.

I lift my arm, showing her the platinum-linked ID bracelet dangling from my wrist.

"My mother gave me this when I was eight. I never take it off. I own a Maserati and crowns, but this is my most precious possession. I understand sentimental value."

She sighs, turning in bed to face me, her hands tucked beneath her cheek. It's my favorite Sarah pose, the perfect mixture of fuck-hot and innocent.

And I want to kiss her so badly my lips throb.

"I overreacted, for . . . several reasons. I'll try not to do that anymore. From now on I should probably imagine what your grandmother would do, first. She's such a strong woman—a very good role model. I can't imagine her crying about anything."

"I saw her cry once."

Sarah moves in closer, her calf resting near mine under the covers. "Did you? When?"

I tuck my arm beneath my head, resting on my forearm, looking at the ceiling, thinking back. "After my parents' plane went down . . . it took a few days for them to find the wreckage. Do you remember?"

She nods, and the corners of her mouth dip with sympathy.

"Those days gave me time to think . . . to concoct a little fantasy in my head. I'd always had a vivid imagination. So, even after they'd recovered their bodies, I didn't believe it. I thought it was a trick—some evil ruse by an adversarial country that was holding them captive. Or, perhaps it was just a mistake."

A sad smile pulls at my lips as I recall the boy I'd been, then. Despite all the toxic shit swirling around us—the complications that come part and parcel with who we are—my parents had done a fine job of keeping me insulated. Protected. And so, unlike my perpetually cynical older brother, at ten years old, I was still hopeful and optimistic.

Still young—and tragically innocent.

"I imagined them on a remote island somewhere, waiting for us to find them. I pictured my dad with a long, scraggly beard building a tree house for them with palm leaves and branches. And my mum, she'd be making little teacups out of coconut shells."

She smiles softly. "Like *Robinson Crusoe*."

"Yes." I clear my throat, scraping the lump that's risen there—because this part is harder. "I was sure, if I could just see the bodies, that I'd be able to reveal the truth. Convince everyone that we had to keep looking for them. So, I had the car take me to the morgue."

Because even though I was still a young lad, I had an old title in front of my name, and there wasn't a driver or staff member who would think of questioning me.

"I almost made it into the cold room where they stored the remains. There were guards, of course, but they were all willing to let me enter. Except for the doctor. Dr. Ramadi was the chief medical examiner—the one entrusted with the VIP cases—heads of state and such. And she stood in front of that door like Gandalf the Grey with a clipboard instead of a staff. And she refused to let me pass.

"I was furious. I stomped my foot like an arrogant little prick and told her, 'I am Prince of Wessco—*your* Prince—so get out of my way.' And she stared right back at me and said, 'You are a child, Your Highness. And your mother and father do not look like themselves. I will not have that image in your mind.'

"It was a standoff for several minutes . . . until the Queen walked through the door. I don't know who called her, but I remember thinking how tired she looked. The Queen never seemed weary, but she was that night. Dr. Ramadi left and my grandmother asked me what in the world I was thinking. And I told her all about my theory—the island and the teacups, all of it. As I did, I started to fall apart; it was difficult to speak. Eventually, I just ended up begging, 'Please, Granny. They're out there—I know they are. Please help me, Granny.'"

I pause for a moment, distracted by the words echoing in

my memory and the shadow of the sickening feeling that twisted in my gut. Helplessness.

"And then, she hugged me. Really hugged me. It was the first time—the only time—she ever did that. Her arms were so strong. She pressed my face against her chest and stroked my hair, and she said, 'Oh, my sweet boy, I would give anything . . . but they're gone, Henry. They're gone.'

"Then she cried. We both did."

I feel Sarah's hand on my jaw, her thumb brushing. Her face close to mine and her beautiful eyes shiny and sad. "I'm so sorry, Henry."

I give her a nod. Then I finish the story.

"Later, I found out that the Queen had thanked Dr. Ramadi for what she'd done. And then . . . she promptly fired her."

Sarah gasps. "What? But why?"

"I asked her the same thing. And my grandmother told me, 'Dissention is not tolerated. You gave Dr. Ramadi an order— and a prince's order is always to be obeyed. Even when he's wrong.' And then she said, 'So be mindful of the orders you give, my boy. One way or another, they will have consequences.'"

Sarah's breath rushes from her, tickling the hairs on my chest. "Wow. That . . . that's . . . heavy."

My mouth quirks up in a smirk. "It is." I tuck a strand of silky hair behind her ear. "And that, love, is why we're all so royally fucked up."

CHAPTER 14

Henry

And the show goes on. It's still a distraction, still entertaining and a hell of a lot better than nightmares and sitting in the library alone at night, poring over boring details and laws and obsessing about just how high the cliff is that I'm sure to drive my country over if they ever actually let me become king.

But . . . being on *Matched* has turned out so differently than I'd first imagined. Now I have Vanessa pick which ladies I should send packing—because I don't really care. For all the filthy sex fantasies I thought I'd be acting out when this started, I'm not interested in any of the ladies anymore.

Well, that's not entirely true. I'm not interested in screwing the contestants silly anymore—not even a little. One particular *sister* of a contestant, however . . . that's another story.

I send several of the ladies packing—including Libby and Jane Plutorch. Jane reacts predictably, which is to say she has no reaction at all. Princess Alpacca and Guermo sneak off and elope in a secret ceremony that we don't find out about until we read it in the papers. Vanessa is thrilled—it'll be grand publicity, she says, when the show airs.

After another week, we're down to the final four: Cordelia, Laura, Elizabeth, and Penny. One morning I'm shooting scenes with Laura down at the beach. We're supposed to be sitting in the sand and cuddling, searching for seashells—it should all be terribly romantic.

But there's nothing romantic about sand coating your balls.

With the water rushing over my feet, I gaze down the beach, spotting Sarah in her baggy workout gear, going through her aikido exercises. And Laura catches me staring.

"She's rather lovely, isn't she?" Laura asks, standing beside me.

I squint, nodding.

"Whoever lands her will be a lucky bloke, I think."

Her comment magnifies the hollowness in my chest.

"Yes." I force a smile. "Lucky."

"Henry—"

Before she can continue, a golf cart drives up and Vanessa Steele springs out and up the beach to us.

"Hey—we have a problem. You have some unexpected guests down at the gate. You should go check it out."

Guests? Who would come here to see me?

I hop in the golf cart and drive down to the main gate. Just in time to hear Franny Barrister, the Countess of Ellington, tearing into a poor, clueless *Matched* security guard.

"Don't you tell me we can't come in, you horse's arse. Where's Henry—what have you done with him?"

Simon, my brother's best friend, sees me approach, his sparkling blue eyes shining. "There he is."

I nod to security and open the gate.

"Simon, Franny, what are you doing here?"

"Nicholas said you didn't sound right the last time he spoke to you. He asked us to peek in on you," Simon explains.

Franny's shrewd gaze rakes me over. "He doesn't look drunk. And he obviously hasn't hung himself from the rafters— that's better than I was expecting."

"Thanks for the vote of confidence."

Simon peers around the grounds, at the smattering of crew members and staging tents. "What the hell is going on, Henry?"

I clear my throat. "So . . . the thing is . . . I'm sort of . . . filming a reality dating television show here at the castle and we started with twenty women and now we're down to four, and when it's over one of them will get the diamond tiara and become my betrothed. At least in theory."

It sounded so much better in my head.

"Don't tell Nicholas."

Simon scrubs his hand down his face. "Now I'm going to have to avoid his calls—I'm terrible with secrets."

And Franny lets loose a peal of tinkling laughter. "This is fabulous! You never disappoint, you naughty boy." She pats my arm. "And don't worry, when the Queen boots you out of the palace, Simon and I will adopt you. Won't we, darling?"

Simon nods. "Yes, like a rescue dog."

"Good to know." Then I gesture back to their car. "Well . . . it was nice of you to stop by."

Simon shakes his head. "You're not getting rid of us that easily, mate."

"Yes, we're definitely staying." Franny claps her hands. "I have to see this!"

Fantastic.

I give Simon and Franny the grand tour, filling them in on the rules and the contestants. When we walk into the great room, where much of the crew has gathered, Cordelia and Elizabeth back away from Franny like snakes making room for a cobra. Back in the day, Franny was Queen of the Mean Girls—but since she fell for Simon, she's much nicer.

She glances at the landing at the top of the stairs.

"Interesting. Are those the Titebottum sisters?" she asks. "Penelope and Sarah?"

My voice softens involuntarily when I gaze up at them. "Yes. Do you know them?"

Franny's expression sobers. "I know *of* them. Quite a bit."

"Good. Now that I think about it, you could be helpful to Sarah. She's terribly shy and you're so . . . not. I'm trying to bring her out of her shell."

"Everyone knows the best way to get a turtle out of its shell is to stick a finger up its arse. Have you tried that?"

I snort. "I would if I could, believe me."

She sighs. "Mmm. All right then, I'll go introduce myself to the shy sweetling."

She climbs the steps, her black heels clicking, to do just that.

I watch as the trio exchanges pleasantries and then Franny loops her arm through Sarah's. "I like you already. Let's be best friends."

As the afternoon fades into night, Penny, Elizabeth, Laura, and Cordelia head upstairs to change for dinner and Sarah tags along with her sister. Apparently, it's a group date night—they'll be filming as I take all four ladies out to dinner to "shake things up," as Vanessa put it.

Simon and Franny sign release papers in case they're caught on camera. Before they start rolling, Sarah comes down the stairs. Her hair is down and shiny and curled at the ends. She's wearing an elegant, form-fitting silk cocktail dress and I lose the ability to speak. Granny would be so pleased.

She looks beautiful, but she rarely looks anything else. The reason I've gone mute is because instead of her typical black clothes, the dress Sarah's wearing is . . . red.

Ruby red.

The color warms her skin and brings out the gold in her eyes.

"Wow," I whisper.

She smiles, cheeks going pink, and flattens her palm against her stomach, fidgeting. "Thank you. It's Penny's. Franny helped me give it a quick alteration—did you know she sewed?"

"Franny is a multifaceted woman."

"Yes."

Then I'm the one fidgeting. "What's the occasion? Hot date?"

Sarah swallows and looks up at me, hopefully. "No. I just thought it might be time to . . . try something new."

"New looks really good on you."

She seems as if she's about to say something else, but then the director calls for filming to begin. Sarah heads off to the sidelines, while Penelope comes down the stairs, with her shoulders back, tits out, and blond head high—in a nice little royal-blue number.

When she reaches the bottom of the steps, I bow and kiss her hand. Penny giggles for the cameras, then takes her spot near the door.

Laura descends the stairs next, in a light-pink, swishy-skirted dress. She looks better than she did a few weeks ago—her cheeks are fuller and her pallor is all but gone. She gives me a peck on the cheek and I return the favor.

And while Penny and Laura are gorgeous girls, my eyes keep drifting over to Sarah, where she chats with Franny and Simon.

I can't stop looking at her.

Then there's a commotion at the top of the landing as Cordelia and Elizabeth argue over who's supposed to come down next. And even better?

They're wearing the exact same dress.

For ladies—especially noble ladies—it's the cardinal sin.

You can screw their man and insult their mother, but you'd better not fucking be wearing their dress.

Cordelia and Elizabeth don't notice right way, but you can tell the moment they do—because right after, they start screaming and tearing each other's hair out.

Vanessa Steele watches the drama with glee—looking like a kid in a candy shop on Christmas Day.

The restaurant is a low-key pub—comfortable like The Goat but more upscale, with a small stage at one end. It's crowded, nearly every table filled to capacity, and there's a loud din of chatter—like background static noise. The reactions of the patrons to me are . . . off, strange. They glance my way but continue their conversations as if they're not surprised a prince just walked through the door, as if they know they're not supposed to be noticing me. And they don't look at the cameras at all.

"Who are these people?" I ask Vanessa as we take our seats.

"Extras. American extras—we flew them in this morning, but the audience won't be able to tell." She wiggles her fingers. "The magic of television."

I sit with the girls at one table, where the cameras focus, while some of the other crew, as well as Sarah, Simon, and Franny take a table beside ours.

I order shots for all of us—tequila. Three rounds later, Elizabeth and Penelope are playing a rock, paper, scissors drinking game. When the drinks don't come fast enough, they wager bets instead. Loser has to pop up on that little stage and sing her heart out.

Penny loses. And then she starts to flip out. "Oh my God, oh my God, I can't sing . . . I'm a terrible singer . . . I can't sing on television—I'll look like a fool. Maybe I can dance instead, a snappy tap number?"

"No." Cordelia points her finger. "We said singing. That was the deal. If you welch, we get to cut your hair off."

Penny frowns and preemptively grabs at her scalp.

"No one's cutting off my sister's hair."

Every set of eyes turns toward the end of the table in surprise. Because the voice is firm and semi-threatening. And it comes from Sarah's lips. I wonder if this is part of her "trying something new" resolution.

Sarah stares Cordelia down. "I'll go up and sing for her."

"You?" Cordelia scoffs mockingly. "You can barely speak. And it's against the rules, anyway."

Sarah doesn't back down—not an inch. "The rules have changed."

Good girl.

Cordelia shakes her head, her face twisting with spite. Then she picks up a glass, holds it out with a straight arm, and drops it on the floor, where it shatters.

When nothing happens, when Sarah just continues to gaze dismissively, the vicious confidence fades from Cordelia's eyes.

"You ought to clean that up," Sarah says, walking past. "Someone could get hurt."

Franny clicks her tongue. "All that arse fucking has made you quite a Nasty Bitch, Cordelia. You should break the seal already—it may help your disposition."

Have I mentioned that I fucking love Franny?

But I'm focused on Sarah, in her little red dress, on the stage, muttering to herself and twisting her fingers into knots and generally looking like she's about to keel over or spew.

I stand and walk up beside her. "How are we doing? Is this going to be Davey 2.0?"

Her throat convulses when she swallows. "Probably. I don't know what I was thinking."

"You were thinking about sticking up for your sister."

Sarah stares out over the crowd, who haven't really noticed her yet—her eyes infinitely big and dark, her face paling by the second.

And she whispers, "I can't do this, Henry."

I disentangle her fingers for her. "Yes you can. I'll be right here the whole time."

Her eyes turn to me and I give her a wink. Then I bring a chair forward and I pick up the guitar that's propped up at the back of the stage, testing the strings and adjusting the amp.

The room goes quiet, everyone watching. Waiting.

Sarah takes the deepest breath and she closes her eyes—not tightly or squeezing—gently, like she's dreaming. And I play the opening notes, soft and sad and consistent.

It's "Hallelujah."

And then she starts to sing, and I'm so fucking proud of her, I want to climb a mountain just so I can shout from it. Sarah's voice is clear and hauntingly gorgeous. In that moment, every person in the audience falls in love with her. And when she sings about standing before God with nothing on her lips but Hallelujah—I fall in love with her a little bit too.

When she gets to the part I've always interpreted as talking about sex—moving in each other and gasping—Sarah opens her eyes, but she only looks at me. And it's like those piercing eyes of hers could capture my soul.

Then they're closing again and she finishes the song as it's supposed to be finished—poignant and unashamed, with broken emotion ringing in every syllable. "Hallelujah, Hallelujah, Hallelujah, Halle . . . luuuu . . . jah."

When her lips close and the final note is still ringing in the air, quiet little Sarah Von Titebottum brings down the house.

And the night doesn't end there—not even close. When we get back to the castle, Vanessa has a surprise. "I thought we needed to up the fun quotient around here, so . . . we're having a party."

She leads us to the great room, where, holy hell—Bartholomew Gallagar, Hannibal Lancaster, Sam Berkinshire, and about half a dozen more of my best lads and old schoolmates are waiting.

"Surprise! Have fun, Henry."

Emily, the host, does an intro to our new guests for the cameras—which are still rolling, rolling, rolling. And then I'm greeting the boys, smacking backs and pouring drinks.

Nicholas despises Lancaster, but I've always found him to be game for a good time.

"You lucky bastard," he tells me, surveying the room. "Have you fucked them all, or are you pacing yourself?"

Sarah's eyes cut over her shoulder, hearing Hannibal and frowning at what he said.

He flips his brown hair out of his eyes and seems to zero in on Cordelia. "I haven't stuck it to a virgin in years. If there are any left, point me in their direction."

I clap him on the shoulder when there's suddenly a noisy row near the door . . . because Sam just saw Elizabeth.

"Lizzy?" he chokes. "What the hell are you doing here?"

Elizabeth unleashes hell.

"Fuck you, Sam! You don't get to ask me questions, you cheating tosser!"

I push my way over to them.

"Henry?" And there's so much accusation in Sam's one word.

"It's not how it looks. I can explain."

But Elizabeth beats me to the punch. "Just wait until the show airs and everyone you know watches me boffing Henry."

It's not true, but she seems to get a thrill over the agony that flashes across Sam's face.

"Get a big bucket of popping corn and watch it with your granny," Elizabeth hisses.

"Are you saying you don't like my granny?" Sam asks, brokenly.

"I'm saying I don't like *you*!" Elizabeth screeches, hair flying out like Medusa.

Then Sam turns my way. "I'm going to rip your balls off."

I hold up my hands. "It's not like that, Sam."

Then, with a roar, he tackles me.

Sarah

Henry looks happy. Well, he does now. After he and Sam Berkinshire rolled around on the floor for a bit, security broke them apart. Sam swore to Elizabeth that the things she'd found—the rubbers and receipts—were items he'd bought for her, to use with her. Then he confessed that the panties . . . he'd bought for himself.

I didn't see that one coming.

And it would seem, neither did Elizabeth—she didn't believe him and is still refusing to speak to him.

But Henry's laughing, teasing, and talking with everyone in the room. He's in the middle of a circle of people, both men and women, recounting stories of his and the lads' antics while they were at boarding school together. The chuckles are loud and plentiful and genuine. He's the center of attention and he basks in it, stretching and blossoming like a lush plant in the sun.

Then, instruments are brought in. Henry grabs his guitar and Sam slips a harmonica out of his pocket. And it seems

Simon Barrister, the Earl of Ellington, plays the drums. His wife, Franny—a lovely, lively character—watches him intently, worshipfully, ready to yell and clap like a teen at a concert. I can see why.

Because when they start to play, when Henry begins to sing the Tom Petty song "You Don't Know How It Feels—wearing low-slung jeans and a plain white T-shirt, his hair devilishly mussed, his arms flexing as he strums the chords, his tattoo on display, his smile sinful—it is the damned sexiest thing I have ever seen.

I couldn't imagine anything hotter.

But then his eyes meet mine and he winks at me, and I'm proven so wrong.

I want to jump him. Literally—throw myself at him. My breasts ache for the touch of those strong hands and long fingers. My thighs clench with raw, randy desire. I want to do things to him—things I can't put into words—and my cheeks flame just thinking about them. I want him to do things to me—everything. Anything he wants.

As the song ends and they start another, I tear my eyes away. I feel light and drunk and just a little bit crazy. My hand fans my face and I pour myself a drink, gulping it down my parched throat. And it's all so overwhelming—wild, but wonderful.

With the sounds of the music following me, I step out of the great room into the cooler hallway, wanting to catch my breath just for a moment. And here I used to think all the swooning heroines in my novels were over the top.

But now I know their reactions were spot on. Now I understand.

And I hope before this night is over, I'll also understand all the sensations—the erotic tastes and touches—I've read about.

The music room is just a few steps from the great room, and the song and chatter from the party still comes through clearly. I run my finger over the shiny black lacquer of the piano, close my eyes and dream of what could happen tonight. I imagine Henry's satisfied groans, his panting breath in my ear, his glorious dirty mouth speaking in a rough voice laden with desire.

And then a voice comes from behind me—and it's not Henry's.

"At first glance, there's not much to you. But close up, you're actually sort of pretty. I like that."

It's one of Henry's friends—the rude one. He's standing between me and the door. And though I want to tell him to go away, or move past him, my feet are frozen. Because there's a look in his eyes that I know well—that I've seen more times than I ever want to remember.

Cruelty.

And it paralyzes me.

"Are you afraid?" he asks, moving closer.

And I can't move.

Then he smiles slowly.

"I like that too."

CHAPTER 15

Henry

This is what I'm talking about. The music is loud, the drinks are flowing, the room is alive with smoke and chatter, and everyone is laughing. Everyone is having a good time. Christ, I've missed this. Hello. old life, long time no see.

I tighten the strings on my guitar, debating what we should play next. Black Crowes? Lumineers, maybe?

That's when one of the cameramen backs into a table. It tilts on two legs before going over, sending the clock, vase, and porcelain dish sliding to the floor with a sharp, loud crash.

Instinctively, I look around for Sarah.

I scan the room once, then again slower and more carefully. But I don't see her. And the unease starts as a whisper, a gentle caress. I lean my guitar against the chair and stand up, turning in a circle, surveying, searching for the dark head and pretty form I'd know anywhere.

But she's not here.

And the unease turns to concern. My palms start to sweat and my heart accelerates . . . because Hannibal Lancaster is nowhere in sight either.

Hannibal, whom my brother hates.

Hannibal, whom Nicholas won't tolerate even looking at his wife, let alone be near enough to speak to her.

Concern surges into panic—the kind that churns and pokes in my gut and makes the hairs on the back of my neck spike. And that's when I make the connection my idiot brain was too stupid and self-absorbed to figure before:

My brother would never, ever hate someone . . . without a very good reason.

I walk over to Penelope, my hand on her upper arm. "Where's your sister?"

She blinks at me before glancing around the room. "I don't know."

Without needing to be told, Penny walks over to where Elizabeth and Sam are arguing in hushed, animated tones.

"Have you seen Sarah?" she asks. When both of them shake their heads, I have to grind my teeth to keep from shouting.

I approach Franny and Simon. "Did you see where Sarah went?"

Franny's sharp eyes dart around. "I just saw her a moment ago."

I tug at my hair, ready to start tearing the walls down, and Simon puts his hand on my shoulder. "She couldn't have gone far, Henry."

My throat tightens, making my voice hoarse.

"But . . . the crash. She's not good with loud noises."

Simon nods, even though he probably doesn't understand. "We'll find her."

"Prince Henry."

It's James. Watchful, eagle-eyed James.

"Lady Sarah went through there." He points to the far door that leads to a short hall and then the music room.

And I could fucking hug him right now. Instead I smack his arm. "Good man."

Then I rush past him.

When I get to the music room, my panic is burned up by rage at what I see.

Hot, blistering rage, the likes of which I have never known.

Because Sarah is on the sofa, her face pale as death and just as lifeless, her eyes blank, with that flat, fucking horrible dullness. And Hannibal Lancaster is beside her—with his hands on her, touching her breasts.

I heave him up and throw him across the room. "Get the fuck away from her!"

And then I'm kneeling, patting her cheek. She's so pale. I would give anything to see her blush right now.

I stand up when Hannibal moves nearer, facing him with Sarah behind me. And I feel the others rushing into the room, but I don't take my eyes off Lancaster.

"What did you do to her?"

He shrugs, tugging on the cuff of his shirt. "Not a thing. One minute she was fine and the next she was totally out of it. I think she's on something, maybe a bad trip."

The vein at my temple throbs.

"A girl goes catatonic and your first thought is to grab her tits?"

"Oh please, she loved it. Look at her, for fuck's sake—it's probably the most action she's ever gotten in her life."

I've heard stories of murderous fury. Crimes of passion. More often than not, the perpetrators can't remember their own actions. They're confused, their mind and memory muddled and unclear.

That's not how it is with me.

I'm fully cognizant of what I'm about to do.

I'm going to kill this motherfucking bastard with my bare hands.

And the dumb shit never sees it coming.

I grab Lancaster by the front of his shirt and slam my fist into the center of his face, again and again.

And again.

And again.

There's a wet crunching beneath my knuckles that should be repulsive, yet only drives me on. I'd like to hear it over and over. But as I draw back for another hit, thick arms come from behind, threading beneath my shoulders and locking behind my head, restraining me.

And James's voice rasps in my ear, "That's enough. You can't kill him."

"Get your fucking hands off me!"

I struggle but he holds tight. And then another voice cuts through the rage—snapping and calculated.

"Henry," Franny says. "There is a time and place for retribution. Now is not that time."

Her dark eyes are velvet with sympathy. With understanding. But then she reminds me of something much more important.

"She needs you, now."

She needs me.

Sarah needs me.

And it's like a switch has been flipped and every cell in my body shifts and repurposes.

"All right," I tell James, pulling away. "All right!"

He releases me and I'm back on my knees at Sarah's feet. Penny is there beside her, holding her hand and whispering gently.

I cup her jaw, her skin cold. "Sarah, look at me."

But she doesn't move, doesn't blink. There's a streak of blood on her cheek—and it's a surprise when I realize it's from my knuckles. It's dark against the whiteness of her skin, like a black stain I've left behind. And I'm suddenly aware of everyone else in the room. The cameras are still filming and all eyes are focused on Sarah. Watching and gaping.

She wouldn't like that.

So I stand, sweeping her up into my arms. I cradle her against my shoulder and push through the sea of bodies to the door. Vanessa stands just inside it, arms crossed.

As I pass her, I growl, "Party's over."

I bring Sarah straight to our room.

Our room.

And I'm grateful it's on the third floor, tucked in the corner of the castle—far away from everything and everyone. Sarah's limp in my arms, like a puppet whose strings have been cut.

"I'm sorry," I whisper, my lips against her forehead. Her glasses are askew, so I take them off. Then I sit on the edge of the bed, feet on the floor, rocking her in my arms. Her skin feels cold, so I hold her tighter.

"I'm sorry. I'm so sorry."

And I am. More sorry than I've ever been in my life. And that's really saying something.

This is my fault. I brought her here. If it weren't for me, Sarah never would have heard of Hannibal Lancaster. She'd be in her simple little apartment, in her tiny town, with her books and her friends, surrounded by people who love her, who would never, ever hurt her. She would be happy . . . she would be safe.

If it weren't for me.

"I'm so sorry."

With an awful, scraping gasp, she comes awake, arms thrashing—fighting.

"It's okay. You're okay." I keep hold of her, smoothing her hair. "You're all right, it's me. I'm right here, I've got you."

She stops fighting and hiccups. "H . . . Henry?"

I keep rocking her. "Yes, it's me. You're all right."

Then her arms are pulling me closer, hands grasping, holding on like something is trying to wrench her away. And she's crying.

No—not crying. Sobbing. Great, heaving, broken sobs that wreck me.

I gather her even closer, rocking and rocking, pressing

my face into the crook of her neck, trying to weave myself around her.

"It's all right, Sarah."

"I . . . I was so . . . afraid."

"I know, but I'm here now. I've got you."

"I hate this," she chokes out, pressing into my neck. "I hate being afraid all the time. I hate it."

And I can't think of anything to say. I can't tell her it's okay, because it isn't. It's all fucked up and wrong. So I give her the only thing I can: me. I let her know she's not alone.

"I'm afraid too."

Her breath catches in her throat, and her lips press into my neck.

"What do you mean?"

She hugs me tighter, resting her cheek on my shoulder, and my hands grasp her closer, both of us shaking.

"I'm afraid of wanting to be king, of wanting to do it well," I rasp out. "Of thinking I might be capable and really trying . . . only to fail. To find out I just don't measure up. I'm terrified of letting everyone down, that they'll all get hurt because I'm such a fuck-up. So I don't bother . . . and it's all because I'm just too damn scared."

I run my hand over her hair, petting her, the way my mother used to when I was ill. Her shuddering slowly eases in the quiet that follows my confession. Her tears taper off to a sniffling trickle.

"I believe in you, Henry," she says so softly. "I believe you can do anything . . . everything you set your mind to, because you care so deeply for everyone you meet. You will be amazing. I know it in my heart and to the bottom of my soul. And I would tell you the truth, I promise—I wouldn't let you try and fail."

And it's miraculous what that does, how her words make me feel. Like I'm a hundred feet tall and a thousand times as strong. Like I'm a superhero or a god.

Like . . . I'm a king.

I run the back of my hand over her cheek. "I'm supposed to be comforting you."

She smiles gently. "You did."

I press a kiss to her forehead and don't even think about letting her go. I shift back against the headboard and hold Sarah in my arms, her head on my shoulder, her sweet breath against my neck . . . until she falls asleep.

CHAPTER 16

Henry

"What's wrong with her?"

When Penelope's topaz eyes go hard and her chin lifts, I know I've chosen exactly the wrong words.

"Nothing. There's nothing *wrong* with her."

"That's not what I meant."

I walk past her through the doorway, into the sitting area of the bedroom. I don't think I've ever been in this particular bedroom. It's covered in shades of rose and fuchsia and pink—nauseatingly girly, as if a Barbie Dreamhouse puked all over it.

Penelope shuts the door and stands in front of me, securing the belt of her robe defensively.

"The fugues," I begin, "when she 'blinks out'—she called it a quirk. It's not a quirk, is it?"

The tightness in Penelope's face dissipates, softens, and something like sadness rises in her eyes. "No."

My heart jackhammers in my chest and my breath skips. Because I knew it before I walked in here—but to hear someone else say it, to hear her sister confirm that there's something wrong with Sarah—something I may not be able to fix, some broken part of her she won't even show me, let alone give me the chance to mend . . . it's horrendous.

"I've seen it happen to men—soldiers with PTSD. They

slip away and get trapped in another place, another time . . . a *bad* time. Is that how it is with her?"

Penelope's lips fold together, her chin trembling. "Yes."

A hundred horrific headlines flash in my head at once. I squeeze my eyes closed but I still see them.

"What happened to her?" My voice sounds tortured even to my own ears. "Please, Penny, I have to know."

Her pale blond hair sways when she gives a little nod of her head, almost to herself, then motions for me to sit on the sofa. And I have to force my knee to stop bouncing with unspent energy, bracing for what's to come.

The fire pops and her voice is gentle when she speaks, like a nanny reading her charge a bedtime fairy tale. Did you ever notice how genuinely fucked up fairy tales actually are?

"Our mother was traditional when it came to marriage. Very old school—"till death do us part," a trousseau she stitched herself, a virgin on her wedding night—the whole damn thing. She was . . . innocent . . . only just eighteen when she married our father. He was thirty-five. Her parents, our grandparents, were cold arseholes; I already told you that. They were pleased to be rid of her. After the wedding, he took her to his estate in Everly."

Everly is more moor than town. Jagged mountains on one side, cold ocean on the other—the weather as harsh and hard as a castle's stone.

"My very first memory is the sound of my mother screaming . . . begging him to stop. He would go into rages for no reason at all. And he was merciless. Sadistic. Things would be quiet for a few weeks after, sometimes a few months . . . but then it would happen all over again. Sarah and I didn't attend school; we had tutors. He said it was because it was the best education, but I think he just wanted control. The handful of servants we had were completely devoted to him—whether it was because they were loyal or terrified, I'll never know."

Penelope stares down at the gray and mauve rug, her eyes glossing over—seeing something I can't.

"We used to hide in the wardrobe. Sarah had read *The Chronicles of Narnia* and I think some part of her prayed it was real, that we could be transported somewhere—anywhere but where we were. We would cover our ears and hold Mother's dresses over our heads to try to muffle the sounds. You wouldn't think you could hear so clearly," she says and looks up at me with tears glinting like ice drops in her eyes. "I mean, it was a fucking castle. But the sounds carried and we heard every slap, every cry."

Her brows draw together and her forehead crinkles. "I was . . . five the first time Sarah did it, so she would've been about seven."

"Did what?" I rasp out.

"The first time she left the wardrobe."

The words drop like lead in my stomach. Like shrapnel.

"She couldn't stand it. I held onto her hand and I begged her to stay. She told me to stay put—no matter what happened, no matter what I heard." Tears fall silently, one after the other, down Penelope's smooth cheek. "And then she went out of the room and started breaking things."

"Breaking things?"

Penelope nods. "A vase in the hallway, china plates in the drawing room—once she pulled a gold-framed mirror right off the wall. Anything that would make a crash. That would take his attention away from Mother. She would go from room to room, until . . ."

It's only when Penelope stops speaking that I realize I've stopped breathing.

"Until?"

Her light brown eyes look directly into mine. "Until he caught her."

My mind is blank. Black. Like the heaviest curtain has come down, blocking out any light or thought or image.

"Caught her." I roll the words around on my tongue. "I don't . . . I don't understand."

Penelope gazes back at me. "I think you do."

The air expels from my lungs.

"Are you . . . are you saying he hurt her? That he . . . beat her? *Sarah?*"

"Yes."

I'm not an idiot. I studied engineering at university and was bored by it. I have a deep breadth of understanding of history and art and military strategy and science. I know words—big and little. I understand their meaning when they're strung together. When they're used to imply, to deduce, to insinuate.

But this . . . this doesn't make any sense. I can't process it.

Or maybe I just don't want to.

"But . . . how?"

How could anyone hurt sweet, darling Sarah? *My Sarah.* She's everything that is kind and good and funny and beautiful and amazing in this world. Why would anyone want to cause her pain? How is that even possible?

Penelope sniffles. "Usually with his fists. Sometimes with the belt. If she fell, he would kick—"

"Stop." Nausea twists and knots my stomach, folding me over. "Fucking Christ, stop."

Because the curtain is lifted and the images that spill out from Penelope's words are sickening and vivid. My thoughts are cut off when I think of something else. Something I didn't put together until this moment.

"She limps," I tell Penelope in a voice colored by ash. "It's barely perceptible, but I noticed. When she's tired, she limps."

"That was the final straw for Mother. He broke Sarah's leg. They were right outside the door of the room I was in when it happened. It was so loud—the snap of it." Penny squeezes her eyes closed. "God, I can still hear it."

I broke my arm once. Fell the wrong way during a rugby match. It hurt like a bitch. And I know just what she means about the sound—it's distinct. Once you hear it, you'll never forget.

"He wouldn't let us leave, wouldn't let Mother take Sarah to the hospital. For three days he kept us in one of the upstairs rooms." Penelope shudders as she breathes and cries softly. "Sarah was in so much pain. And then, Joseph, the driver— he had only been with us a few months—he helped us escape when our father fell asleep. I remember he swept in and scooped Sarah up in his arms and told us, 'Down the back steps, the car is waiting—hurry now.' And the most terrifying moment was when the three of us were loaded into the back and Joseph had to run around to get to the driver's seat. We were so close . . . I kept watching the door, waiting for my father to burst through and kill us."

Penelope's face has lost all color now. She rubs at her eyes and cheeks with weary hands. "But he didn't. Joseph drove us to the hospital and they set Sarah's leg, but it never healed the way it should have. Auntie Gertrude took us in, had her lawyers arrange the divorce, and they managed to convince our father that if he ever came near us again, details of his actions and photos of Sarah's bruises would be made public. He was in Switzerland the last I heard, and I hope every day that an avalanche falls on him."

My chest feels like it's filled with concrete. And I want to cry. I haven't wept since I was ten years old, but I could now. For her. For the fucking injustice of it. I want to fall to my knees and shout at the sky. I want to curse God to his face.

I want to slash and burn and maim and kill.

And it's that last thought that finally gives me the focus I so desperately need. I take a few deep breaths then stand up and put my hand on Penelope's shoulder, squeezing. "Thank you for telling me."

She gifts me with a shadow of a smile. But as I step toward the door, she clasps my hand in her chilly grip. "Henry. You can't . . . you need to leave my sister alone. You can't toy with her. I know she seems strong and in some ways she is, but inside . . . she's so fragile. Sarah is genuine and good and . . . not like us."

Penelope Von Titebottum and I are cut from the same selfish cloth. Wild. Needy. We know how the game is played, how to turn all heads our way. We thrive on it—the attention, the adoration of others. I mean—look at this fucking show I've jumped into.

Without a care in the world.

Without a thought for my country or my responsibilities or even a second of concern for the feelings of the women who've signed up for it. The whole point is to get them to fall in love with me—to think they have a chance at living royally fucking ever after, while the whole world watches.

All because I wanted a distraction.

And if a few hearts are shattered in the process? That's just too damn bad. Because this is who we are.

What did my brother tell me once?

We can't change who we are.

"No." I tell Sarah's sister. "She's not at all like us."

My hands shake as I walk down to the great hall—to the Fantastic Wall of Death.

The mace is the first thing to come down. The rusty spiked ball and chain. I give it a test swing.

That'll do.

Next is my grandmother's namesake—the battle-axe. It

comes with a sling so it can be strapped across the back, and the blade is still razor sharp.

Then it's the jewel-handled sword. It's heavier than you'd expect. I thrust forward and imagine running it through a stomach, then watching patiently as the acids leak out from the wound into the body cavity, eventually eating away at the vital organs. It's a slow, ghastly way to die.

Perfect.

After carefully selecting four additional harbingers of death, I clink and clank my way up the steps to the third floor. When I walk into the room, Sarah is awake, sitting on the sofa. She's changed into nightclothes and a soft white robe, and her voice is thick with sleep. "I woke up and you weren't here."

Her eyes drift over my arms and chest, laden with weaponry. "What are you doing?"

"I'm leaving."

Her brows pinch. "Where . . . where are you going?"

When I speak, I barely recognize my own voice.

"I'm going to find your father, and then I'm going to kill him. Badly. I thought it'd be rude not to ask if you'd like to come along and watch."

CHAPTER 17

Henry

She gives me that look. I'm familiar with it now. It tugs at the flesh of my heart.

It's a small smile, a pitying shake of her head as if to say, *silly, silly boy*.

"Henry, you can't kill my father."

"Oh, I can." My voice is low and dark and viciously certain. "Believe me, I can."

She reaches out and takes my hand.

"Penny told you."

My chin jerks, nodding.

I replay every interaction Sarah and I have had, noting every sin and overstep. Did I ever frighten her? Was I ever too rough? I think about the night I broke her book, the things I said, and I want to hit my own fucking head with the mace.

"I should have been more careful with you."

She looks up, eyes round and innocent. "You *are* careful with me."

She takes the sword from my hand and sets it aside. She slips the strap that holds the battle-axe on the back of my shoulder and lays it on the table. One by one she disarms me, and I let her. Then she leads me to the sofa by the hand and sits down.

"I don't think about my father anymore, Henry."

"But that's not true. Every time you slip away, it's because of him."

She licks her bottom lip, and her forehead furrows as she thinks over what she wants to say.

"When you hate someone, they're a part of your life; they get to take up space in your thoughts, every day. They claim your focus and, in a way, they have control over you. What happened to me, happened; no one can change it now." Her voice grows stronger then, more determined. "But he doesn't get to have anything else. Not a second more of my time or my energy or my thoughts. My life is mine, Henry . . . and it's a good life."

She looks down at our hands, clasped together.

"So you see, if you kill him for me, it will all be dredged up again. I've put him behind me. And I'd like him to stay there."

I bring her hand to my mouth, kissing the back, forcing myself to be gentle, because the rage still lurches and swirls inside me like lava.

"It's not fair."

Sarah smiles then and it's sad.

"You had a mother and father who loved you more than anything else in the whole world. And they were taken away too soon. Life isn't fair, Henry. Not for any of us."

No. Not fucking good enough.

I hold her face in my hands. "It should be for you."

I lean down and kiss her forehead. Then I stand up.

"And if I can't make it fair, then I'll make it even. An eye for an eye. See how he likes it when I break his fucking—"

Sarah stands up and presses her lips against mine. It's so unexpected, I freeze. But then, as her mouth moves over mine, I begin to thaw. Her mouth is so soft, so very sweet. The kiss is almost chaste—at least it's the most chaste I've ever had. Unpracticed.

And yet, it still manages to make my heart pound against my ribs like an animal in a cage.

"What are you doing?" I whisper, when she pulls back just a little.

"I'm distracting you." She looks up at me uncertainly. From behind those ridiculously prim little glasses with those big, dark eyes that could bring me to my knees. "Is it working?"

My tongue traces my lower lip—tasting her.

And craving more.

"I'm not sure. Keep trying—I'll let you know."

She smiles quick and relieved . . . and then she reaches back up, wraps her arms about my neck, and kisses me.

Her two lips envelop my lower one, then the upper, all eager, pleasing sweetness. And it's good—I don't think any kiss has ever felt so good. I could do this for days.

My hands find Sarah's lower back and I pull her in close, tight against me. Then, gently, I open my mouth and she mirrors my movement, opening for me. And it's like my blood has turned to gasoline, and the touch of our tongues is the spark.

I delve deeper, harder—more demanding—taking the lead, but she meets me every step of the way. I cup her head in my hands, holding her still while I plunge and devour. A beautiful moan seeps from her lips and I devour that too. I can't catch my breath and my heart does its best to break through my ribs.

But then I squeeze my eyes tight, and stop . . . panting against Sarah's neck.

"Sarah, maybe we shouldn't. Maybe we should just—"

"I'm sick of being afraid, Henry. And I'm so tired of being alive . . . but not really living. I want this; I've wanted it for a long time. I want . . . you." It's only then that hesitation dims her eyes. "Do you want me too?"

I grip her arms. "More than I've wanted anything or anyone in my entire life."

Sarah takes my hands in hers, lifts them and presses my palms to her breasts. They're soft and full and absolutely perfect.

"Show me."

Beneath her robe, her bedclothes are paper thin. I trace my thumbs across her nipples, feeling them harden and peak. I want to suck on them until she's mindless. I want to lick every inch of her skin and watch her flush with desire. I want to feel her fingers squeeze my arse and her nails rake my back.

There's so much I know—deviant, filthy, lovely moves. And I want to teach her every damn one.

I wrap my arms around Sarah and lift her right off her feet. With a groan, my mouth is back to hers. Her small hands cup my jaw as I carry her toward the bed. I stop against a wall on the way, knocking a frame sideways, lifting her leg in one hand and wrapping it around my hip so I can thrust against her.

Her head tilts and her back arches, and she writhes beautifully against me.

And it's the damnedest thing. Here I am, pressed up against Sarah's softness, hard as stone and hot as fire, but the thought that floods my mind is . . . my brother.

Nicholas.

I didn't understand before, not really. How he stood up there that day and upended both our lives. How he changed everything . . . gave in . . . gave it all up.

But now . . . now it makes sense.

Because I would give up a crown for her. I would give up my name, my title—I would trade my country, forfeit my birthright, lie, kill, cheat, and steal, for this.

For her.

A chuckle rumbles in my throat at my own cluelessness. How stupid I was.

But now I know. And nothing will ever be the same.

Sarah draws back when she feels me laugh. "What is it? Am I doing something wrong?"

I caress her face and brush back her hair.

"No, you're perfect. It's all so fucking perfect."

Nicholas was right. I'll have to tell him one day soon that he was right.

Love is stronger.

When I get us to the bed, we fall upon it, rolling and thrusting and insane. My hands are everywhere. Pushing up her top, pulling at her pants, kissing her warm skin the moment it's revealed. Sarah gasps and pulls at my clothes too, beautiful and wild, not a trace of shy innocence in sight. She lifts her arms and her shirt is gone.

And her breasts. Oh, perfect, pale, full breasts, with dark pink nipples that beg for attention. I'm happy to oblige. I kiss my way around the gorgeous globes, nibbling and sucking, and Sarah's hands bury in my hair, yanking in the best, neediest way.

When I close my lips over one nipple, she gasps—high-pitched and loud—then it tapers off to a long whimper. I flick my tongue, suckling hard until her hips are lifting, seeking friction. It's crazy and fast, desperate and rough . . . but we can't seem to slow down.

Sarah pushes on my shoulder, rolling us over so she's on top, straddling me. She moves on instinct, perfectly positioned on my cock, rolling her hips. She lifts my shirt off, her hands roaming and her lips kissing across my chest. She licks the groove in the center of my abdomen, over and over again—she really seems to like that part. Her hair falls all around my torso, tickling like silk feathers.

And I want to take my time, I want to know every freckle on her skin . . . but first I have to make her come. The desire is like a runaway train, unstoppable and raging.

I roll us back over so that Sarah's beneath me. Then I lift up onto my knees and enjoy the sight of her on her back, knees open, lust and yearning making her eyes shimmer. Holding her gaze, I deliberately unbutton my trousers. Her eyes drop as I yank them off without leaving the bed, but I keep my black briefs on.

Too much temptation if they were off and as hot as she is, I don't think she's ready to take things quite that far. She reaches for me, pressing her hand on the thick, hard outline of my cock beneath the fabric, and my eyes roll back in my head.

I push against her hand, hips thrusting, because it feels so fucking divine.

Then I'm skimming her sleeping pants down her shapely legs and throwing them over my shoulder. And Sarah lies beneath me, in a simple pair of white cotton knickers . . . and nothing else. Her chest rising and falling, her lips swollen from my rough kisses, her breasts high, nipples tight.

Without taking my eyes from hers, I move on top of her, spreading her legs wider, looking deep into her eyes, gazing at her beautiful face. I line my cock up against her, right against her clit, and I can feel how hot and wet she is, even through the cotton.

And then I thrust slow and long.

"Henry," she whimpers from deep in her throat. "Henry."

And nothing has ever sounded sweeter.

I pull my hips back and thrust again.

She whimpers and her head lolls to the side.

"Like this?" I rasp.

Sarah's head bounces in a jerky nod and her hands knead my arms. She lifts her hips up to meet mine and then I'm bending, pressing her into the bed. Kissing her rough and wild, claiming her plump mouth as surely as she fucking owns me.

"Henry, Henry, Henry," she chants against my lips, in time with the movement of my cock against her. The pressure is perfect, the pleasure racing up my spine and down my legs, settling in my pelvis and tightening balls.

Sarah screams when she comes, scratching and wild and beautiful. With an arched back she raises her hips and stiffens—everything tight and clenching. I pump harder and then I'm with her, coming in a hot, pulsing stream that makes my mind go white with bliss.

And after, we kiss and touch and giggle—both of us a sweaty, sticky mess and too damn happy to move.

Later, after I've gotten a cloth from the bathroom and cleaned both of us up, I lie on my back with Sarah cuddled against me.

"We should talk."

She turns on her side to face me, even while her eyes scrunch closed.

"Talking isn't my strong suit."

I trace the bridge of her nose with the tip of my finger.

"That's not true. You're getting better at it."

My instinct tells me that with Sarah, simple and direct is the best way to go.

"I like you," I whisper, pressing a kiss to the tip of her nose, her chin, her smooth brow. "I like you so much."

She cups my jaw, caresses my neck and shoulder.

"I like you too. So much."

I've had sex with hundreds of women, some whom I actually cared for . . . but this right here, is one of the most intimate moments of my life.

"I want to take you out. Take you everywhere. I want to show you everything. Now that I know what's underneath your clothes," I run my hand up her stomach, kneading her breast, and she moans sweetly, "you can wear all the black you want and I won't tease you a bit."

She smiles and I feel invincible.

"I like it when you tease me."

I nibble on her lip, her chin. "Have you ever seen the library at the palace?"

"No."

"You'll love it. Two floors, more books than you could read in three lifetimes. And I want you to meet my grandmother."

"All right, Henry."

"I want to buy you things. Everything."

I want to drape her in jewels and silks . . . and crowns.

"I don't need things," she says softly, eyes beautiful and dark.

I pull her closer, my hard, demanding cock pressed against her pelvis.

"Which makes me want to buy them for you even more."

Sarah wraps her arms around my neck, toying with my hair. And before she speaks it, I feel the word—the world—trying to rise up between us, wedge us apart.

"But . . ."

But the show—this damned show that I don't even care about—that I never did. *But* the crew that fills the castle at this very moment and the contracts I've signed. *But* the other women—including her own sister—who I'm still expected to entertain and engage for the next two weeks.

Fuck me.

I think of all the times Granny's lectured me about my responsibilities, about duty and honor and the importance of following through with my commitments.

Christ, this sucks.

But I want to do the right thing. I don't want to be that stupid boy anymore—the one who ditches and makes excuses and mucks it all up.

Honor means something different to me now. Something more. Because Sarah deserves a good man, an honorable man. Steady and reliable and true.

And I want to be that man for her.

"But, I'm bound to two more weeks of filming. I've given them my word and I speak for the House of Pembrook."

I feel her nod. "That's not a small thing."

I look into her eyes. "I don't want to keep filming. You know that, don't you?"

Sarah sighs, and her expression is so open, so damn trusting. It humbles me.

"I do, yes."

"If I could, I'd stay right here in this bed with you. Do you believe that?"

"Yes. But you can't."

"No. I can't."

What a shit-show. And it's all my own stupid doing.

Where the fuck is that mace?

"The other girls, Henry . . . you won't touch them?" she stiffens against me. "Not like this. I won't put up with that."

"No, of course not. I'll barely look at them, I swear. All my touches—my hands, my lips, my cock—they all belong to you now, sweet Sarah."

She grins. "That's good to know."

But then her eyes narrow. "Have you touched them? Like this?"

I chuckle at the thread of jealousy in her tone.

"No. I'm practically a monk. It seems fate has been conspiring from the very beginning for us to end up right here."

"Good."

Wanting to make sure we're clear, so there are no misunderstandings, I reiterate, "So I'll do what I have to do, go through the motions, honor my commitment for the next two weeks. But we'll have this, here in this room; we'll be together. Yeah?"

She gives me a nod and I want to sigh with relief.

"Yes."

Now that that's out of the way, I lean forward and kiss her again, sliding my tongue against hers. She presses back eagerly, honest and so damn perfect. My lips trail up her jaw to her ear and she shivers against me.

"I want to make you come again, Sarah."

She nips at my earlobe. "Yes, please."

And I laugh. "So polite."

Then there's no more talking. There's only moaning, and gasping and writhing and coming. Until, much later, exhausted and spent, we both fall asleep.

CHAPTER 18

Henry

The next morning, I wake with my nose buried in the soft skin of a fragrant neck and strands of hair tickling my face. I give Sarah a squeeze and nip at her shoulder, but she just moans sleepily.

Poor thing—I kept her up very late, doing very, very bad things.

And I can't stop bloody smiling about it.

I slip out from under the covers, shower and get dressed. It's a location shot today; Laura and I will be hiking all day. Before I leave, I kneel beside the bed and brush back Sarah's hair, then run my hand up and down her arm, until eventually her long lashes blink and her eyes open.

She inhales. "Henry? What time is it?"

"Early. You can go back to sleep. I just didn't want to leave without saying goodbye. How are you feeling, sweets?"

I've never been with a virgin. And while last night wasn't the big "first time" for Sarah, it was a lot of little firsts. As the experienced one, I want to make sure she's all right with that.

She stretches and the sheet falls down, exposing her elegant neck and perfect tits—my mouth goes dry and my head goes blank.

"I feel . . . hungover," she says. "Drained." And then she

smiles naughtily. "And randy. I think you've created a monster, Your Highness."

My head drops to the bed with a thud. Why am I leaving this room again? Oh, that's right, my dick reminds me—because I'm a double damned fool.

"Hold that thought." I kiss her, quick and playful. "And don't move from this spot. We'll pick up right here when I get back to you tonight."

Sarah

It's a gloriously indulgent day. After Henry leaves, I fall right back to sleep and don't wake until noon. Penny comes to check on me, to makes sure I'm all right after last night. She explains that Lancaster was tossed out after Henry beat him to a bloody pulp. I'm not usually a vengeful person but in this case, I'll make an exception.

Penelope also says that Elizabeth is leaving with Sam this morning. She wanted to stay, to go through the motions, like Henry said—for the sake of the show—but Sam put his foot down.

"Good for them," Penny says, and I agree.

After she leaves, I shower and dress and grab a quick bite at the food service table and then head straight back upstairs, to be lazy. I lie in the nook and read, resting my forehead against the cool glass of the windowpane, but my mind keeps wandering from the story back to what Henry and I did last night.

Now I see what all the fuss is about.

I'm not completely clueless. I know what an orgasm is and

have been happily giving them to myself for years. But getting one from Henry . . . just *wow*.

He's bold and confident; I think that's my favorite part. The way he moves, how he touches me and himself—how he's sure of just what to do. And he knows it. It's beautiful and thrilling at the same time. And I like that we talked afterward, cleared the air. It'll make it easier. He's the Crown Prince, the star of the show; I can't very well expect him to quit like Elizabeth. I need to be understanding. And I am. Truly.

Plus it's only two more weeks. It'll be like no time at all.

It's after six and already dark when the bedroom door opens. Henry leans back against it, watching me. His eyes shine with an intense, almost dangerous light. Everything about him is tight and coiled—his jaw, his shoulders, his clenched hands.

A shiver ripples under my skin as he stalks forward, like a jaguar or lion—all smooth grace and lethal power. He grips the back of his shirt as he goes, sliding it up and off, revealing the tight, sinewy muscles of his arms and abdomen. Lounge pants hang low on his hips, displaying a dusting of golden hair that trails a path beneath the waistband. And the image of rubbing my cheek, my lips, against that hair springs to mind. Will it be soft? Wiry? Would Henry moan if I blew on it or would he grip my hair and move my mouth to more interesting places?

When he reaches the bed, he wraps his hand around my ankle and jerks me down to the edge. "I've been thinking about this all day."

It's only when I speak that I realize I'm breathless. "About what?"

And the man who will be my king sinks to his knees before me.

"About tasting you. I'm going to lick you until my tongue gives out. Any objections?"

Oh God...

His lips slide into an adorably crooked half-smile. "Speechless, love? Was it something I said?"

His hands slide up my skirt, grasping my panties and skimming them off my hips and down my legs. His movements are sure and confident.

Then he looks at the beige silk material in his hand, almost curiously. "How do you do that? Make something so plain look so hot I could come in just two pumps?"

Then he presses my panties to his face and inhales—his eyes sliding blissfully closed.

Oh my God...

He doesn't remove my skirt, but pushes it up to my waist—exposing me to the cool air and his simmering gaze. My heartbeat pounds in my ears, not swift and erratic, but in a deep, hard, steady rhythm.

Henry kisses my calf, then behind my knee. "I need your words, sweet Sarah. Do you want me to lick you?"

"Yes," I whisper so softly I can barely hear myself.

"Say it. Say, 'Put your mouth on me, Henry. Taste me, kiss me, fuck me with your tongue.'"

I'm going to die. He's going to kill me with words and excitement and need.

"Yes, all of it." I swallow and try to give him what he wants. "Taste me, Henry. Fuck me w—"

I don't finish—because with a deep groan, he's on me. Mouth sucking and licking, hungry—starving. And it's amazing. Dizzyingly divine. My skin feels electrified and warm, wet, pulsing pleasure pumps through my veins. I let my head drop back to the bed because I can't hold it up, and my legs spread wider, hips writhing. Wanting him, wanting this, wanting to let him do anything and everything just so long as he never stops touching me.

"It's so good . . . so good . . . Henry."

My words are incoherent like my thoughts and I don't really know what I'm saying.

He cups my bottom and holds me up to his mouth. I feel his teeth against my soft lips, his tongue lapping up and down, tracing firm circles around my clitoris again and again.

But then he shifts his mouth, nibbling the tender skin of my upper thigh. "Give me your hands," Henry says, his breath hot against me.

I lift my arms and offer my hands. He puts them right where he wants them—between my legs, fingers holding me open to him, my thumbs at my cleft, exposing my most sensitive flesh.

"Stay just like that," Henry rasps. "Fuck, look at you." He licks me with the very tip of his tongue. "Such a pretty, pink, tight pussy."

Ohmygodohmygodohmygod . . .

"You like those words, don't you?" His finger drags across my slick opening, slowly circling and circling. "They make you wet."

"It's so . . . dirty," I pant, but I don't feel at all embarrassed.

"That's why it's fun." He presses a kiss to my clit and I moan so loud. "Because you're so fucking sweet."

Then Henry lifts his eyes to mine. "Now, Sarah . . . watch."

Slowly, he licks me from bottom to top. On the second pass, he stops at my opening and presses inside. He thrusts in and out, deep and hard, fucking me just like he said . . . with his tongue. I whimper and he moans. And it builds inside me, cresting—the intensity—the pleasure. I try to keep watching, because that's what Henry wants, but it's just all too much.

My legs tremble on his back, thighs squeezing. I writhe and I beg.

"Please, please, please, oh please . . ."

So close.

So . . . close.

His tongue is replaced with fingers, long and thick. And when his lips close over my clit, sucking gently, my muscles clamp down on those fingers and my mind goes white as shattering pleasure wracks through my body. Wave after wave makes my back bow and my mouth scream.

After a time, when the grip of my orgasm wanes to languid contentment, Henry kisses his way up to my lips. His kiss is hard and dominating, with teeth and tongue.

And yes, I taste myself on his lips—just like in the books.

But there's no shame or disgust. It's arousing, erotic, and perfect—because everything with Henry is perfect. And I feel so incredibly tender toward him. I wrap my arms around his neck and back, anywhere I can reach.

"That was . . . amazing," I say.

Henry's lips nuzzle my neck and a chuckle rumbles in his chest.

"That . . . was only the beginning." He leans away just long enough to pull my shirt over my head and push my skirt off to the floor. Then he rolls onto his back, hooking me under the arms and effortlessly lifting until I'm straddling his chest.

I should be embarrassed—I mean, my crotch is practically in his face. And it seems Henry wants to go from practically to literally.

He crooks his finger, looking carefree and young and heartbreakingly happy. "Hold onto the headboard and bring that sweet pussy up here."

And I laugh, because who says that?

"Are you sure?"

"My tongue isn't even close to tired. And I need more of you, Sarah."

He's so damn comfortable, so sure and confident in his own

skin. And he makes me feel that way too. Beautiful and bold. Brave. Like I could do anything—say anything—be anything.

But at the moment, all I want to be is his. So I wiggle forward and follow my prince's command.

Henry

In secondary school, my friends and I made up a drinking game called "The Way I'd Go." The idea was to think of the grandest, best way to die—like drowning in a vat of ale or blowing up the chem lab for the betterment of all student-kind. I've just discovered the ultimate, most sublime way to die: with Sarah Titebottum sitting on my face.

That's the way I'd go—hell yeah.

Her pussy is perfect. She smells like fucking roses and tastes like sunshine. In the last hour and a half, she's come three times. I think I've sprained my tongue.

Totally worth it.

Sarah sighs contentedly, snuggling up against my side, her pretty eyes closed.

I stare at the ceiling and try not to think about how painfully hard I am or the throbbing weight of my heavy balls. It's possible my cock could actually burst—which hurts to even think about—that's how hard I am.

Sarah's palm slides along my chest.

"Henry?" she says, soft and sweet.

"Mmm?"

"I want to do that to you."

My eyes spring open. And I actually get harder. But I have

to be sure she's saying what I think she's saying—I'm in no state to be messed with.

"Do what?"

She leans up on her arm, looking down at me with cheeks flushed. And there's a new directness in her eyes, an audacity that I don't think was there yesterday. It makes her even sexier.

"I want to put my mouth on you." She glances down to where my briefs are tented so high it should be funny. I purposely kept them on so I wouldn't get carried away. Sarah naked is one thing—both of us naked and rubbing on each other is entirely too dangerous.

I should ask her if she's sure. I should tell her she doesn't have to.

But what I actually say is, "Fuck me, Christ, yes please."

She giggles and I feel it in my aching cock. Then she dips her head and starts peppering kisses across my collarbone. Soft, whispery brushes of warm lips. She flicks her tongue over one sensitive nipple, pulling a moan from me.

"I feel drunk, Henry. Wild. And I want to make you feel every bit as good as you made me feel. I want so much to give you that."

I lift up again, pulling her to me, kissing her wet and deep. "You do, Sarah. Christ, everything you do—feels incredible."

She moves lower, and I start to pant. Her tongue licks at my abs and swirls around my navel and I have to fist my hands in the sheets to keep from grabbing her head and fucking her mouth. And when that wet, pink tongue dips below the waistband on my briefs, I almost lose it.

I need a distraction. So I ask stupid questions that I already know the answers to.

"Have you ever done this before?"

She giggles against my skin. "No."

And I bask in hearing it out loud. In the knowledge of being her first.

Her *only*.

It feels so greedy, so fucking possessive—mine, mine, every inch of her is mine. If she could read my thoughts she'd probably call me sexist—maybe misogynistic—but I don't care.

It's awesome. And if thinking that makes me a pig, well . . . *oink, oink*.

"But I've read about it. Some romance scenes are very . . . detailed."

When she tugs on the waistband, I lift my hips—she skims off my briefs in one swoop and my freed cock taps against my stomach.

"Detailed how?" I grind out, trying not to lose my fucking mind.

She gets comfy on her elbows, adjusts her glasses, and gazes at my dick like it's something to be figured out. It enjoys the notice, thickening and twitching, attention whore that it is. Sarah grips me at the base and brings her mouth closer—close enough that I can feel her warm breath on me.

"Well, the books say this is the most sensitive part, especially this little ridge here."

She swirls her tongue around the tip, then licks at the ridge in question. My skull digs into the pillow and it's so good it's almost painful.

"That's true," I moan.

Then she kisses up and down the shaft, talking as she goes.

"And, they always mention massaging the testicles, how that makes it better." Her voice turns teasing. "Should I test that theory?"

Cheeky girl

All I can do is nod. And then I whimper when she cups my sack in her hand, causing hot, weighted pleasure to light every nerve in my body.

"What do they call it?" I wonder. I have no idea why. "Can't see Jane Austen writing the word *cock*."

It's possible I just want to hear the word from Sarah's lips.

"Depends on the book," she says, licking me from base to tip, swirling around the full, aching head, before licking her way back down with her hot, wet tongue. And then she does it again.

"Not Austen, but some books call a cock, a cock."

So bloody good

"Others call it a rod or a sword . . . and the woman is the sheath."

"Sounds painful."

Sarah giggles, and then slips the head of my dick into the wet cavern of her mouth and I groan.

She removes her mouth, stroking me slowly.

"And this," she brushes her thumb across the tip, rubbing at the pre-cum, "is sometimes called the 'pearl of desire,' and they always say it tastes sweet or salty." And then she fucking licks me. "Mmm . . . it is a bit salty."

And I'm gone.

"Take me in your mouth, Sarah. All the way. Suck it hard. And fast. Now."

And she does just that. Envelops me in her tight, wet mouth, sucking and laving—wrapping her little hand around what she can't take, pumping hard.

"That's good, so good, love."

Gently, I cup the back of her head, holding her steady, and then I thrust up between her full, hot lips. "Fuck, fuck, fuck . . ."

When the pleasure hits, intense and quick, I pull out of Sarah's mouth. Then I cover her hand with mine, showing her how to stroke fast and tight in the end. And with a guttural groan, I come and come on Sarah's hand and my stomach, thick and hot.

When I can, I lift my hand and motion her closer. I kiss her lips then, soft and tender.

Then she leans back, smiling proudly. "I think blow jobs are fantastic."

And it would be adorable . . . if it weren't so hot.

"I can't tell you how happy I am to hear it." I choke out.

She dabs her finger in the come on my stomach, rubbing it between her thumb and her forefinger. And it makes me think of all the places I want to come on her.

"Next time, I'd like to try swallowing, Henry."

Next time, she's probably going to kill me.

And there's another way I'd definitely go.

CHAPTER 19

Sarah

My and Henry's relationship goes wonderfully . . . for three days. That's when I make a mistake, a crucial error in judgment: I leave my room. While he's filming. While he's filming with other women, including my sister.

It begins in the dining room, where Henry's having breakfast with all three of the remaining contestants—Penny, Laura, and Cordelia. Henry's in a rowdy good mood, smiling and laughing . . . and teasing with them all. And that's how it starts. There's a bitter taste in the back of my throat as I think, *He should be joking with me, and only with me.*

The rational part of my brain reminds me: we discussed this. He asked me if I believed him when he said he didn't want to continue filming and I said I did.

So why am I wondering now if perhaps he wasn't being entirely truthful? If maybe, just maybe, he likes having three beautiful women fawning over him during the day—the pig—and a different, starry-eyed woman in his bed at night.

He certainly seems to like it now.

Laura's eyes close in ecstasy as she eats the omelets prepared by the chef brought in by the show. And then she says, "Henry! You have to try this, it's unreal!"

It's fucking *eggs*.

But she scoops some omelet onto her fork . . . the same fork she just used . . . and offers it up to Henry.

And that's what pushes me over the edge. I have to walk away. I don't wait around to see if he eats off her fork. Christ, it's like a bad idiom.

Just before I turn around, with my fists clenched at my sides, Henry catches my eye, and whatever he sees on my face makes him stop mid-chew and drop the smile from his lips.

But he doesn't follow after me. He just keeps eating breakfast and filming.

Things continue downhill at lunchtime—like an avalanche. They're filming outside, around the perimeter of the castle. It's cool and windy, but the sun is warm. Henry's walking with Cordelia and her flatulent little dog, Walter. He grips Walter's leash and they chat as they stroll, grinning, making such a pretty picture together.

He doesn't hold her hand or put his arm around her. He keeps Walter firmly between them at all times, like a drooling little buffer, so even when Cordelia leans in for a kiss, he's able to lean back, turn his shoulder. and pick up a ball to play fetch.

I know all this—I see it.

But it doesn't help the absolute wretched feeling inside as I watch them together. It's a yearning, like my soul is trying to pull out of my body, and it's a crushing pain, like my heart and my lungs are being squeezed by an invisible vise.

After his walk with Cordelia, Henry comes straight for me

in the courtyard, his brow weighted with worry. He puts his hand on my arm and as easy as that, my stomach flutters and swoons. She's a weak, spineless organ and it doesn't take much to please her.

"What's wrong with you?" Henry asks.

I open my mouth to answer, but he doesn't let me.

"And don't say 'nothing.' I know there's something. You're looking at me like you want to burst into tears and kick me in the balls and you can't make up your mind which to do first."

I chuckle, because it's like he's reading my mind.

"It's this, isn't it?" His eyes flick around us, at the cameras and crew. "That's what's bothering you."

And I haven't lied to him up until this point, so why start now?

"Yes."

Henry nods and his face tenses with consternation. But before he can say anything else, Penelope is there, wrapping her arms around Henry's, looking adorable in snug cut-off jeans and a casual maroon top, without a clue about the conversation she just walked in on.

"Come on, Henry! It's our turn in the kitchen. They're having us make chocolate lava cake! I love lava cake but I've never made it a day in my life . . . it's going to be an epic disaster!"

And then my little sister looks between us.

"What's going on? What's the matter?"

And it's my sister. Of all people, I should be able to stand watching Henry with my darling sister.

I shake my head and look into Henry's eyes. "I'm being silly. It's fine."

He hesitates.

"Truly, Henry, it's all right."

"What's all right?" Penny presses. "What the hell is going on with you two?"

And I see the moment when Henry decides to go

forward. His face breaks into a smile and his voice changes—with obviously faked enthusiasm, but I'm the only one who recognizes it.

"Nothing's going on, Pen. Sarah wants to explore the tunnels below the castle—supposedly there's an old dungeon down there, maybe a tomb or two—but she's too scared to go alone."

Penny squeals. "Oooh, that's creepy! Well, Henry can take you after filming, but count me out! I won't be able to sleep another night in this old place again."

She tugs on Henry's arm.

"Come on, they're waiting for us. And you have to wash up and change."

He lets her pull him along, glancing back over his shoulder once to look at me.

Turns out, watching Henry play house with my sister makes it worse, not better. When she flicks confectionery sugar at him flirtatiously, I want to vomit. And when he wipes a bit of batter off her cheek with a cloth—a strictly platonic move—I realize I'm done. Finished. I can't watch this anymore. I don't want to.

And more than that, I can't hide in my room knowing that scenes like this—and worse—are going on outside of it.

I feel his eyes follow me when I turn on my heel and stomp upstairs.

Henry

Two hours later, I find her in our room, packing, with John Cale singing "Hallelujah" softly in the background from her mobile. Watching Sarah slowly gather her things, seeing her precious books packed in the satchel by the door, all ready to go, makes me fucking livid. Furious. Does she really think she can just walk away?

Does she actually believe I would let her?

I want to throw all her things out the window into the ocean and tie her to the bloody bed—and I know how unhinged that sounds, which is why I'm not saying it out loud.

I don't want to control her; I just want to keep her. Her gentle spirit, her kind loveliness has become the center of my world and I'm not sure I know how to function anymore without it. I take it back—I don't want to tie her to the bed, at least not right now.

Right now, I just want to tie Sarah to me.

I cross my arms, leaning against the closed door. She jumps when I speak, like she didn't know I was here.

"What are you doing?"

My voice is calm, but I know my eyes are bright and intense, and there's a visible frantic energy in my limbs, because we both know exactly what she's doing.

"I'm going to go home now."

I nod, watching her every move. The soft sway of her hips, that lovely tight bottom that was made for biting, the gentle slope of her jaw that's now tense with her frustration.

She lays a stack of sweaters in the suitcase and I move forward, quick and sharp. And a second later, her sweaters aren't in the suitcase anymore—they're strewn all over the room, because that's where I tossed them.

"Hey!"

Glaring at me, she picks one up, shakes it out, folds it, and places it in the suitcase—and then it's back out again, flying over my shoulder.

"Stop that!"

I move in closer, going nose to nose. "*You* stop it. You're not going anywhere."

She throws her arms up. "Why not? Penny's been on her best behavior—there's no reason for me to be here!"

"I'm the reason!" I shout back. "I need you here!"

Sarah looks away, off to the corner of the room. "I can't do it. I can't stand it. I thought I could but I can't. Watching you with them makes something ugly and painful spring up inside me. Maybe you could come to me when it's all over and then we can see if there's something between us . . ."

If there's something between us? Has she lost her fucking mind?

"I'll quit the show. Today."

That brings her up short—she genuinely wasn't expecting it. She actually thought I was going to just let her walk out the door. I can't decide if that's more funny or sad.

"I don't think you can do that."

"I can do anything I want . . . it comes with the title."

"Vanessa will be furious."

I shrug. "That's why we keep lawyers on retainer."

Sarah moves closer, slowly, cautiously, looking up at me.

"You would do that? Quit, just because it makes me upset?"

I almost laugh. "Of course."

"Why?"

And then I'm the one peering down at her, with perplexed, puzzled eyes.

"Because I'm in love with you, sweet silly girl."

She goes still, just . . . looking at me. And wetness rises in her eyes.

I press my palm to her jaw.

"Didn't you know that? Can't you see it, Sarah? I'm absolutely gone for you."

Her breath shudders as she inhales. "I wasn't sure. I'd hoped, but . . ."

I slip her glasses off and set them on the bedside table so I can kiss her eyelids, tasting tears.

"I love you."

Then I kiss each cheek and her dainty little chin. "I love, love, love you."

I kiss the tip of her nose and her plush, perfect mouth.

And then we're falling, falling onto the bed. I push aside suitcases and clothing, making room, but my lips never leave hers. I slip both my hands beneath her head, holding her and lifting, our tongues stroking, swirling. And then I angle my mouth across Sarah's, and my hands skim over soft flesh and into her hair and back down again. She pulls at the hem of my shirt, raising it up my spine—I lift my arms, helping her.

And then her hands delve into my hair, stroking and gripping. Her lips are at my collarbone, across my chest, up my neck and my jaw.

I pull her shirt up and off, and flick the clasp at her bra so it falls away, and we're skin to heated skin.

And there are no words. We don't need them. Our hands speak for us—desperate and holding. Our tongues show our wet worship and our eyes speak our confession—our adoration for each other.

When we're completely bare, I slide down Sarah's body, sucking at her peaked, pink nipples. Her back arches and her legs spread and I slide lower, kissing and licking her pussy until she's whimpering and writhing on the bed and tugging at my hair. Then I slip back up to her, face to face. Her fingers spread across my cheek, holding me close as she kisses me with all she is and gives me all she has.

I dip my hand between her legs and I moan into her mouth

when I feel how wet she is, so tight and sweet. And then it's not my fingers tracing her lower lips, opening her—it's the hard, full head of my cock. I use it to spread her wetness, to rub her clit, and when I know she can't stand a moment more, when she needs to feel me every bit as desperately as I ache for her, I take myself in hand and press inside her.

I groan at the sensation of her impossible snugness. At the sucking, greedy clamping of her pussy clenching at the head of my cock. Breathing raggedly, I withdraw. I glance up at Sarah's face. Her eyes are lowered, watching with panting breaths as I push into her again, further this time. And she moans, longingly, deeply, hungrily.

I feel her nails dig into my arms and her hips rise, needing more. Needing everything.

I press my cock into her tightness again, this time not stopping. Smoothly, gently, I push forward, sliding in.

I don't ask if she's all right; I watch her beautiful face, her closed eyes, smooth and unflinching as she absorbs every sensation.

And fuck, the sensations are overwhelming. She closes in around me, muscles wet and gripping, cradling me inside her.

With my elbows on the bed, I hover above her, nose to nose, breath to breath. And then I pull back my hips, and thrust hard and quick—so I'm fully, gloriously buried.

Sarah's mouth opens on a short cry, her neck arching. I slant my mouth across hers, swallowing her moans, licking her lips and sucking her tongue. And then Sarah opens her eyes and they shine with joy and heat and aching desire.

She licks her lips and runs her fingers through my hair.

"You're inside me," she whispers against my mouth, and it's almost too much. "You're inside me, Henry."

I nod helplessly. Then I twine our fingers together and raise our hands over her head. And then, pressing my mouth to Sarah's, kissing her like it's the end of the world, I move.

Steady and gentle, I roll my hips around and around, rubbing her clit with my lower pelvis near the base of my cock. She moves with me, her hips rising and circling.

And it's so fucking beautiful. So fucking right.

Anything that came before is nothing. This is all that matters. This brave, stunning girl in my arms is all I will ever need.

My mind goes weightless and my body takes over. Circles turn to thrusts, harder than before, her slick pussy and keening moans make me crazed. Sarah clenches at my arse, pushing me deeper.

"Henry," she gasps, her fingers sliding up and grasping onto my shoulder blades with a fraught urgency. "Henry."

I wrap my arms under and around her, pulling her closer, letting her know I've got her.

"That's it, love. That's it," I croon. "You're going to come, you're going to come right around my cock. That's my love."

My hips don't stop moving, rubbing against her, thrusting deep inside her.

And when that perfect, sobbing, blissful cry erupts from her lips moments later, when she presses her temple against my cheek and goes taut and stiff because the pleasure is wracking her body and it's too intense to move . . .

That's when I let myself go. I bury my face in Sarah's neck and pump hard and quick—and then I'm filling her, coming in powerful pulses that reduce my voice to grunts and groans, and my heart to a pounding wreck that belongs to this girl alone.

After, I lift my head and feel the caress of her hand against my ribs. I kiss her lips and her nose and wipe the tears that leak from the corners of her eyes.

And Sarah looks into my eyes and whispers, "I love you, Henry."

And it's the most perfect moment of my life.

"We didn't use anything."

Probably not the most romantic post-coital thing I've ever said. But condoms are the golden rule of royal intercourse, and this is the first time I've broken it.

Sarah nods against my chest, where she rests her head.

"I know."

"It's my fault. I should've thought of it."

"I could've thought of it too. I was a virgin, not an idiot."

"I've been tested; you don't have to worry."

"I'm not worried."

I turn on my side so I can see her eyes. "What are you thinking right now?"

"It's the wrong time of my cycle for a baby. But, I read once that there's a word for people who only use the rhythm method for birth control."

"What's the word?'

"Parents." Sarah grins.

I chuckle, then blow out a breath and look back at the ceiling. "I would be okay if you were pregnant. I mean . . . it wouldn't be ideal in the grand scheme of things, my grandmother would shit a brick and it would make the ridiculousness that can be my life even more chaotic. But I would take care of you. And I would be all right with it . . . happy, excited even. Is that insane?"

She takes her time thinking about it. "If it is, then we're both certifiable, because that about sums up my thoughts too."

Sarah snuggles in closer, drawing pictures on my chest with her fingertip, and I like how she feels right up against me. "I think this is how it is when you're in love. And nothing seems too big or too scary, because you know whatever happens, you won't be facing it alone."

A few moments later, I leave the bed and run a cloth under

the warm water at the bathroom sink. Then I come back and gently wipe the pink-tinged fluid from between Sarah's legs. A muted blush rises on her cheeks as I tend to her, but she doesn't object. After doing the same to myself, I slip back under the covers and wrap my arm around her.

I kiss the top of her head and comb my fingers through her hair as she drifts off, her breath coming in steady, tickling brushes against my neck. But I don't fall asleep. I stay up, watching her—because she's so beautiful, and good. My darling girl.

I've never had someone who was just mine, body and soul—mine to protect and hold and love. And that's what Sarah is . . . she belongs to me now. We belong to each other.

I dress early the next morning so I can speak to Vanessa, and tell her that I'm out. It takes me a bit of time to actually go, because Sarah's lips are terribly distracting. I can't seem to stop kissing them.

But, eventually, I force my feet to walk out the door.

And less than five minutes later I march back through it—unbuttoning my trousers and taking my clothes off as I go. It's important to be efficient.

"What's happening?" Sarah asks.

"Get naked, right now. It's food poisoning."

"What?"

"They all have it—something from the food service table last night. Everyone who ate there has it."

And everyone ate there—the producers, the crew, Penny, Laura, and Cordelia . . . everyone except Sarah and I.

I slip out of my shoes, and my trousers and pants hit the floor. My cock juts out, firm and ready and swaying a bit as I move, like it's saying hello.

"Why do you still have clothes on?" I move up to her. "Here, I'll help you." Then I'm undressing and kissing her. "We have hours, probably days." I lean over her and kiss her longer, deeper, thrusting into her pretty mouth the way I'm going to be thrusting into her very soon.

"We can do this for days, Sarah."

I unbutton my shirt quickly, but when I try to tug my arms out of the sleeves, my hands get stuck in the cuffs. So I yank harder, sending the buttons flying. Sarah laughs at me, at my eagerness. But I'm more than eager—I'm borderline desperate, with this insatiable craving to touch her, to fuck her, to hold her, to be near her. It's out of control in the best way, like she's the fabled good drug—a positive addiction—and I'll do anything for a fix.

Shirtless and smiling, I lift her up and set her on the dresser gently, feeling like I want to be anything but. She's probably tender from yesterday and God, I'm like an animal, wanting to rub and rut with her, even if we both starve to death.

"Tell me to slow down." I step between her legs and hold her face in my hands. I lean down and kiss her in quick, needy brushes—sipping at her lips. "Tell me to stop, Sarah."

Her brows come together and her head shakes, like the words make no sense. "No, please." She reaches around my waist and locks her legs about my hips, drawing me close and hot against her. "Don't ever stop, Henry."

CHAPTER 20

Henry

Sarah has a tiny russet freckle an inch below her navel. She has two on the inside of her elbow, and a small dotted constellation across her left shoulder blade. A thin, colorless scar traces her right shin bone, as long as my index finger, and another marks the outside of her left thigh, beneath her hip. I note every mark, each perfect imperfection, while we hide away in our room and I explore every inch of her skin. Hours later, there's not a place I haven't kissed or licked or nuzzled and caressed.

She lays on her back now, lashes low, watching me with dark, seductive eyes that make my cock throb. Again.

But . . . not yet . . . my mouth is having too much fun. I press my teeth against the tender flesh of her thigh and Sarah's legs open wider, all on their own. I press a kiss to her soft, full outer lips and a rosy flush springs up on her chest, spreading beneath her skin, all the way down to the tips of her toes.

I was right . . . she does blush everywhere.

I drag my finger up her hot slit and then through her damp brown curls to her clit, rubbing slippery, firm circles. "You're so wet." I marvel.

And she hides behind her hands, murmuring, "I know."

I tug at her wrists and her eyes flutter to me. "Don't ever,

ever be embarrassed about that. It's beautiful." I slide the tip of my tongue up and down through her wetness. "Doesn't it feel beautiful? I love it. It means I get to keep fucking you, sweetheart, for hours and hours . . . for as long as I want."

Her sweet pussy gets even more slick and I chuckle deep in my chest.

"You definitely like those words, don't you?"

I take her in the shower. Her hair is longer, darker when it's wet and the steam from the water dusts Sarah's flesh with a dewy, glowing sheen. I lift her in my arms, press her back against the cold tile and pump into her in steady, measured strokes. I swivel my hips, rubbing back and forth over her stiffening, needy little clit.

Sarah runs her fingers along my jaw, gazing into my eyes, while her breasts bounce with every thrust. She traces my lips with her thumb and I nibble and suck at her fingertip.

"I love you, Henry," she says, tenderly but clear. "I just . . . I just love you."

The words make my knees turn to warm jelly and while her tone doesn't demand a response—I give her one just the same. "And I love you."

Then heated pressure streaks down my spine, gathering low in my stomach. Sarah's orgasm takes her quietly—a simple open-mouth gasp, a clamping of her pussy, driving me into my own release. I push into her one last time, her cheek against the hallow of my throat and mine pressed above her head against the dripping shower tile.

Eventually, we have to eat, and I don't want to bother the staff with requests or see anyone. So, in the middle of the night Sarah slides into her robe and I put on only my sleeping pants, and we sneak down to the kitchen and forage for food. Then we bring our loot—water, a bottle of wine, a block of cheese, a loaf of fresh bread, and a bag of Cook's biscuits—back to the room and have a picnic on the bed.

The wine makes us drowsy. She feeds me with her fingers and I lick the crumbs that fall on her lap. And we speak in hushed tones about small things—birthdays and favorites colors—the small shards of information that, while almost insignificant individually, together make up a large piece of a person.

We don't sleep fully, but steal quick naps in between vigorous rounds of love-making. I rest my head on Sarah's chest, while she sings soft, bawdy old ballads and runs her fingers through the damp strands of my hair. I can't get enough of her voice and she's a bit obsessed with my hair. Other times, she rests on me, limp-limbed and come-drunk, and the only sounds in the room are our synchronized breaths and the matched thrum of our heartbeats.

The sun rises and falls outside the window, but neither of us notice. And I'm not the only one who has fun exploring flesh.

Just after I've felt the pulse of Sarah's orgasm around my fingers, and licked her sweet honey off them for the third time, I'm on my back—and Sarah's down between my spread knees, putting her mouth to fabulous use.

She nuzzles the delicate skin of my thick cock with her nose.

"It's so soft," Sarah purrs, her breath hot against me. "How can it be so soft and hard at the same time?" She licks up and down, getting thoroughly well-acquainted and enjoying herself in the process.

She nibbles at the skin of my thigh, making me jerk. Sarah blows at the hair on my lower stomach, making me laugh. She wraps her lips around the head of my dick, suckling with her mouth and rubbing with her tongue, until there is nothing left in my brain.

She's sucked every thought straight out.

Then, the sheets rustle as she moves lower and I feel the flat of her tongue, wet and hot, drag up and down the seam of my sac—and it's so fucking good my heart practically tears away from my body.

"Sarah," I groan. "Come here."

She shakes her head, shiny dark hair swaying. "I'm having fun where I am."

And then she opens that pretty mouth, and uses it to lave and suck on my balls.

"Jesus, fuck." I groan, writhing with pleasure.

My words encourage her, and while her mouth stays occupied, her hand tightly wraps around my shaft, like she knows I like it, and strokes me in long, firm pumps. When I curse again, Sarah moans and I feel the vibration down to my fucking soul.

And that's when I snap, when I decide I can't stand another second of not being inside her.

Sitting up, I grab Sarah under her arms and haul her against me. I place my hand in her hair, wrapping the strands tight around my fingers, gripping with my fist, and Sarah's palms splay against my face, fingers digging—each of us holding the other willingly captive. While our mouths devour each other, teeth clicking, tongues swirling and stabbing.

It's rough—the roughest I've let myself be with her and she releases moans of pleasure.

Then I grab her hips, drag her right over my dick, and

plunge up into her, hard and full. We both moan and it's fucking gorgeous. But I notice when her brows pinch and eyes squeeze in a small, quick grimace.

With one hand against the nape of Sarah's neck and the other at her spine, I still her, making her meet my eyes.

"Are you sore?"

She smiles with a shrug. So bloody beautiful. "Only a bit."

I swallow hard, and skim my palm up over her ribcage, to her breast. "We can stop, Sarah. There's other things we can do . . . I don't want to hurt you."

"It doesn't hurt, not really."

I lower my head, licking at the tight berry of her nipple—bringing it to my mouth for a suck.

"Not really?" I say with my lips around her, biting just so. "What does that mean?"

Sarah's chin lifts for a moment, neck arching—giving me more of her tits. But then she reverses course, pulling her breast away with a wet pop and bringing her own mouth down to the sensitive skin where my shoulder meets my neck.

And then she bites me. *Really* bites me. Not breaking skin but definitely leaving a bruise.

"Does that hurt?" she asks, so sweetly. Then she does it again.

I hiss, and my fingers grasp at her thighs. "Yes."

She kisses the sting, licking at her teeth marks.

"Do you want me to stop?"

This time she sucks as she bites down, and my cock twitches inside her.

"No," I pant.

Sarah lifts her head and kisses my lips. "That's what 'not really' means. That it hurts only a hint but feels so good, it doesn't matter. I want more."

And she's so hot and wet and tight around me, my eyes roll closed. She wraps her arms about my neck as I grip her hips and guide her forward and back, slowly, moving her up and down on my cock, before skimming my hands over her thighs and letting her take over.

"I don't . . ." she whimpers against my ear. "I don't know how."

"There's no how, love. Move however feels good. Any way you want."

She closes her eyes and bites her lip. Then she swivels her arse, testing the feel of it. And Christ, she's a quick learner. Her chin dips and her spine curls, "Oh . . . oh that's . . . you're so deep this way, Henry."

My lips drag across Sarah's collarbone. "Yes, so fucking deep."

I drag the tip of my finger down the column of her spine, then back up again, as she rides me. Her breaths come harsher, and her hips move faster and she's lovely, wild in her passion—chasing the peak for us both.

Sarah's pelvis loses its rhythm, shuddering and jerking, thighs trembling where her knees dig into the bed.

I suck at her earlobe, craving the sound of her voice.

"Are you going to come, sweets? Come hard for me? All over me?"

A high pitched gasp escapes her throat.

"Say it," I rasp harshly. "Say it now."

Sarah's arms tighten around my shoulder and her voice floats from her mouth.

"I'm coming . . . oh, oh . . . I'm coming."

I skim my finger down her back, resting it at the top of the cleft of her arse—and then I press down—and Sarah's muscles tighten everywhere at the new sensation. And then she's flying, coming, spasming with a tight cry all around me—wrenching a deep, soul-ringing orgasm from me, along with her.

I pulse inside her, over and over, like it's never going to stop.

But when it does, we're two sweaty, sticky, messy, kissing,

laughing . . . loving things—all wrapped around and inside one another. I brush Sarah's damp hair back from her face, look up into her eyes and in a weak voice say the only word that's appropriate.

"Hallelujah."

CHAPTER 21

Henry

Eventually, the time comes when we have to stop. And that's after two days. Most of the crew has recovered from the food poisoning and we're set to resume filming. Down at the docks. It's to be a sunset cruise, dinner and dancing—very romantic. I was an idiot to think I could go on as if nothing had changed when everything had.

And if I'd been in Sarah's position? Knowing that she was spending time—hours and hours—with other men? It wouldn't have taken me a few days to break—I would've ripped their fucking arms off within minutes.

After a hot shower, I dress and then gaze down at her sleeping form on the bed, her hands tucked under her cheek, a smile playing at her rosy lips. And this time, I just don't have the heart to wake her. I brush her forehead with my thumb and kiss her there. With a sigh, she snuggles down under the blankets, and that's how I leave her—warm and safe and happy.

It's gray skies that greet me outside, and storm clouds gathering over the water. Vanessa's already down at the docks when I arrive; I find her in the white staging tent, making notes on a clipboard. She looks up when I come in.

"Good, you're here. And early—that's a first."

She speaks quickly to one of the crew members, and then he leaves and we're alone.

Vanessa's skin is a pasty pale and she looks even thinner, sharper than when we first met. It's obvious she had food poisoning too. "How are you feeling?"

She shrugs. "I'll live. But we're on a super-tight schedule now—there's no wiggle room for screwing around, okay?"

"Yeah, about that . . ."

"And I was thinking for tonight's glass-slipper charm ceremony—you should send Penelope home."

"Why Penny?" I ask, just out of curiosity.

Her ice-blue eyes seem almost white in this lighting—devoid of any color. "Because that leaves Laura and Cordelia for the final episode. Beauty versus the Bitch. It'll be like Team Edward and Team Jacob all over again—people will eat it up."

"Penny's nice."

Vanessa shrugs noncommittedly. "She's more of a party girl. She's nice, but Laura's a fucking saint." She makes a note on the clipboard. "So you're good with that?"

I fold my arms and lean back against the table. "Vanessa, I'm not going to film any more episodes."

Her eyes snap up. "What the hell are you talking about?"

"Things have changed. This isn't a good fit for me anymore."

"This is about Penelope's sister, isn't it? The quiet one." She shakes her head. "Always the fucking quiet ones. Fine, whatever—I really don't care what you do at night or who you spend your time with, but you are going to hold up your end of the agreement. I have given months of my life for this show—you're not screwing that all up for me now, Henry."

I knew she'd be pissed, so I keep my voice calm and direct. "I've already made my decision."

But then Vanessa says something that stops me cold. "For Sarah's sake, you may want to reconsider."

Slowly, I move closer to her. "What does that mean, exactly?"

She crosses her arms, elbows pointing. "It means Sarah Von Titebottum signed a release—any footage we have of her is ours to use however we like. And I have a lot of it. I could tell a very interesting story about little Sarah. How she schemed and connived her way into the show as her sister's assistant, even though we didn't want her. How she seduced and stole you, not just from the other girls but from her own sister. You'd be amazed at the picture that a little editing and some background music can paint. The other girls will back me up—at least some of them—and by the time I'm done, anyone who watches will think Sarah is a nasty, selfish, vapid, backstabbing bitch."

My jaw clenches tight enough to snap. "But none of that is true."

Vanessa shrugs. "This is reality TV, Henry. What does truth have to do with it?"

My palms go damp and anger pricks under my skin like electric sparks.

Vanessa paces the room, then looks at the ceiling and speaks almost philosophically. "I don't think that would go over well with your people, if you actually decide to marry her. And if you don't, the tabloids will have a field day. Which will probably exacerbate her 'problem'—those spells she has." She shakes her head. "It would be very difficult for her."

Then she slides forward, her voice lightening. "Or, you can finish the last two episodes." She gestures toward the boat. "A few hours on the boat with Laura, dinner in front of the fireplace with Cordelia, and then the finale. No one will be surprised if, after the finale, you part ways amicably with whoever gets the diamond tiara—it happens more often than not in this business. You'll honor the agreements you signed, and we both get what we want. And then, you and Sarah will be free to ride off into the sunset. Happy endings all around."

My fists clench with frustration, the way a cornered animal coils before striking. But more than that, there's an overwhelming drive to keep Sarah safe. To protect her—always—at any cost, especially from the problems I've brought on myself. I don't want anyone to suffer because of my shitty choices—not Nicholas or Granny or Wessco—but especially not her.

Never her.

"So . . . what's it gonna be, Your Highness?"

Two hours later, I'm on the boat, out on the water with Laura. We sit at a perfectly set table, having brunch with the cameras rolling. I tried calling Sarah—I keep trying—but the mobile reception is rubbish. Before we set off, I told Vanessa to explain, to tell Sarah that I'll speak to her as soon as I'm back this evening. But I trust Vanessa as much as I'd trust a boa constrictor that promises to play nice with a kitten.

"What are you doing here, Henry?"

I sip my orange juice and Champagne, wishing for something stronger. Because this all feels so fucking wrong. "What do you mean? I'm having brunch with you."

Laura's head tilts and her lips curve with sympathy.

"But you're in love with Sarah."

I glance sharply at the camera. We're miked, and this isn't part of the script. It's not the way the show is supposed to play out and I don't know if it will end up blowing back on Sarah.

"I . . ."

"I've been in love, Henry. I know what it looks like."

"It's complicated."

Laura's face shines with kindness and understanding. "No, it's the simplest thing in the world. The sky is blue, the earth is round . . . Henry loves Sarah. Isn't that right?"

And it finally hits me what she's doing. From the beginning this was Vanessa's show—the story she wanted to tell. The rest of us were just pieces on the chessboard. But Laura is giving it back to me. Giving me the chance to tell the story—our story, Sarah's and mine—even if just this once. They might edit it out, but at least it will be said.

"Yes. I love her."

Laura's eyes well with tears. "Good."

I cover her hands with mine. "I'm sorry." And I don't even know what I'm apologizing for.

She wipes under her eyes, then waves me off. "Don't be silly, I'll be okay."

"Yes, you will be." And for the first time since this whole thing began, I forget all about the cameras—and it's just me and a friend, chatting. "One day, you're going to find a man who worships the ground you walk on, who makes you so happy. He's out there, right now somewhere, just waiting to meet you."

She shrugs. "I had that. Maybe we only get it once."

I squeeze her hands. "Horseshit." I think of Sarah and all she's been through, how strong she is, how she makes her own happiness. "Sometimes life is unfair, Laura. But you can't give up. You need to just keep moving forward and happiness will find you again. I believe that."

She smiles. And then a gust of wind blows hits us, knocking the flowers and glasses over on the table.

"We'll have to move this inside," the cameraman tells us.

The cameras get lowered and Laura and I stand up. Without warning, the boat tilts and Laura crashes into my chest. I hold onto her, bracing my back against the outer wall of the cabin to keep from falling over.

She looks up into my eyes. "Henry . . ."

Her expression is blank and her face pale. She swallows hard. "Henry, I . . ."

"Yes?"

That's when she opens her mouth . . . and throws up all over me.

Well . . . *fuck.*

Sarah

I'm not concerned when I wake up alone. I run my hand over the empty spot in the bed—Henry must have left early this morning to find Vanessa and decided to let me sleep in.

I've earned it over the last few days.

I roll onto my back, staring at the ceiling, replaying those days in my head again and again. The way his hands skimmed and grasped at my skin—possessive and desperate. The words he gasped and promises he whispered.

He loves me.

Henry Pembrook loves me.

And what I feel for him, I can't even put into words, it's so huge. Excitement bubbles under my skin and warmth heats in my belly. Nothing will ever be the same. I was happy with myself before—with my little life. But this is different. It feels like I'm on the edge of a mountain cliff, the wind whipping my hair, the sun blinding—but there is no fear. Only exhilaration, pure and right. I'm not going to fall. I can't.

Because Henry has shown me how to fly.

Eventually, I stretch my arms above my head—making my poor, overtaxed muscles groan. The soft, tender place between my legs throbs in a delicious, well-used sort of way. I go to take a long, hot shower. As I drag the soapy cloth over my breasts and up my thighs, it's Henry's hands and mouth that I see. That

I feel. And I smile when I discover tiny bruises and bite marks on my skin. Proof that it wasn't just a dream. Wasn't a fantasy inspired by reading someone else's imaginings in a book.

This is my story.

Penny is waiting for me on the sofa when I step out of the bathroom. She's a bit pale from the food poisoning, and gray rings shadow beneath her eyes.

"How are you feeling, Pen? Better?"

She takes one look at my face, and says, "I'm going to cut his cock off!"

I guess she's feeling better.

Then she doubles over onto the couch, groaning dramatically. "Tell me you did not let Henry Pembrook pop your cherry. Say it isn't so!"

"Well . . ." I start. But that's all she lets me get out.

"Bloody hell!" After a few more moans and groans, she sits up and takes my hand gently. "I'm sure, as far as first times go, Henry made it good. But he's not for you, Sarah. He's not the sticking kind. I mean, look at where we are—this show. He's been flitting from one girl to the next. What do you think he's been doing on all his 'dates' with the other girls? You actually believe he didn't get his freak on in the sodding hot springs? With *Cordelia*?"

"He didn't. We talked about it."

She throws her hands up. "Oh, well you talked about it— that settles that, then. Because Lord knows, boys never lie. Especially rich, spoiled, entitled, *royal* boys. They're the most truthful of all."

I smile and shake my head at her. Because she doesn't understand.

"He loves me, Penny."

She scoffs. "Of course he does. Did he tell you that when he was balls deep or right after he came?"

I shake my head again. "No, it was before, but—"

"Before? Do you know how many men have told me they loved me before—just to have a chance to stick it to me?" She ticks off her fingers as she lists the names. "Let's see, there was Barry Windstormer, Alfred Sullivan, Timothy Englewood—though he was hung like a bull, so totally worth it—Ryan Fitz—"

"It's different with Henry and me." I squeeze her hand. "He loves me. I know him, Penny, in a way no one else does. What we have is new . . . but it's deep and real. I'm sure of it."

My sister closes her mouth, but still looks unconvinced.

"Once upon a time, Mother was sure too."

I flinch.

"We're all sure, Sarah, until the bastards prove us wrong." She runs her hand up my arm. "I just don't want to see you get hurt. I don't want you to be another notch on the crown—and I don't want to see you become fodder for the tabloid rags; we both know that would be especially awful for you. And when the show airs, the publicity—"

"Henry's quitting the show. It's not going to air because he's not going to finish it. He's speaking to the producer right now."

Penny's eyes widen. "He told you that?"

"Yes. See—they're not all bastards, and actions mean more than words."

The rumble of cars floats in from outside, from the driveway leading up to the castle. I spot the familiar string of SUVs.

"He's back."

I throw on a black sweater and slacks, and pin my hair up into a damp bun. Then I rush downstairs to show Penny how wrong she is.

Down in the foyer, Vanessa Steele flips through a stack of papers, giving directions about lighting and setup to the crew scurrying around. I look behind her toward the door, but Henry doesn't walk through it. And I don't see him anywhere.

"Where's Henry?" I ask.

She spares me a quick glance. "He's on his date with Laura."

I've never been punched in the stomach, but the words make me want to fold over like I have been. I feel Penelope standing behind me listening, her emotions building like a volcano ready to erupt.

"Did he speak with you?" I ask Vanessa.

"Briefly, yes, before he went out on the boat."

I feel my face starting to flame, but I try to be strong. "Did he say anything to you about me? About the show?"

She flicks her wrist, checking her diamond watch. "I don't have time to chat, Miss Titebottum—I have a show to plan." She glances over my shoulder. "Make sure you're dressed and ready for tonight's shoot, Penelope. And you should wear that dark blue dress—it's a good color for you."

Vanessa moves to step past me, but my hand lashes out, grabbing her arm.

Because I will not be dismissed.

And then I look at her face, searching her eyes.

"You're lying."

She gazes back at me for a few seconds and then she sighs. "I got the vibe from Henry that he felt things would be easier this way, for everyone involved. He said he would speak to you when he gets back later. And that's the truth."

She pulls out of my grasp and walks away.

Back in my room, Penelope vibrates beside me, like a small blond tornado that wants to obliterate everything in its path. "Fuck. Him. He doesn't deserve you. I could literally kill him for this."

I try Henry's mobile again, but the call goes straight to voicemail.

"It must be some kind of misunderstanding. I'm not going to panic, Penny."

"How could it be a misunderstanding? He said he was going to quit and he obviously didn't. Don't be simple, Sarah. He spent the weekend screwing you into a trance and now he's where? With Laura Benningson. On a boat. Probably telling her the same things he's told you. The poor, misunderstood Prince. He knows women, Sarah. He knows it's the broken ones we try hardest to fix."

I feel sick. My stomach twists and drops. And for the very first time, I feel . . . used.

Penelope looks around the room, her face tight and sharp, the wheels spinning furiously in her mind. "We should just go. Pack up our things and leave. Right now."

My voice is hollow, like an echo of myself.

"You signed a contract, Penelope."

"Fuck the contract; I don't need them. Jerry the cameraman has a brother-in-law who's an agent in LA. He sent him my head shots and video and he wants to fly me out there next month." She grips my hand. "And even if he didn't, you're more important to me than this."

My back stiffens. "I'm not going to run away. If Henry's feelings have changed, he can have the decency to tell me to my face."

"There's nothing decent about him! And it's not running away; it's telling him to piss the hell off! That he can't mess with you, like you're some lovesick fool. He may have taken your cherry, but who cares—at least you'll have your pride. Come on, Sarah. Be strong."

Is that what being strong means? I don't think so. To me it means having faith in Henry, until he gives me a real reason not to. I'm not ready to give up on him yet and I tell my sister as much.

Penny sighs, her shoulders falling, reining in her inner

drama queen. "You came here because of me—all of this is because of me. And if you end up hurt because of it, I'll never forgive myself."

I hug her.

"There would be nothing to forgive. I'm a big girl, Penny. I'm responsible for my own choices. No one else."

And so is Henry.

I put "Hallelujah" by John Cale on repeat on my mobile and I sit in the nook, not reading, but gazing out the window. Waiting. A storm's come in, the rain and wind pelting the castle and the ocean waves roaring against the rocks. Penny eventually falls asleep on the sofa. They canceled the evening filming. A crew member told my sister that they decided to take the boat farther off-shore, to wait out the storm instead of trying to make a run for the shore. Worry stabs at me as I watch the waves crashing, violent and angry. I hope he's okay . . . please God, let them be all right.

And then I realize that I've prayed for "them" and suddenly a whole different kind of worry pierces me. Because Henry's not on that boat alone. He's with Laura—gorgeous and fun and truly a nice person, Laura. Despite what I've said to Penny, I'm not a fool.

He wasn't supposed to be on that boat. He promised me. Why did he go?

As the lovely song repeats, I think about all the things that have happened the last few days. So many changes.

And I feel like I'm falling after all—like my wings have been clipped.

I'm afraid and unsure about everything. It's not just about Henry. I miss my flat. I miss the library and the simple joy of my books. I miss the consistency and assurance of knowing how each day will begin and end. I crave it, deep inside, the way a tiny turtle craves the warm protection of its shell.

The night passes faster than I imagined. And when the sun has risen full above the horizon, and John Cale's voice goes quiet, I wipe my tears and wash my face.

Big-girl knickers time.

CHAPTER 22

Henry

What a fucking night! An awful disaster of a night. On a boat. In a storm. With a food-poisoned, seasick puking woman, begging me to hold her hair and make it stop the whole damn time.

Move over, Stephen King—I'm the master of horror now.

As we drive up through the gate, all I can think about is a hot shower and that bloody perfect big bed, with Sarah, warm and naked, tucked up tight against me.

I help Laura from the car and into the castle; she's weak-kneed and weary. But inside the castle door, it's chaos. Crew members bustling and shouting, and . . . Willard.

Why in the hell is Willard here?

Out of the corner of my eye, I see Vanessa Steele, motioning to a cameraman to pick up start filming. Before I can say a word, little Penelope Von Titebottum advances, and then she takes a damn swing at me.

"Arsehole!"

I step back out of reach, but just barely.

Sarah comes down the stairs then, looking small and frail. And across her shoulder is her old satchel . . . filled with her books.

"Sarah . . . what's happening?"

Her skin is so pale, her eyes huge and dark as she looks me up and down. "You're back. Are you all right? Was anyone hurt? I was worried about the storm."

"No, we're fine. We're all fine."

Something shifts in her features then. "You said you weren't going to go. You said you would quit, Henry. And instead, you were gone all night—I think I deserve an explanation."

I rub my forehead. "I was going to quit, but . . . this way is easier. It's only a few more days, Sarah. It's better this way—trust me."

"Better for whom, Henry?" Tears well in her eyes and I want to die. And her tone drips with betrayal. "I waited for you. I believed you, like a fool. And you were off with Laura all night, doing—"

"Doing nothing!" I shout, because—*fuck me*. "Nothing happened between me and Laura."

Of course, there's a lull in the ruckus, just enough for Laura's voice to carry as she tells Cordelia, "Henry was wonderful. He held me all night."

Sarah blanches, then accusation resumes its place in her expression.

"While she vomited her intestines up!" I yell. "All over me! Here—smell me—I reek of puke, not pussy."

There's a loud gasp and a squeak, and both Sarah and I turn in time to see Laura's head loll, her eyes close, and her knees give out as she faints dead away. Luckily, it's Willard to the rescue—he moves quickly and catches her before she hits the ground. Slowly, he lowers down to his knees and after a moment, Laura opens her eyes, blinking up at him.

"You caught me."

"I did," Willard replies gently.

"I'm Laura."

"I'm Willard. Feel free to fall into my arms anytime."

Laure covers her mouth with her hand. "I smell terribly."

He gazes down at her—already totally enamored.

"I don't mind."

Penelope breaks the tender scene when she comes up beside Sarah, hands on her hips. "Well? Did he quit?"

Sarah's voice has the ring of a death knell. "No."

Sparks practically shoot out of Penny's eyes—right at my fucking forehead.

"And he's not going to? He's going to continue to take up with the other girls?"

"I'm not fucking taking up with them," I object. "It's not like that."

Only Sarah seems to think it is. "Yes."

"I knew it." Penny shakes her head. "I'm glad I called Willard beforehand. We'll send the staff for our things. Let's go, Sarah."

I grab Sarah's arm. "It's not like it sounds, I swear. I can explain."

She makes a visible effort to control her breathing. "No, I think . . . I think Penny's right. Some perspective will be good for me. It's all so much at once. I won't stay here if you're going to . . ." She looks away, choking on the words. "I need some space away from all this."

She means space away from me. And *space* is just another word for banishment.

And for a moment I lose my mind.

"Fucking hell!" I kick the table at the bottom of the staircase—sending a crystal vase tumbling over and crashing to the floor, emitting the sound of a gun blast as it shatters into a thousand pieces.

And Sarah's lovely face pales to stark white. Her eyes glaze over and her body goes still as death.

And it feels like my ribs crumble into dust.

Because she's gone, lost in a hell of her father's making . . .

And I'm the one who sent her there.

Anguished words are torn from my lungs. "Sarah . . . no . . ."

Before I can pull her into my arms, Penny's there, wrenching her away and screaming.

"Get away from her! You stay away!"

Penelope's eyes are wild, and her mouth is drawn back in a feral snarl, ready to tear to pieces anyone who gets near the sister she loves so much.

We're frozen in our places for only a few moments, but it feels much longer. And then that horrific rasping sound comes from Sarah's throat as she comes to, gasping and panicked, grasping at Penny. Then she lifts her head and looks at me.

I move forward again, but Sarah falls back, away, dragging Penelope with her. She holds up her hand to me. "Stop."

And it's all so fucking awful. How is it possible for things to go from perfect—the most perfect moments of my life—to ruins?

I keep my voice calm and steady. "Sarah, please, just . . . please."

I'm not even sure what I'm begging for.

"Stay . . . stay away from me."

And with one last agonized look, she turns around and, with Penny, walks out the door.

I move forward, but my steps turn to stumbles, and before I know it I'm on my knees. Maybe it's the exhaustion or maybe it's the knowledge that the one relationship in my life that I thought I'd finally gotten right, the only woman I've ever loved, who I would cut my fucking heart out for . . . doesn't want to be anywhere near me.

Laura's on her feet now, standing off to the side, and I watch as Willard turns to follow Sarah out the door.

"Willard!" I call. "Wait."

Soft brown eyes swimming with pity look down on me. "I'm sorry, mate. She's my best friend. Maybe . . . just let her catch her breath, you know?"

And then he leaves too.

I don't know how long I stay there on my knees, with my head in my hands. I feel people moving around, hear their whispers, but then there's a rush of cold air from the door, and one clear, furious voice that I know all too well slices through my haze.

"What in the name of all that is holy is going on here?"

Granny's home.

Fuck.

I lift my head and watch her walk toward me, like a god of thunder and lightning and destruction. Halfway across the foyer, Vanessa Steele intercepts her.

"Queen Lenora, I was hoping we would cross paths. It's an honor to meet you."

And she holds out her hand.

Big, big, *big* mistake.

The Queen lifts her chin and looks down at Vanessa's outstretched hand with eyes so sharp it's a wonder it's not sliced clean off her arm.

"Do you know who I am, girl?"

"Ah . . . yes . . . you're the Queen of Wessco."

Her words are crisply enunciated and dripping with venom.

"You do not offer us your hand. You *bow.*"

And like many a stronger person before her, the producer buckles . . . and bows. My grandmother steps passed her dismissively. Coming straight for me.

But the strange thing is . . . I don't feel any guilt or shame or intimidation. It's like there's a small pellet of steel in my stomach, snowballing and spinning, growing thicker and larger. And even though I've screwed up massively, I have no compulsion to explain myself—not now. Not even to the Queen.

All I feel is the resolve to go somewhere alone and figure out how to fix this mess.

And that means Granny's just going to have to wait.

"Henry, what in the—"

I get to my feet and lift my hand.

"I'll speak with you shortly, Your Majesty."

Her eyes widen and her chest puffs up as she inhales, like a dragon about to breathe fire.

"Shortly?! You will explain—"

I look into her eyes and say in a tone that brooks no argument—one that I've never used with her in my life, "Not. *Now.*"

It's possible I've stunned her into muteness, or caused a stroke. Either way her mouth snaps shut. And I turn on my heel, walk to the library, and close the door behind me.

For the next hour, maybe two, I sit in the chair facing the fireplace, watching the flames dance and lick at the stone that holds it.

And I contemplate. Consider. For the first time in my life.

It's helpful.

I see it all so clearly, like reading a map—every mistake and wrong turn. But I don't get bogged down by the errors. I refuse to sink into self-pity and loathing, doubt and regret. Not this time—not ever again.

That was the old Henry. And I'm really not him anymore.

Rock bottom changes you. Glimpsing heaven changes you more.

I've touched perfection, I've felt its arms around me and though she's slipped away, she's out there, just beyond my reach. Waiting for me to get off my arse and get my shit together. To prove myself. To become the man . . . and the king . . . she deserves.

And staring at that fire, I swear to myself and my parents, to God and—fuck it—the devil too, that I will not let her down.

"Henry."

I didn't hear my grandmother come in. She stands beside my chair, gazing at me, not with anger or disappointment in her stormy gray eyes—but something else. Concern, maybe. Curiosity?

"We must discuss what went on here. What have you done, my boy?"

I give her the truth. Without deflection or excuse.

"I've made a mess of things, Granny. But . . . I'm not going to do that anymore."

She regards me for several moments and then softly says, "All right."

"I'm marrying Lady Sarah Mirabelle Zinnia Von Titebottum."

The words come out quiet and true. The earth is round. The sky is blue. I'm marrying Sarah.

She doesn't know it yet, but . . . one step at a time.

"From what I know of her, she's a bit shy, but we can work on that. She's a lovely girl."

"Yes, she is." I look back toward the fire. "She was a virgin when she met me. She's not anymore."

My grandmother folds her hands at her waist. "I see. There are ways to get around that part of the law. A physician's sworn statement should do it."

My voice is soft but steady. "I don't want to get around it. I want to change the law. We won't marry until it's done."

"But why does it matter?"

"It matters to Sarah . . . so it matters to me. And when I put Mum's ring on her finger, I want the world to know it's because I've chosen her. Not because she fits the bill or checks the boxes, but because she's magnificent. And I'm lucky enough that she's willing to put up with me."

My grandmother snorts. "Changing the law will take time. And it requires a vote in Parliament. That means . . . politicking."

"I know. I was hoping you could show me how to be good at that. Will you help me, Granny?"

She blinks down at me. Like she's never seen me before, as if she's relieved and grateful for what her eyes behold. "Yes. Yes, I can do that, Henry."

I put my hand over hers and give it a little squeeze. It's not a hug, but it's a start.

"Thank you."

Not long after that, after I've explained the entire situation to the Queen, it's time to clean house. I find Vanessa in the library, for the first time looking frazzled, shuffling papers.

My voice is soft but with a hint of lethal.

"What did you say to her?"

She lifts her pointy chin. "Nothing that wasn't true."

I straighten my shoulders and look down at her, demanding, "What did you *say*?"

"Come on, Henry. You know how this goes. Drama sells. And your tryst with the sister? That's some high-flying drama right there."

"Do you think this is a game? Just a show? This is my life."

She folds her arms and tightens her stance. "You're a prince. Your whole life is a show."

"Not anymore." I shake my head. "I'm done. We're done. This is all finished. You take your footage and do whatever you like. You want to eviscerate me on television? Have at me." Then I lean over her. "But I'm warning you now, and it'll be the only warning you get—if you go after Sarah, if you disparage her in any way, I will ruin you. I will use every resource at my disposal—and I have a fucking country behind me—to destroy you and everything you touch. Are we clear, Ms. Steele?"

Her eyes dart across my face, gauging my resolve and my sincerity. Vanessa may not be particularly pleasant, but she's not stupid.

"I want an exclusive."

"What?"

"If things pan out between you and the bookworm, it'll be the story of the century, and I want it. I'll sit on the footage and when you announce your engagement, I'll put together a documentary." Her eyes rise, seeing the headlines. "It'll be like a goddamn fairy tale. How the prince was tamed by the quiet girl. How, after going through a dozen mattresses, he found his perfect pea. I want an interview to go with that story—with you and Sarah."

I turn the offer over in my head, weighing the options.

"I'll give you an interview, but I won't speak for Sarah. If she wants to participate, fine—if not, you settle for me."

"Agreed."

"And I want final approval." I point my finger at her. "You don't air a second of footage until I see it in its entirety and approve."

She thinks it over and then she holds out her hand.

"Deal."

We shake on it.

And it looks like I'm not so shit at politicking after all.

An hour later, she brings me the new contracts. I sign on the dotted line and hand them back. "Now, get your equipment and get the fuck out of my castle."

Later, after Fergus closes the castle door firmly behind him, my grandmother stands beside me in the foyer, brushing her palms like she's scuffing off dust.

"Well . . . I'm glad that's over. Will you join me in the library for a glass of sherry?"

"Yes. There's more we need to discuss." I look her in the eye. "You're not going to like it."

She just nods, stalwart and unshakable as she's always been. "I'll tell Fergus to bring the extra-large glasses."

CHAPTER 23

Sarah

Three weeks.

It doesn't seem so long. Only two more than one. *Three weeks.* It doesn't sound so long to say it out loud. Only two syllables. But in some ways, the last three weeks have felt endless. Filled with self-doubt and questioning of what I should have done differently—what I should do now and next. The exhausting inner debate. Do I call him? Do I wait for him to contact me? Is he still filming? Should I go back to Anthorp Castle? Is he still there or is he behind the palace gates? There hasn't been a word about him on the news or in the headlines. Why hasn't he called? Does he ever think of me? When I told him I needed time and space, I didn't think it was over. I didn't believe that was really the end. Should I have stayed longer? Did I judge too quickly, did I leave too soon?

But it hasn't all been regret and self-pity.

I stopped crying after four days.

I stopped checking my mobile for a text or missed call after ten.

After sixteen, I stopped looking up and down the street when I stepped out of the library, searching for a black SUV and wild green eyes.

After eighteen, I accepted that Henry wasn't coming for me.

I still dream of him, though. Every night, in bed, I hear his voice and imagine his long fingers plucking at the strings of that old guitar. I see his smile in my mind and can swear I smell him on the bedsheets. And then the dreams come, but there's not much I can do about that.

Because sometimes, life is very much like a book—we don't get to write our own ending; we have to accept the one that's already on the page.

Slipping back into my life was easy, because it was ready-made, like a child's bin of LEGOs—the pieces designed to seamlessly interlock. Organized and scheduled.

But at the end of the first week, day seven, something strange happened. Something that turned out to be not so bad.

I began to look for ways to deviate from my routine. To move away from the consistency I'd once craved. I went into work early and left after sunset—not just to keep busy, although that played a part, but more because I was yearning for something . . . different. Something new. I satisfied the itch with small things at first: rearranging the furniture, hanging new drapes, walking a different route home each day, offering to sit with baby Barnaby from upstairs so my neighbors could grab a bite, popping over to Mother's for dinner randomly instead of the staid Wednesdays and Sundays.

One night, Annie took me to a pub two towns over, to meet her new boyfriend, Wade, who thankfully isn't at all a douche-canoe. The place was a bit rowdy, crowded, and loud. But I didn't mind so much.

Another time, it was dinner and dancing with Willard. The funny part was, I kept glancing at the band while they played, because there was a pushing, pulling sensation inside me—and I had the maddest urge to pop up on the stage and grab the microphone for a song or two. I didn't actually do it, but I thought about it.

And I wasn't afraid.

Because once a shell is broken, it can't be put back together again—not really, not in the same way it was. The cracks will always be there.

That's the Henry Effect.

And it's miraculous. Freeing. And despite how it all shook out in the end, I will always love him for that. I will always be grateful. And I will always remember the sweet, teasing prince who changed me for the better.

The symposium. My Waterloo.

The second week I was back at work, Mr. Haverstrom asked me if I would be presenting after all, now that my Palace business had concluded early. He told me he understood if I declined, because I hadn't had the time to prepare a presentation.

He gave me an easy out. And I could've taken it.

But I didn't.

So here I am. In the largest conference room in Concordia Library, facing a packed room, over two hundred filled chairs and more attendees standing along the back wall. All eyes on me.

Willard and Annie are in the front, as close as they can be for moral support . . . and to catch me if I pass out. I know my cheeks are bright, flaming red. My knees are trembling and my stomach spins like a top. As I step up to the microphone, the panic surges right up to my throat, threatening to swamp me.

So, I close my eyes and breathe deeply, and then . . . I picture Henry Pembrook naked.

And I laugh. Because he was right, the wanker. It does work.

An hour later, I'm wrapping up my presentation on the importance of promoting child literacy, especially among young girls. I've kept my head down, eyes on my notes, so while it probably hasn't been the most engaging of talks, I didn't pass out or Davey on any of them, so I consider it a grand victory.

I just have to get through these last few lines and the Q&A.

"In conclusion, I'd like to end with these final thoughts: Reading brings knowledge and knowledge is power; therefore reading is power. The power to know and learn and understand . . . but also the power to dream. Stories inspire us to reach high, love deep, change the world and be more than we ever thought we could. Every book allows us to dream a new dream. Thank you."

They clap.

And I close my eyes and sigh, deflating with relief. *I did it, I really did it.* Willard blows an obnoxious whistle while Annie fist-pumps, and it's wonderful. I only wish . . .

A yearning ache begins in the center of my chest, then spider-webs outward like a crack in a windshield.

Because I wish Henry were here. He would love this—it would blow his mind. And then he'd make a teasing comment that there are others things I could blow. Or maybe I'd say it—he always did bring out the dirty in me.

I shake my head, trying to dust off the melancholy. And I look out over the sea of clapping hands and nodding heads . . . and then my heart stops mid-beat.

My first thought is: he's cut his hair.

It was almost down to his shoulders the last time I saw him. Thick and soft, wavy and wild. But this is nice too. Short and clean, professional and powerful-looking, with just the right length in front, with a few strands falling over his forehead in a roguish sort of way.

His suit is beige, his tie light green, his shirt crisp white—so sharp and handsome—like a broker on Silver Street.

He's clapping heartily—with those strong hands that I adore. His gaze is alight with admiration and his smile . . . his smile is so tender my eyes prickle with wetness.

I blink and look away . . . and then I remember to be pissed off at him. *Three. Weeks.* Three fucking, awful weeks. I lied when I said they weren't so bad—they were bloody hell. And he shows up now? Here? For what, exactly?

I don't have to wonder long.

Because the moment Mr. Haverstrom calls for questions, Henry's hand shoots up high and straight, like he's a child in class who can't wait a second more to use the lavatory.

I ignore him.

The only problem is, he's the only one raising his hand.

"Questions? Anyone?" I look left and right, tilting my head to check all around. "Anyone at all?"

Henry clears his throat. Loudly. "Ahem."

And several heads swivel toward him.

But I'm still ignoring him, shuffling my papers. "Well, since no one has any questions—"

"He has a question," Willard says, clear and grinning like a traitorous Cheshire cat.

I'm going to smack him when this is over.

But, first I'm going to deal with Henry.

"Yes, you there in the back," I say like I've never seen him before in my life. Like he isn't our future king. "What is your question, sir?"

His eyebrow hitches, as if he's saying, *"So that's how you're going to play this?"*

Murmurs of recognition ripple through the room, but Henry doesn't seem to notice.

"My question is about Heathcliff."

And his voice . . . I've missed his voice—strong and rough, but teasing and sweet. Oh balls, I'm melting like a cheap candle.

But I don't let it show. I cross my arms.

"The fat orange cat, you mean?"

The corner of his mouth kicks into a smirk. "No. From *Wuthering Heights.*"

"Ah, I see. Go on."

"My question is, why didn't someone shoot the bastard? Were guns not around in that time period?"

My head shakes on its own. What a ridiculous question! "No, firearms were used, but . . ."

"Then someone should have definitely shot Heathcliff in the arse. He was a thoughtless, abusive, mean son of a bitch."

"Some feel his one good quality is his love for Catherine. That's what redeems him."

Henry shakes his head, his expression sober. "He didn't deserve her."

"Well," I lift a shoulder, "Catherine wasn't exactly a saint either. And I'm sure the debate over Heathcliff's worthiness will continue for as long as people read the book. Thank you."

I turn to the rest of the room. "Other questions?"

Aaaaand up goes his hand. Quick and strong and, again, the only one raised.

I don't try fighting it this time, but sigh dramatically. "Yes?"

"It's about Mr. Darcy. He's kind of a snob—he's got a stick up his arse. A big one."

My own eyebrows rise above my glasses. "You've got a thing for arses today, don't you?"

He chuckles, totally unashamed. ""Well . . . tight bottoms are a few of my favorite things."

And he can still make me blush like no one else.

"But that's a discussion for another time. My point is, Mr. Darcy is a prat—I don't get it."

"Well, if you had read the book—"

"I did read the book." His green eyes watch me intensely. "I read all of them."

And butterflies go berserk in my stomach.

"Oh."

I shake out of my stupor, and refocus. "Well, Mr. Darcy and Elizabeth Bennet are two sides of the same coin. He is painfully reserved and she is uninhibited but they both make their assumptions and end up getting it wrong. In the end, they must put aside their prejudices and their pride and be honest with themselves and each other to make it right."

He gazes at me, soft and gentle, like he never wants to stop.

"Hence the title, I guess."

"Yes." I nod.

He rubs his knuckles against his jaw. "Now about Colonel Brandon from *Sense and Sensibility*."

And I smack my hands down on the podium. "No. You can say what you want about Darcy or bloody Heathcliff and hell, you can tear into every Dickens hero written—I never liked any of them. But you will not besmirch Colonel Brandon! I won't allow it."

Henry finds my outburst amusing. "I'm not going to besmirch him. I like Colonel Brandon."

"Then what is your question?"

Slowly, stealthily, he drifts forward up the aisle.

"The way I see it, Marianne messed up. Brandon was there all along, but she let herself be distracted by the wrong things. It wasn't written on the page, but I'm guessing she had to apologize and he had to forgive her."

My throat is dry and my voice is like sand. "Yes, I suppose that's true."

Closer and closer he comes.

"My question is, if their roles had been different—if Marianne had been the man and Brandon the woman—do you think she would have forgiven him? Taken another chance on him, trusted that this time, he wouldn't mess it up?"

My head swims the nearer he gets.

"I . . . I'm not—"

"I mean, if he completely threw himself into the groveling. Pulled off a stupendous grand gesture, something really public and humiliating."

He's right in front of me now. Close enough for me to touch him.

"I don't think she'd like that, the public part," I say softly. "She's still a bit . . . shy."

Henry nods, and his voice is low and raw and desperate.

"Then what if he just stood in front of her and said, 'I'm sorry. And I miss you. I want to be a better man for you and because I love you so much, I actually believe I can be.' Do you think she'd give him a chance then?"

My eyes go blurry and I blink because I want to see him clearly. "I think . . . I think that could work."

Henry smiles, and it feels like my heart is flying out of my chest.

"Good."

I nod, crying and grinning at the same time.

Then I hear Willard on the sidelines: "Are we supposed to keep pretending they're actually talking about the book?"

"Wait," Annie responds, "they're not talking about the book?"

Willard pats Annie's head. "You're so pretty."

We're stuck in the library for almost an hour after my presentation. As soon as one person recognizes Henry, the news spreads like wildfire and everyone wants to meet him. Most of the people here are visitors to Castlebrook; I don't think the regulars would be so swept up in the celebrity of a visiting prince.

Security does their best to control the crowd and Henry is gracious, but I can tell he's impatient. He keeps looking over at me, almost to assure himself I haven't run off.

Though it's only a short distance to my flat, James drives us there. When they first close the door behind us, and it's just

Henry and me in the backseat, he tells me fervently, "I'm so proud of you. You were absolutely brilliant up there."

And my smile spreads far and wide across my face. "Thank you. I'm happy you were here to see it."

We're quiet then. James takes the long way around, with extra turns and diversions to lose anyone from the library who tries to follow us. And Henry holds onto my hand the entire time.

Inside my flat, I slip off my shoes and hang my coat in the closet, and Henry stands in the middle of my parlor, looking too big for it, larger than life.

And there's something different about him. He's still the Henry I know. The wild lad with a dirty mouth is still there below the surface. But the way he carries himself has changed, like there's a veneer of . . . nobility that wasn't there before.

He turns in a circle, noting my framed covers on the wall, running his finger along my prized bookshelf.

There's so much to say, but I can't for the life of me figure out how to start.

So I ask, "Would you like tea?"

"Yes, tea would be lovely."

I nod, and on jittery legs move into the tiny kitchen. And just like our first real conversation by that big tree on the hill, instead of going mute, I babble.

"I have peppermint and chamomile. But that's probably too bland for you, isn't it?" I take the pot and canisters out of the cabinets and set them on the counter. "I have this fruity, exotic blend that Annie convinced me to try—it's not my taste at all, but you may—"

Henry puts his hand over mine, standing so close behind me, I can feel the heat from his strong chest and smell the scent of his shirt.

"Sarah," he says against my ear, raising goose bumps along my neck. "I like peppermint tea."

And it's absolutely insane, but that small, insignificant

confession breaks something open in my chest—which I didn't even realize I was keeping tightly shut.

I turn my head, looking at him over my shoulder, and he's right there, near and real and here.

"You do?"

Henry nods.

"It's not too plain for you?"

He shakes his head, swiping a tear from my cheek that I wasn't aware had fallen.

"It's my very favorite."

His arms come around me then. And I sink back against him. I feel his lips on my hair, as he inhales deeply—breathing me in.

"I've missed you so much," he whispers. "Every day."

"Where have you been? What took you so long?"

Henry straightens with a sigh, like he has to force himself to back away.

"Tea first. Then we'll talk."

I'm not sure I like the sound of that. But I put the pot on and a few minutes later, we're seated on the sofa, drinking peppermint tea.

Henry sets his cup carefully on the table and rubs his palms on his slacks, like he's nervous.

"I fucked up, Sarah. I thought I was doing the right thing for us at the time, finishing out the show, putting it behind us. But I was wrong. Just like . . . Mr. Rochester."

Warmth spreads through my chest. And I laugh out loud.

"You really did read the books."

Henry nods. "Every one." He reaches out, squeezing my hand. "It made me feel closer to you. Knowing you had read the same letters, that you knew the words by heart."

"But Henry, if that's true, why did you wait so long to come here? Why didn't you call or text or even write me a letter?"

"I had to be sure I was doing the right thing, I didn't want to risk hurting you again. And there were . . . arrangements that had to be made. Things I had to get in order."

"What things?"

He waves his strong hand. "That's not important now. What matters is that I'm here, for you. Nothing's changed for me and yet, everything is different. How I see the world, the part I want to have in it, it's all different because of you. And I'm ready now—I can be the man you deserve. Steady and consistent, unselfish and adoring. Your very own Colonel Brandon."

It seems so foolish now. A silly girl's thoughts. Henry doesn't compare to Colonel Brandon—he's so much more. He's real and true and wild and romantic, all the things I once thought only existed in books.

"I've spoken to Grandmother about us; she can't wait to meet you. And . . . I want us to be like Jane and Guildford . . . only without the whole head-chopping part."

I laugh and start to cry.

"I want to change the world with you at my side, holding your hand. I love you, Sarah, and whatever happens, I promise there won't be a day that I don't love you with all that I am."

He takes my hands and leans in close.

"Will you have me, love?"

I shudder in a breath and my face is wet with tears. I shake my head at him, silly boy.

"Have you? Are you mad? You are every dream I never let myself believe could come true."

And then I'm in his arms, kissing his face and holding him close. He lifts me up and carries me to the bedroom. He lays me down and strips me bare and I run my hands up and down his beautiful chest. And we make love, over and over again.

Outside the window, tiny snowflakes begin to fall, but we don't notice. Because we're lost in each other and no matter where we are, from this moment on—whether it's in a drafty castle, a grand palace, or a little flat in an old, quiet town—it will be Henry and I, together for always.

CHAPTER 24

Henry

For the next seven days, my life is perfect, because I slip seamlessly into Sarah's. She still goes to work at the library—I meet her boss, Mr. Haverstrom, and her git of a coworker, Pat. I chat football with George the bachelor retiree and flirt with Maud, the nearsighted widow volunteer. But mostly, while at the library, I just watch Sarah—basking in the joy of seeing her in her element, soaking up every smile and laugh and committing them to memory.

I also fuck her in the aisles, late at night after closing—and the reality of it, the naughtiness of lifting the sexy librarian's skirt and pressing her up against the shelves, the way her moans and my grunts echo off the walls, like an erotic symphony . . . it beats the hell out of my fantasy.

And we don't stop there.

I make love to Sarah in her shower and she rides me hard on the floor of her parlor. I take her in her tight, tiny kitchen, from behind, with her beautifully bent over the counter, and she sucks the life out of me, on her knees in her hallway, while I hold her head and thrust wildly into her eager mouth.

Sarah cooks us dinner while I kiss and nibble and maul her . . . and she makes me hard with her blushes and dirty jokes while I wash up the dishes afterward. I play my guitar for her and she hums her little songs and some nights, she reads out loud while I drift off to sleep, with my head against her soft breast.

I meet Sarah's interesting mother and wiggle my way back into Penny's good graces. She likes me again, which is nice since she's leaving for the States soon—Los Angeles, to pursue her acting career.

One Saturday afternoon, we test the strength of Sarah's bed frame, fucking rough and loud and sweaty, but afterward, it's all tender touches and sweet whispers. On the radio, "Little Wonders" by Rob Thomas comes on and Sarah sighs.

"I love this song."

I brush my hand up her stomach. "I love your tits."

Sarah swats me on the head, laughing. But when I cover her nipple with my mouth, sucking and flicking with my tongue, her giggle turns into a long, serrated moan.

"And I'm glad you love the song, sweets."

And it's all so grand and perfect.

But the clock is ticking like a time bomb, and there are things I have to tell her that can't wait any longer. So the next day, Sunday, I make us peppermint tea and sit down in the chair in her parlor and put it all out there, as gently as possible.

"I have to tell you something. You're not going to like it."

She squints behind her glasses, cautiously.

"All right."

I pull her up and arrange her in my lap, her arse over my groin, her legs together, dangling over my thigh, my arms around her middle, holding on tight.

"I've reenlisted."

She goes very still and her lips pale.

"You're the Crown Prince . . . you can't . . ."

"Turns out, I can do a lot if I set my mind to it."

"But the Queen—"

"Is not happy with me, but she understands that this is something I need to do. It'll be a real deployment this time, in a regular unit. I'll be registered under an assumed name, so I won't put the other men in danger." I give her a squeeze and try to joke. "You'll have to help me come up with a fitting pseudonym—Finley Bigdick the Third or John Thomas Longhorn."

She doesn't laugh. She doesn't even smile.

"The press will be told that I'm on safari in Africa, then climbing Everest, and finally, on a research mission in the rain forest. I'll be portrayed as quite the heroic adventurer. But you can't tell anyone—not Penny or Willard or Annie or your mum. No one can know."

Sarah just looks at me and her expression slowly breaks my heart.

"Why are you doing this?"

I push her soft hair back and hope she can understand. "Because if I'm going to be a king, I need to know how to lead. And I think . . . I think I could be good at it."

Her hands slide up and down my chest, grazing, like she wants to be sure I'm still here with her.

"Where will they send you?"

"I don't know yet. I'll find out when I report for duty . . . in two weeks."

"Two weeks? Why didn't you tell me sooner?"

"I didn't want to risk manipulating you. I didn't want to pressure you into taking me back."

She snorts. "You picked a hell of a time to be noble, Henry."

"I know." I scoff, shaking my head at the craziness of it all. "And . . . I'm sorry. I realize this isn't what you want . . . but it's what I have to do."

"For how long?" she asks quietly.

"Two years."

She flinches, and I rush to tell her the rest.

"Extra precautions will have to be taken to keep my location under wraps. We won't be able to text or Skype or call. It's not just about my safety . . . you understand, don't you?"

Her voice is clogged with sadness, but she nods. "Yes."

I bring my hand to her jaw, needing to touch her, and the flutter of her pulse taps against my fingertips. Then, in a rough voice, I promise and swear, "But I'll write you. I'll write you every day. Pages and pages of lovely words and filthy thoughts."

Sarah smiles, even as a tear trickles down her cheek. "You'll write me letters? Real letters that I can touch and smell and hold?"

"Real letters." I pull her closer, whispering, "Paper and ink. I've been told there's nothing else like it."

Three days later, I wake up alone in Sarah's bed. It's early, still gray outside, without the full brightness of the winter sun. Not needing to be anywhere anytime soon, I pick up my guitar and strum a few chords.

Just a bit later, Sarah appears in the doorway—her hair delightfully windblown, eyes shining, the tip of her nose pink from the cold. It makes me want to bite it—and that thought makes me want to bite her everywhere else. I set the guitar down and she bounces onto the bed and her coat feels like ice as I skim it off her shoulders, because she's wearing entirely too much clothing.

"I've done something," she tells me, excitedly. "You're not going to like it."

"Anything that puts a smile like that on your pretty lips, I'm sure I'll like very much."

"I doubt that."

Then she holds out a handful of papers. I look them over and my own smile drops fast and hard. She was right—I don't like it at all.

"No."

"Henry—"

"Absolutely fucking not."

The Blue Coat Association is Wessco's equivalent of the Red Cross. Volunteers travel to disaster and war-torn areas to deliver food and medical supplies, build homes—whatever the populace needs. Six months ago a BCA facility was mistakenly hit by friendly fire, killing all thirty-three people inside.

"I'm going to start a reading program; they're very excited about it. I'll be teaching the children in the encampments to read and organizing donations from libraries. I can start with Concordia, but they're hopeful the program could expand to libraries all over the world."

My jaw clenches and I shake my head. "You're not doing this, Sarah."

"I've already signed up."

"Then we'll unsign you."

Her mouth goes tight and her eyes harden.

"I didn't ask for your permission and I'm not looking for it now."

I feel the frustration swelling inside me. And the fear.

"I'm going to be your king."

"But you're not yet."

"I'm going to be your husband."

She holds up her hand. "Huh, look at that—no ring. And it wouldn't matter if there were, because if you think I'm going to stand in Saint George's Cathedral and promise to obey you for the rest of our lives, you haven't been paying attention."

I don't want to make her doubt herself, but I'm desperate enough to say, "There may be explosions, loud noises. You still don't . . . you still have a hard time with those."

Her eyes dim—and I hate myself.

"I've explained the situation. They're willing to work with me on it. Make whatever accommodations are possible."

I cup her face in my hands. And my voice turns strangled.

"It will be dangerous."

Her hands encircle my wrists, holding on.

"But you make me want to be brave."

Something bends inside me, on the verge of breaking. And my eyes sting and blur. Because I have lost people I love—I know that it happens, and how it feels.

And I can't lose her.

"I don't want you brave; I want you safe. I want to lock you in a tower, like in one of your books, so no one can hurt you. And you'll be safe and happy and mine."

She rubs her thumbs in calming circles on the inside of my wrist. "Only the villains lock ladies in a tower."

"Then you make me want to be a villain."

She bites her lip, thinking of her response. She's come so far since the first time we met—she's already one of the bravest people I know. And the strongest. And even though this conversation scares the shit out of me, another part is of me so damn proud of her. For standing up, for not backing down or giving an inch—even to me. Maybe especially to me.

"Ask me why, Henry."

"I don't give a flying fuck why."

"Yes, you do. Ask me."

My throat gets too tight to swallow.

"Why?"

Sarah's dark eyes go shiny. She smiles as she replies. And it's beautiful.

"Because if I'm going to be a queen, I need to know how to be the voice for people who can't speak for themselves. To comfort people, be their friend and their champion. I want to change the world with you, Henry. To take what I know and what I have been given and make a difference." She blinks, and a tear falls from her eye to her soft cheek. "And I think . . . I think I could be good at it."

Cursing, I pull her against me, holding on too tightly.

"You'll be amazing."

After a time, I lean back and look into her eyes. "If anything happens to you, I'll die. I'm not exaggerating." My voice is strangled and wetness trickles from my eyes and I don't give a damn. "You are woven into my soul and you are wrapped around my heart. And if anything happens to you, both will wither and die and I won't even care."

"It's the same for me." She touches my face softly. Sweetly. My beautiful, sweet girl. "I guess we'll both have to make sure nothing happens to us, then."

I pull her against me, still terrified, but loving her enough to let her do this.

"What a pair we make."

Sarah tilts her face up and kisses me. "A perfect match."

Two days later, I have an itch for a new tattoo. Castlebrook doesn't have a tattoo shop—no shock there—so Sarah and I venture out, driving three hours north, close to the capital. I wear a cap and sunglasses to try and go undetected, but the presence of security men surrounding the shop would give us away if anyone was paying attention. Luckily, the place is empty when we arrive.

I pull up the photos on my mobile and show the artist the one I want. It's a close-up of Sarah's face—I took it a few days ago, on her balcony. The sun was rising and we'd been too busy fucking to even think about sleep. She's looking away from the camera, glasses on, her hair perfectly bed-mussed. It's the image that comes to mind whenever I've thought of her since, and it's the one I want on my right forearm, so I can gaze at it when we're apart.

I have the work done in an area cordoned off by a black

curtain, while Sarah waits, reading, on the other side. Because she's especially beautiful when she's surprised.

And I am not disappointed.

She gasps when she sees her face branded on my body, her pretty hand covering her mouth, making my cock go stiff and hard and aching for her.

I had new details added to the tattoos on my left arm as well. "The words have new meaning for me now," I say as she rests her head against my bicep, her eyes glinting and her cheeks flushed—because my ink makes her so very wet.

Duty is written beside the royal coat of arms, *Honor* beside the military crest, and beneath Sarah's picture, *Love.*

"Duty, Honor, Love," I tell her. "But the greatest of these is love. The Bible said that."

"Actually, First Corinthians says, *"And now these three remain: faith, hope and love. But the greatest of these is love."*

I shrug. "Well then, I fixed it for them."

She laughs, her eyes drifting to the wall of tattoo photographs—examples and suggestions.

"I want to get one too."

"My grandmother is going to have a coronary." I shake my head. "It's one thing for the future king to have a tattoo; she'll see the future queen having one as something altogether different."

Her back straightens with quiet strength. "It's the twenty-first century. And that means what's good for the king is good for the queen. Her Majesty will come around."

I kiss her forehead. "If you want one, sweets, then you'll have one, whether the Queen approves or not. Do you have any idea what kind you'd like?"

"I do, yes." She grins, excitedly. "But you'll have to wait and see. No peeking."

She disappears behind the curtain, speaking to the tattoo artist in feverish whispers.

A bit later she reappears, a small white square bandage on her right wrist. She takes my hand and pulls me closer, adorably giddy.

"I wanted it right here, so I can look at it and touch it anytime I like," Sarah says. And then she peels back the bandage.

It's a simple drawing, an open book with two blank pages, except for one word at the top:

Henry

"My story hasn't been written yet," she reaches up, tracing my jaw, "but I know it begins with you."

And I'm so fucking honored and grateful, so absolutely in awe of her and so much in love with her I barely know what to do with it. So I do the only possible thing I can in the face of such a gift. I bring Sarah into my arms and kiss her.

In a blink, the morning arrives when I have to report for deployment—when I have to leave Sarah. I try to get her to stay at her flat, snuggled under the covers, but she pleads and insists on coming to the airport with me. I want every moment with her that I can have, so I give in.

The sun isn't quite up yet and the air is frigid. On the tarmac, outside the plane that will take me away, Winston, the head of Palace security, meets us. I introduce him to Sarah.

"Sarah, this is Winston, the head Dark Suit. He'll be making sure you're looked after while I'm gone."

Winston bows respectfully. "An honor and a pleasure, Lady Sarah."

She gives him a nod, smiling graciously but shyly, as she tends to be with new people.

I squeeze her elbow and tell her I just need a private moment with Winston. And then I take him aside.

"You're aware of Lady Sarah's plans to join the BCA?"

"I am, Sir."

"You're arranging her security?"

"Yes, Prince Henry."

My voice is as cold as the air. "Your job is to protect the royal family, to secure the future of the monarchy, is that correct?"

He nods, his eyes tireless and unyielding, like a machine. "It is."

"Take a good look at her, Winston. Without her, there is no future for this monarchy, do you understand?"

He bows just slightly. "Completely, Sir."

"I want her covered in security. Only the best men. If she chafes at it, have them go undercover, but I want her protected at all times. No matter what. Is that clear?"

Again, he nods. "Do not trouble yourself about it, Prince Henry. Lady Sarah will be as secure as the Queen herself."

And a small measure of comfort slips into place. I'm not a fool, and there's a terrible conflict that comes with being who I am and loving someone so much. A price. Because by loving Sarah, I'm bringing a level of attention and scrutiny—even danger—into her life that wouldn't be there without me. The only reassurance is that I have the resources to protect her from it. Men like Winston and James, and the hundreds of other noble security men and women who would die to keep me, my brother, my sister-in-law, my grandmother—and now my Sarah—safe.

I tap Winston's shoulder and with a bow, he heads toward the plane.

And I return to Sarah's side, gazing at her face, burning this moment into my mind. I push up the sleeve of my coat and unclip the ID bracelet at my wrist, then I open Sarah's hand and pool the platinum into her palm.

"Keep this safe for me, will you? It'll be good to know the two things most precious to me are in the same place."

She nods and smiles up at me at first, so lovingly . . . but then her face tightens and crumples as she starts to cry. She wraps her arms around me and I hold her close.

"I'm sorry," she says against my coat. "I didn't want to cry."

I kiss her hair, rocking us gently. "You go ahead and cry all you like, love. You're crying for both of us."

For a few more final moments, we hold each other.

And then it's time to let go.

I kiss her softly, deeply. And as I look into her beautiful eyes, I remember words from a lifetime ago. Words that comforted me when I needed comfort more than anything.

I press my palm to Sarah's cheek and smile. "We're going to be all right, you and I. Yeah?"

She takes a deep breath and gives me a smile back.

"Yeah."

EPILOGUE

Sarah

Three years later

Henry kept his promise. He wrote me a letter a day, every day that we were apart, and it turns out he's a fantastic writer. Most were romantic, naughty—the kind a typical soldier would pen to his girl back home. A few were heartbreaking, a place for him to find solace, to pour out his grief after a difficult battle and the losses that all too often accompanied them. Some were philosophical, a way to sort out his own thoughts and beliefs by conveying them to me. And there were others that were hopeful, that spoke of the future—our future, as well as the future of our country and people and the kind of leader he aspired to be.

And I matched him letter for letter. I found I was bolder, dirtier, in my writing . . . although with Henry's instruction, I've come pretty far on the dirty talk front too. In the moments that he needed my comfort, when the words were too difficult for him to write and he needed my open arms but I wasn't there to hold him, I would send him pages and pages of I love you's— because sometimes there's nothing else that can be said. Other letters spoke of the work I did, the children I met and how all children are the same, no matter where they live or the language they speak . . . they all have the enormous capacity for resilience and hope and to give and receive love. And there were the letters that I wrote of my own dreams for Henry and me, for our children, and the source of strength for our people I hoped one day to be.

All of our letters, his to me and mine to him, are stored in the private safe at Guthrie House. It's odd to think that one day, many years from now, someone could read our letters the way George and Martha Washington's are studied, as a part of history. For us, they were simply words from Henry to Sarah and back again—but we now understand and accept the place we'll one day fill in the world. It's who we are, and we're at peace with it.

When Henry's enlistment was up, he surprised me—found me and came to me—where I was stationed with the BCA. To others, he looked like any rugged, bearded soldier, but I knew him in an instant. Those eyes, that smile—I ran and threw myself into his arms, and that's when we were both reassured that two years apart had only deepened our passion for each other.

These days, Henry lives at Guthrie House, already working with Parliament and the Queen, to change and better Wessco. And I have my own flat here in the city. Mother complains about the crowds and the noise every time she visits, but she comes anyway. Penny's had a few small parts in several moderately successful television shows and one hugely successful commercial for tooth-whitening cream. She's on a billboard in LA for the same product—and she takes a picture of it at least once a week and sends it to me, because she still can't believe it.

I spend my days working in the Palace library, and as a member of several literacy-promoting charitable organizations. I still struggle with new people and places, but it doesn't hold me back—and like I once told Henry, we all have our quirks.

As for Henry, he gets my nights. Almost all of them, all the time. It's different here in the city than in Castlebrook—

the paparazzi are relentless, and there's nothing they'd like more than to get a shot of Henry or me doing the walk of shame in the morning, after having spent the night together. We have to be sneaky.

Lucky for us, sneaky is still Henry's specialty. They haven't caught us yet.

In fact, I was just with him last night, talking about the speech he's giving to Parliament right now. I told him if he was nervous he should just picture me naked, and he said he needed a refresher . . . and there wasn't much talking after that.

I now sit with Prince Nicholas and the Queen, and listen as Henry gives the position of the House of Pembrook on Wessco's potential military engagement. He writes the speeches himself, in coordination with his grandmother, and as I said . . . he's quite the writer.

As he concludes his remarks, Henry slowly meets the eyes of each seated MP.

"This is not an action I take lightly. I have seen the cost of war, and I ache for the loss of every soldier as if they were members of my own family—because they are."

And then his voice changes. Surges in strength and resonance.

"But the world is not always gray. There are moments in time when the line between right and wrong is stark and clear. And each of us must make our choice. It has been said that evil flourishes when good men and women do nothing. And so I ask you to stand with me today, beside me and beside the sons and daughters of Wessco as we declare in one resounding voice, *I will not do nothing.*"

The chamber fills with a cacophony of clapping hands— thunderous applause—and every member of Parliament rises to his feet. To stand with His Royal Highness, Crown Prince Henry.

Later, Henry steps from the platform and makes his way through the throng of chattering Parliament members, shaking hands and nodding as he goes. When he arrives at our seats, his brother immediately embraces him, smiling broadly.

"Well done, Henry. You sounded like an actual politician."

"No," the Queen interjects. "He sounded like a king."

It's the truest compliment she could give, and Henry . . . blushes.

A wicked sense of vindication tickles my stomach, because I've definitely rubbed off on him. Loving Henry has made me wild and brave, and his love for me has made him humble and calm. What a funny pair we are—better than any storybook couple I've read about, and for me that's the truest compliment I could ever give.

Henry turns to Olivia and hugs her warmly. "Look at you, Olive." He gazes at her midsection, where a round burgeoning baby bump strains against her blouse. "I'm going to have to start calling you Pimento—you're all stuffed."

Olivia laughs. And then we file out to the waiting cars and drive to the palace.

Henry

After my speech, Sarah, Nicholas, Olivia, Granny, and I retire to the yellow drawing room for tea. And I broach the subject that's been on my mind a lot lately.

"I want Sarah to move into Guthrie House after New Year's."

My grandmother practically chokes on her tea.

"Absolutely not."

"Why not? She practically lives there now anyway; we may as well make it official."

The Queen raises one sharp eyebrow. "Your definition of *official* and mine are very different."

I shrug. "The law's on the verge of being been changed—and then there'll be no reason to pretend we don't 'get busy' every chance we get, in every room of the Palace."

After intense lobbying by the Queen and me, we almost have the number of votes in Parliament needed to revise the law. We're hopeful it'll be done within the next year, two at the most, and then I and all future heirs will finally be free to marry whomever we choose. And the first child Sarah and I have—whether it's a boy or a girl—will be next in line to the throne.

"TMI, Henry," Olivia quips.

"Thank you, Olivia," my grandmother says. "My thoughts exactly."

The Queen sets down her teacup. "Small steps, my boy. Tradition still demands propriety. The fact that Sarah accompanies you to functions of state and family affairs would've been scandalous just ten years ago. You're not even engaged."

I wave my hand. "A technicality."

Nicholas chuckles. "You sound awfully cocky for a man who hasn't popped the question yet."

"Just realistic." I wink at Sarah. "I'm irresistible."

My little duck rolls her pretty eyes.

"Be that as it may," the Queen says dryly, "we must set a good example for the young ladies of Wessco." She pats Sarah's hand. "Explain it to him, dear."

My grandmother and Sarah have grown very close in the last

year. Granny's taken Sarah safely under her wing and become a wonderful, strong mentor to my lovely girl.

Not unlike Emperor Palpatine and Darth Vader.

"Oh, I don't know, Queen Lenora," Sarah replies. "I'm a modern, independent woman. Living with Henry before marriage could be a very good example for the women of Wessco. What's the phrase? 'Try it before you buy it'?"

"'Try it . . .'" the Queen sputters.

And then she looks at Sarah's face.

"Are you teasing me, Sarah Von Titebottum?" she asks sternly.

Sarah's expression sobers, but the sparkle in her eyes remains.

"Yes, Your Majesty. Sorry. Your grandson is a terrible influence."

In more ways than one.

I wiggle my eyebrows suggestively and Sarah throws me a mock frown before reassuring the Queen.

"But I agree with you: I won't be moving into Guthrie House until after the wedding. We've enjoyed so much support from the people, we shouldn't risk offending the more conservative citizens . . . no matter how tempting the idea may be."

My grandmother nods. "Well said, child."

And I pout. "But that will take so *long*. I don't want to wait."

The Queen has no pity. "Then I suggest you get the ball rolling, Henry. If you like it, you should put a ring on it." Then she adds proudly, "I told Beyoncé that once."

We all laugh. Because apparently the Queen has a sense of humor.

Who knew?

But still . . . it's good advice.

Sarah tells me the best happily ever afters end with a wedding. But if you've seen one royal wedding, you've basically seen them all—glossy commemorative magazine cover–worthy photos of the stunning white dress with lace sleeves, the dashing groom in his military uniform, the gold, horse-drawn carriages, the crowds, the adorable flower girls.

The real story is the one that comes before. The one that only a handful of people get to know and even fewer get to see.

For us, it happens at The Horny Goat. Sarah looks stunning in a dark plum dress. She still doesn't like to stand out, still is not a fan of loud colors, but these days her fashion choices are more vibrant and fearless—just like her.

I like to think I had something to do with that.

Nicholas and Olive are with us, Penelope and my brother's bouncy sister-in-law Ellie Hammond too, as well as our friends—Simon and Franny, Willard and Laura, Annie, Sam and Elizabeth. Macalister and Meg are behind the bar, and James and big Mick are at the door, joined by two members of my brother's security, Tommy Sullivan and Logan St. James.

The gang's all here.

Onstage, in a chair with my guitar, I tap at the microphone and the crowd goes hushed.

"My father used to put together jigsaw puzzles in his spare time; it was a hobby for him. Huge, complicated puzzles with thousands of pieces. I remember pushing my toy cars around on the carpet while he sat at a table in his study, patiently putting together one piece after the next."

I see Nicholas smiling softly, because he remembers too.

"And sometimes, there were pieces, just one or two, that were odd, that didn't seem to fit in anywhere. He would put them off to the side and I would think, maybe there's something wrong with them, maybe they're broken. But then . . . he would find the piece they fit with, their match—and when the two pieces were joined, you could see what they were supposed to be. Where they fit and how important they were to the whole picture."

I scan the crowd, searching for my Sarah's dark eyes, and when I find them they're already filling with tears.

Because she knows what's coming.

"The official account of tonight will be very proper and appropriate and . . . fucking boring. But that's okay. Because those of you here, those of you who mean the most to Sarah and me, you'll know the true story of how it all happened. That once upon a time, a pitiful lad met a shy, lovely lass and together they became something more . . . something strong and beautiful and forever. And one night he sang her a song, in a fantastic rickety old pub—a song with a question in it. And after he played the very last note, she said yes a thousand times."

My lips slide into a grin. "At least . . . that's how I'm hoping it'll go."

I bring my fingers to the strings and play the opening notes of "Marry Me" by Train.

And as I sing every word, lyrics about forever not being enough time and wearing out I love you's, about love showing the way and promises to sing to her every night, I look at Sarah the whole time and she doesn't take her eyes off me for a moment.

She's already nodding when the last guitar notes ring out, when I leave the stage and stand before her and sink down, not on one knee but two—and I offer her my mother's ring—a flawless, oval diamond upon a bed of glittering smaller diamonds, set in a shiny platinum band.

"I love you, Sarah. You already know that, but I promise to tell you and show you every single day, just the same. I promise to keep you safe, always, so you're never afraid to be bold and brave . . . even when it scares the hell out of me. I will cherish your sweetness, and be inspired by your strength and kindness. And I promise you a life filled with adventure and excitement and fun, and enough laughter and love to fill the pages of a thousand books."

I smile up at her, my throat tight with emotion and my heart close to bursting.

"Will you marry me, Sarah?"

And with happy tears streaming down her face, my beautiful girl goes down on her knees with me, and she takes my face in her hands and whispers, "Yes, Henry. Yes, I'll marry you. Yes, yes, yes, yes . . ."

I pull her against me, and we seal our words with a long kiss. And the claps and cheers of those who know us best and love us most fill the air.

And that, that's the story you won't see on television or read in the history books. The tale of an unruly prince who found the queen of his heart, and learned how to be a King.

DON'T MISS THE NEXT BOOKS IN THE ROYALLY SERIES!!

Royally Endowed

A boy from the wrong side of the tracks…

But these days he covers his tattoos with a respectable suit. He's charismatic, good looking, smart and trustworthy—any girl would be proud to bring him home to her family.

But there's only one girl he wants.

She's his living, breathing fantasy. For years he's known her, sometimes laughed with her, once shared a pint with her…he would lay down his life for her.

But she doesn't see him—not really.

A girl endowed with royal relations . . .

She dreams of princes and palaces, but in her quest for happily ever after, harsh truths are learned: castles are drafty, ball gowns are a nuisance, and nobility doesn't equal noble intentions.

In the end, she realizes her true heart's love may just be the handsome, loyal boy who's been beside her all along.

BOOK #1 IN THE ROYALLY SERIES AVAILABLE NOW!

Royally Screwed

Nicholas Arthur Frederick Edward Pembrook, Crowned Prince of Wessco, a.k.a. "His Royal Hotness", is wickedly charming, devastatingly handsome, and unabashedly arrogant—hard not to be when people are constantly bowing down to you.

Then, one snowy night in Manhattan, the prince meets a dark-haired beauty who doesn't bow down. Instead, she throws a pie in his face.

Nicholas wants to find out if she tastes as good as her pie, and this heir apparent is used to getting what he wants.

Dating a prince isn't what waitress Olivia Hammond ever imagined it would be.

There's a disapproving queen, a wildly inappropriate spare heir, relentless paparazzi, and brutal public scrutiny. While they've traded in horse-drawn carriages for Rolls Royces and haven't chopped anyone's head off lately—the royals are far from accepting of this commoner.

But to Olivia—Nicholas is worth it.

Nicholas grew up with the whole world watching, and now Marriage Watch is in full force. In the end, Nicholas has to decide who he is and, more importantly, who he wants to be: a King…or the man who gets to love Olivia forever.

CPSIA information can be obtained
at www.ICGtesting.com
Printed in the USA
BVOW11s2044190217
476552BV00001B/1/P